ANOTHER 365 DAYS

Praise for KE Payne

me@you.com

"This book fell together perfectly and Immy's journey was one I will read over and over. I know I will be keeping a look out for more books by KE Payne in the future." —*Dreaming in the Pages*

"A fast-paced read [which] I found hard to put down." —*C-Spot*

"A fresh, clean look at first girl/girl love and all of its baggage."—*Queer YA*

"A wonderful, thought-provoking novel of a teenager discovering who she truly is."—*Fresh Fiction*

365 Days

"One of the most real books I've ever read. It frequently made me giggle out loud to myself while muttering, 'OMG, RIGHT?'"—*After Ellen*

"Hilarious! Please, KE Payne, write a sequel, would you?" —*Queer YA*

"The writing is crisp and clever; the characters are simple yet multi-dimensional; and the storyline is fresh but familiar. Ms. Payne artfully captures the confusion and concerns of a young woman coming to terms with her lesbian libido, as well as life with her family, the inconvenience of schoolwork, morphing dynamics with friends, the torment of waiting for a text, an email, or a call, and the near-consuming fear of losing it all."—*Rainbow Reader*

"Payne captures Clemmie's voice—an engaging blend of teenage angst and saucy self-assurance—with full-throated style."—Richard Labonté, *Book Marks*

By the Author

me@you.com

365 Days

Another 365 Days

ANOTHER 365 DAYS

by

KE Payne

A Division of Bold Strokes Books

2013

ANOTHER 365 DAYS

ISBN 13: 978-1-60282-775-2

This Trade Paperback Original Is Published By
Bold Strokes Books, Inc.
P.O. Box 249
Valley Falls, NY 12185

First Edition: January 2013

Credits
Editors: Lynda Sandoval and Stacia Seaman
Production Design: Stacia Seaman
Cover Design by Sheri (graphicartist2020@hotmail.com)

Acknowledgments

I'm so pleased to have had the chance to write *Another 365 Days*. Something about Clemmie Atkins stuck with me the first time I "met" her, and I knew we weren't quite finished after *365 Days*. I have a lot of people to thank for allowing me to follow her chaotic life for another twelve months.

Firstly, I'm very grateful to all the amazing people at Bold Strokes Books that have made this book possible: Radclyffe for accepting me into the BSB fold in the first place, Stacia Seaman for hunting out all my silly mistakes, Sheri for yet another awesome cover, and to my editor, Lynda Sandoval, for her invaluable advice and input.

A huge thank you, too, to Sarah "Smartie" Martin for always being willing to read my work, despite being so busy with all her own stuff, and for offering up so many fabulous suggestions. I really do appreciate you giving up your time to read *Another 365 Days* over and over, and for all your feedback that let me know I was heading in the right direction with it.

Lastly, but most importantly, a massive thank you to BJ for her unwavering support. I don't think I could do this if I didn't have you by my side, encouraging me and saying all the right things just when I really need to hear them, although a few more coffees when I'm writing wouldn't go amiss…

Wednesday 2 January

Was woken up by the sound of Mum singing 'Dancing Queen' down in the kitchen at 7 o'clock this morning. Staggered down to be greeted with the sight of her 'boogying' (her words, not mine—no one under the age of twenty-one would even dream of using such a word, Mother) while washing up, using the washing-up brush as a makeshift microphone. It's most unbecoming for a woman her age to be wiggling her bottom to ABBA whilst up to her elbows in Fairy liquid.

She is 43, after all. She should know better.

I don't know what she's got be so cheerful about anyway. Not only does she have to go back to work tomorrow, but I saw at least three new grey hairs on her head that weren't there yesterday AND she's still got to come with me into town to buy me another top for school. This is despite me reminding her at least four times over the Christmas holidays that the sleeves on my current ones are too short and make me look like I've just been released from a Young Offenders' Institute. I pointed out all three details to her, adding a bit of a tone to the first two for good measure and the singing face was promptly replaced by her usual grumpy face. Mission accomplished, I returned to bed where I managed to squeeze in another two hours' sleep before going over to Han's this afternoon. Result!

Went to Han's house after lunch 'cos she'd told me she wanted me to come shopping with her for another eyebrow ring 'cos she'd rubbed at her eye while sitting on the toilet that morning and knocked her original one off, managing to flush it down the toilet for good measure, and if she doesn't get another bar in her eyebrow *tout suite*, her piercing hole will heal over and she'll have to pierce it again with a hot needle. Every time she tells me a tale like this I'm even more grateful I'm not an EMO and don't have to cope with the 'accessories' that she and her fellow EMOs favour. My cool leather bracelet with skulls on is the only accessory I need, thank you very much.

Thursday 3 January

Mum left the house at 8 this morning muttering darkly about teachers and training days. I pulled the duvet up over my head and tried to forget the fact that I have to go back to school tomorrow too. Han came over just before lunch and was greeted with the sight of my sister, Her Royal Bloody Highness, sitting in the lounge in her nightwear, namely a skimpy T-shirt that said 'Drummers Do It With Rhythm' (a Christmas present from Joe) and not much else. I thought Han made a pretty good effort of not looking at my sister's legs, but I noticed her staring hard at the TV every time HRBH crossed and uncrossed her legs.

#revolted

Friday 4 January

Whose dumb idea was it to make us go back to school on a Friday?? The only good thing about having to go back was that it was awesome seeing everyone again after aaaaages away! Alice had been to Germany for the whole of the Christmas holidays and she'd brought us back some German cake to all try, which was very nice of her (nicer than the cake anyway, which was yuk, yuk, yuk!). I asked her if she had a nice time in Germany but she didn't really say much back to me.

Anyway, not content with making us go back on a Friday, the school decided today to dump about ten years' worth of work on us. Okay, so I know I have to take important exams in the summer (not my choice) but was it necessary to remind us, like, every five minutes today, of the importance of working hard this year? I know I've gotta work hard! I don't WANT to have to work hard, but I know I've got to—I just don't need every bloody teacher in the school reminding me, thankyouverymuch.

Especially not on my first day back.

Saturday 5 January

Went into town with Mum today to look for some new clothes. I wanted slashed sleeveless T-shirts with naked women on them, ripped jeans, a distressed leather coat, and some new Converses. What did I come home with?

A jumper, three pairs of knickers, and some ibuprofen.

I think there was a breakdown in communication somewhere along the line there, don't you?

Sunday 6 January

Han came over to ours after lunch today with Toffee. We took her and Barbara for a walk up into the woods at the back of the house and had *a session* up against an old hazel tree, which felt very naughty (kissing always feels different outside, I dunno why!) but totally awesome at the same time.

As I'm writing this, I've just realised that was my first *session* of the year, and…dang, it felt good!!

Monday 7 January

Back to school again. Groooooan!

Han told me on the way home tonight that she's getting a new Art teacher this term. She's a bit pissed off 'cos she thinks it'll muck up her chances of doing well in her exams 'cos her previous Art teacher, Mrs. Greene, was 'the only one who understood her tortured soul and didn't complain when she drew pictures of skeletons with worms coming out of their eye sockets or spitting cats hanging themselves from the Statue of Liberty and weird shit like that'.

According to Mrs. Hallam, the new teacher is called Miss Smith and they're all very pleased to have her come to work at the school 'cos she's something quite big in the textile world, having won some tapestry award in 2006. Great! So she's going to be some old fuddy-duddy with a neat line in cardigans and saggy boobs like Boxing Day balloons, who can join all the other old fuddy-duddies that work in this godforsaken school!

Tuesday 8 January

Went over to Han's after school tonight and chilled up in her room. I told Mum that we had a project to do for school, but, to be honest, the only task I was focused on tonight was having a darn good feel up under Han's jumper.

So I have a hot girlfriend! Whaddya gonna do?

Wednesday 9 January

Mrs. Unwin told us in assembly today that Han's new Art teacher starts next week. She asked us all, regardless of whether we took Art or not, to 'give Miss Smith a rousing St. Bart's greeting and welcome her into our happy little fold'. She told us for, like, the HUNDRETH time, that it was quite a coup for us to have Miss Smith 'cos she's thought of very highly, apparently, in the world of tapestry.

Whatever.

Thursday 10 January

Alice's birthday is this Saturday so I nipped into town after school with Han and bought her a birthday card and an HMV music voucher for £10 'cos I didn't know what else to get her.

Han asked me why I still bothered with sending Alice a birthday card bearing in mind we hardly speak any more, but when I pointed out—quite impatiently really—that I'd been friends with Alice for, like, years and there was no way I'd ever forget her birthday, she shut up.

She wandered off to the DVD section of HMV on her own and for a moment I panicked that I'd pissed her off, but she came wandering back over with a big grin on her face, waving a copy of *Saw IV* at me, telling me we could watch it together at the weekend, and I knew she was okay.

Friday 11 January

We got told in registration today that we've got to start telling the school where we want to do our work experience once our exams are over in the summer. We got told about work experience last year but as usual I forgot all about it and so haven't got a clue where I want to go.

I asked Mrs. Schofield what would happen if I didn't do work experience and she told me I'd have to come into school and do 'tasks' instead. I asked her what sort of 'tasks' and she said, 'Helping out around the school. Tidying up, that sort of thing.'

Had visions of having to serve the little year 7s their lunches and I know I'd look like a right tit in a tabard so put my mind to thinking about where and when I can do this work experience stuff.

Saturday 12 January

Today was Alice's birthday. I sent her a *Nappy Birfday* text but I didn't hear anything back from her. We haven't really spoken much since Christmas when I rang her just as she was about to head off to Germany for two weeks and poured my heart out over Han to her. I don't think Alice likes me any more, but I can't say I blame her, the way I treated her last year.

Doesn't stop me from missing her, though.

Sunday 13 January

Great Aunt May came to our house for lunch today, so it meant we all had to eat lots of mashed food 'cos Great Aunt May can't eat anything that requires excessive chewing due to her false teeth.

She told us she'd seen something in the *Gazette* advertising Polish dancing and thought she might give it a go. She said when she met Great Uncle Roy during the war he'd taught her some Polish dances 'cos he'd been friends with some Poles and they'd taught him, and she thought it might be nice to try it again all these years later. She said, 'He wooed me with his magnificent Polonaise, you know. One look at that and I was putty in his hands,' and her eyes went all rheumy at the thought of it.

I'm not sure what sort of dances Polish people do, but I just hope it's not the same as those funny old Cossack dances they do in Russia 'cos one rapid squat by Great Aunt May and she'd be in traction and support knickers for a month.

Monday 14 January

OMG what a strange day! It was Miss Smith, the new Art teacher's first day today. We had a full school assembly to welcome us all back from our Christmas holidays, so most of the teachers were there looking really pissed off, and like they wanted to be anywhere but back here at school (I know the feeling!) Anyway, Mrs. Unwin introduced us to Miss Smith and asked us all to give her a warm welcome to the school, and to help her 'find her feet in her first few weeks with us here'. Then she asked Miss Smith to come up onto the stage so we could all welcome her and at that point Han leant over and whispered, 'What colour cardigan do you s'pose the old girl's wearing?' which gave me a fit of the giggles and a steely stare from Mr. Pritchard, who was sitting nearest to us.

Then, this, OMG, like, DROP-DEAD GORGEOUS woman walked up on to the stage and smiled at us all as Mrs. Unwin led us in a soft ripple of applause. Han's eyes were like saucers and I noticed she was breathing just that little bit faster than normal as she muttered, 'THAT'S Miss Smith??? Dear God, pinch me 'cos I must be dreaming!' I glared at her but could only agree with her, really. Okay, so Miss Smith is old (maybe 30, I guess) but not as old as we thought she'd be, and she sure as hell wasn't wearing a cardigan!!

From the brief glimpse I got of her, I'd say she was probs 31, 32. She's really tall, has long black hair, a figure to die for, and definitely looks like she's the sort of teacher you don't mess with!

Made a mental note to try and have a proper look at her sooner rather than later.

Tuesday 15 January

Met Alice in the corridor at school today. It was a bit awkward at first, like it seems to have been just lately, but I persevered and asked her if she had a nice birthday and she said she had. At least she's talking to me. She thanked me for the card and voucher and I asked her if she'd spent it yet, wanting to add that Han had bought *Saw IV* for £8 on Saturday and that might do fine, but figured that Alice isn't really a *Saw IV* kinda person so stayed quiet.

Alice said she hadn't bought anything with it yet but she had her eye on a Lil Wayne CD. A small part of me thinks she said this on purpose 'cos she knows that even a hint of rap music makes me want to stab my ears with a blunt Lil Chef fork. It would certainly be less painful, anyway.

Alice looked like she wanted to say something else to me (probs tell me she was going to buy a bloody Kanye West CD with the change—that'd *really* tip me over the edge), but instead she just smiled and walked on down the corridor.

I miss her being my friend. (Despite her lousy taste in music.)

Wednesday 16 January

Dear God, Miss Smith was wearing a leather skirt today!!! The woman is pure sex on legs.

Thursday 17 January

Great Aunt May has signed up for Polish dance lessons!!! She's going with Ariadne Dawkins for moral support, and for the fact that Ariadne can touch her toes without leaking so Great Aunt May says she can do all the difficult moves. The first lesson's at the church hall next week. Great Aunt May's very excited about it. She says anything that gets her a bit of exercise at her age has gotta be a good thing, plus it means she hasn't got to spend yet another evening in the communal lounge at Autumn Leaves listening to Eric Stapleton talking to his imaginary friend, Gerald.

I texted Han just before going to bed and told her about Great Aunt May and her dancing. She thought it was well funny! Started thinking about Han after I'd turned my light off and began getting horny, but then images of Great Aunt May trying to touch her toes swam into my head and my horns were blunted within ten seconds.

Friday 18 January

Copped a good look at Miss Smith in school today. Cor, flipping heck! I tell you what, she's as fit as a blimming butcher's dog! She was wearing heels so high you'd need a ladder to climb them; last time I saw shoes that high, old Mrs. Russell was attached to them, clip-clopping down the corridor at 100mph, and lemme tell you, there was NOTHING fit about Mrs. Russell (yuk, yuk, yuk!!)

Miss Smith has these amazing eyes, like piercing blue, almost like those Siberian wolves that you see on the Discovery Channel! And she has this perfectly arched eyebrow, which Han says she puts to good use in her Art classes when she's not too happy about something. Han also reckons she's got this dead cool kickass attitude and she reckons she's the best teacher she ever had! Why didn't I ever choose Art? Why did I have to stick with French and Mrs. Howells and her goddam halitosis and dicky hip? Damn, damn, damn! Life's so bloody unfair at times!!!

Actually, maybe it's a good idea I'm not taking Art. If Miss Smith was my teacher, every time she walked past me as I was trying to paint I'd probably get so distracted I'd end up painting the desk or something. Or my hands would be so shaky the examiners would think my work had been drawn by a five-year-old.

Saturday 19 January

Woke up to snow this morning!!! It, like, NEVER snows in England, so I was really excited! I heard Dad saying about how it used to snow all the time in the winter when he was small (back in the Dark Ages, otherwise known as the 1980s) and how global warming or something meant it doesn't snow as much.

As long as this global warming thing didn't melt the snow today I didn't care. I rang Han and asked her if she wanted to come tobogganing with me over the fields. She thought about it for a while, wondering if frolicking in the snow was what EMOs did, but then decided that even those who were emotional hardcores like her needed to let their hair down once in a while, and if she didn't wear too much eye make-up she wouldn't look too daft zipping down the slopes, shrieking like a banshee.

I dug out my sparkling, bright red toboggan that Mum and Dad bought for me when I was, like, 10 and which had been hanging in the garage gathering dust. Dad spotted it and started going on about 'the youth of today' and how, when he was my age, he used to toboggan down slopes in an old coal sack filled with snow. Mind you, the way he talks sometimes, I wouldn't be surprised if he wasn't made to wear Hessian sacks instead of shirts too. Sometimes I think that man was born old.

Anyway, Han came round with her full-length distressed leather coat on, which Mum promptly advised her to leave at our house and gave her a pink anorak to wear instead. Han's face was priceless, but she didn't say anything to Mum 'cos she's too shy. I noticed the anorak got left at the end of our garden before we went over the fields, though.

The slopes were, like, full of old people acting like teenagers!!! I thought tobogganing was something only people under 20 did, but noooooo! I watched these overweight, puffing men struggle up the slopes only to fling themselves heavily down onto their tiny, weeny sledges and glide back down the slopes at 3 miles per hour. The thought struck me that if you can't even go down a slope at 3mph without screeching and grunting and puffing with exertion, then you're too bloody old!!! Go home and have a cup of cocoa by the fire and leave the fun to us young ones. Saddos.

Sunday 20 January

Snow all but melted! The snowman that me and Han built in the garden yesterday now looks like Gollum from Lord of the Rings. Barbara won't go anywhere near it.

Monday 21 January

Met up with Han, Alice, Matty, Caroline, and Ems at lunchtime today. It's 'Spanish Fortnight' in the canteen all this week so today we had a choice of paella, Spanish omelette, or sausage and mash (for those that don't like foreign food). I chose paella 'cos I figured I could have omelette any time at home, but as Dad won't touch prawns 'cos he says he couldn't eat something that spends its life swimming around by sewage outlets with its little prawny mouth open, it's not likely Mum will ever have a crack at cooking it at home.

Tuesday 22 January

Miss Smith is as cool as hell, I've decided. I was waiting for Han after her Art lesson today and Miss Smith saw me hanging around in the corridor outside the art studio. She beckoned me in, telling me, 'Rather than standing there looking like a spare piece, you can help me clear some of this mess up,' and casually threw a roll of cleaning cloths at me before sauntering back across the studio! I thought I'd died and gone to heaven, but also thought next time I wait for Han I'll make sure I wait further down the corridor 'cos I got Vibrant Sapphire paint splashed over my blouse and knew I'd get a load of earache about it when I got home.

Which I bloody did.

Wednesday 23 January

Great Aunt May is writing a letter of complaint to the *Gazette*. She says she and Ariadne went to the church hall for their first Polish dance lesson last night and the hall was full of—and I quote—'harlots, sluts, and strumpets wobbling their bits and pieces at us.'

She said it was only when the tutor approached them with a pole, 'waggling her tassels in our faces and asking us if we could lift our legs up higher than our shoulders', that they realised that they'd enrolled into a pole-dancing lesson, not a Polish dancing lesson.

Apparently Ariadne was well up for it, but Great Aunt May is of the old school, and politely declined. She said that she hadn't lifted her leg any higher than her pelvis since 1983 and if she wanted to bend and flex her body round a broom handle, she'd do it in the privacy of her own front room, thank you very much. Chance would be a fine thing! I hear her knees crack every time she sits down, so God knows how she thinks she'd be able to wrap anything round a pole without it popping out of joint.

Thursday 24 January

I think it's just as well that Miss Smith teaches in an all-girls school 'cos if there were teenage boys in this school they'd all be walking round with stiffies. Today she was wearing skinny black jeans and high heels (and a top, of course). I did a double take when I saw her sashaying down the corridor to the Art studio, but then I noticed that Mr. Troutt did too. And Mr. Pritchard, and Mr. Harman, and Mr. Dawkins.

And Miss Bletchley-Smythe, the librarian.

Who knew?!

Friday 25 January

Went over to Han's house for tea tonight. Mum graciously allowed me to go 'cos it wasn't a school night (she's so totalitarian sometimes) but secretly I think she was pleased to have the house to herself for a few hours 'cos Dad went up to see Great Aunt May and HRBH was over at Joe's, where she seems to spend most of her time now.

As I was getting ready to leave the house at 5 p.m. I heard the sound of the radio being cranked up so loudly that I could hear it from my room.

When I came down to complain, I saw her pouring herself a glass of wine and dancing round the kitchen. She told me it was some band she'd loved when 'she was my age', called Whoomph, or Bam, or Bong, or Wham, or some dumb name like that. She said 'didn't the lead singer, some bloke called Michael something or other, have a lovely voice in the days before he started sniffing things up his nose and crashing his car into shop fronts at three in the morning?'

I had NO idea what the hell she was on about, but I blame the wine for her ramblings. Personally I think 5 p.m. is far too early for her to start drinking.

I hope she's not going through a mid-life crisis, even if, at 43, she's way past her mid-life now.

Saturday 26 January

OMG soooooooo embarrassing tonight! Me and Han bought this, like, gay DVD in the bargain bucket at HMV in town today (well, I say WE bought it, what I mean is SHE bought it while I waited outside the shop just to make sure no one we knew came in). Anyway, we had the real deal tonight: takeaway, some beers, and a gay DVD under the duvet (I mean, we watched it under the duvet, not the DVD was under the duvet. That would just be silly).

So we were watching this film, called *My Best Friend Anna*, or something like that, and, well, this girl's 'Best Friend Anna' became her 'Best Friend Anna Who I Like To Shag', and boyyyyyyyy did she like shagging her. A lot.

Anyway, we had the sound turned down, like, dead low, even though Mum and Dad were downstairs watching some Z-list celebrities do ballroom dancing, and we'd just got to a juicy bit in the DVD when THE most embarrassing thing happened!!! Mum knocked on the door but did that thing that parents do when they, like, knock...and then come straight in anyway. I mean, WTF?? What's the point of knocking then coming in? You might just as well come straight in, save the skin on your knuckles for something more important, like punching someone.

So she came in, just as Best Friend Anna was getting the top of her thigh kissed by someone who *quite clearly wasn't a bloke* aaaaaaand could I reach the bloody remote to switch it over? Nooooooooo! Why would I be able to? That would have been far too easy, wouldn't it? Luckily though I did manage to grab it just in the nick of time, dangling out of the bed in a most unladylike manner before Mum got close enough to the TV to see what was going on, and hastily changed channels, smiling sweetly and offering her a prawn ball from my bed, while Han sat red-faced next to me.

I don't think Mum suspected a thing, although she did ask why Han and I would want to watch a documentary on quantum physics when *Shameless* was on the other side.

Sunday 27 January

Han texted me late last night after she'd gone home and asked me if Mum had said any more about the DVD. She hadn't, and I could practically sense the sighs of relief coming down my phone from Han when I texted her back and told her that Mum was totally oblivious to anything and hadn't even noticed that:

a.) We were in bed together,
b.) We were watching a roodie in bed together,
c.) Han's face went the colour of a London bus the minute Mum walked in.

Sometimes I wonder if my mother thinks of anyone other than herself.

Monday 28 January

Woke up this morning wondering whether I should start talking to Mum about stuff. I've been thinking loads about what happened on Saturday night and I feel like crap every time I remember the blind panic when she came in the room, and how I hate all this secrecy, even though we got away with it this time.

Even thinking like that makes me hate myself sometimes: *even though we got away with it.* Why should I have to get away with anything? Godddd life would be SO much easier if I didn't have to creep around like I was doing something bad all the time!

Sometimes I wish she'd talk to me, like other mothers do. I mean, why hasn't she twigged? Why have I got to offer the information to her? And, to be honest, how the hell do I even begin to start a conversation with her about it?

'Hi, Mum. Erm, I'm gay, okay?'

'Gay?'

'Yes. Gay. This is why I've never had a proper boyfriend—Ben doesn't count—, why I show absolutely no interest in boys whatsoever and why I always lock my door when Han comes up to my room. The other night was a temporary lapse in concentration and nearly ended with you seeing My Best Friend Anna having a right good going over, because I like watching films about girls loving girls because, erm, I'm a girl who loves a girl.'

Hmm. I can see I'm going to have to work on the approach technique on this one.

Tuesday 29 January

Waited for Han after school but she was late—again. This is the third time it's happened in as many weeks and it's beginning to piss me off. She's only late on Tuesdays when she has Art last lesson and it's getting to be damn obvious why she's only late after Art and not any other lesson. All the rest of the week she can't wait to get out of school, but on Tuesdays…she seems to like staying behind more, and it's really starting to bug me.

Wednesday 30 January

Han caught up with me behind the Science block today as I was heading over for my lesson. She grabbed my arm and pulled me away from view and we just kinda held hands for a bit, just 'cos, well 'cos we could and we wanted to.

It was dead sweet, leaning up against that wall, while the wind swirled around our feet, blowing dust and empty crisp packets at us, just holding hands. I'd been pissed off with her yesterday for staying behind after Art, but standing there today, holding hands and looking at each other, was just awesome.

Totally loved up tonight.

Thursday 31 January

Today was the last day of 'Spanish Fortnight' in the canteen so we all went down to see what delights Morag the head cook could conjure up. There was something called 'gazpacho' on the menu today which Ems said was some kind of cold soup. I wondered if I could ask for mine to have a 2-minute spin in the microwave, but Ems said it was supposed to be cold. She said Spanish people liked to eat it cold 'cos on really hot days it made it refreshing; I looked outside the window and saw a force 10 gale howling round the yard and figured I didn't need refreshing today, thank you very much. Besides, it looked a bit strange, all green and lumpy, a bit like a small child had sneezed into the bain-marie so I opted for pie and chips instead 'cos the only other Spanish option was paella again and I didn't want to inflict prawns on my stomach for a second time in less than two weeks in case it rebelled.

Friday 1 February

Han and I were walking behind Miss Smith down the corridor today. She was wearing this blouse which clung to all her bits and pieces. I can't see old Mrs. Unwin putting up with that for long. Anyone who outdoes her in the tight-blouse stakes is a condemned woman. She still looked bloody fit though (Miss Smith, not Mrs. Unwin—yuk, yuk, yuk!!!)

Saturday 2 February

Me and Han went into town today and met up with Ems, Ryan, Matty, and Caroline down in Pizza Hut. Why Ryan had to come as well is anyone's guess 'cos all he did all afternoon was fiddle about on his phone, taking photos of Ems and the pizza he was eating (but not at the same time) and then putting them on Twitter, or Facebook or something. Twat.

He told me and Matty that that Ben twit I went out with last year had just broken up with some girl called Amber who he'd been seeing since Christmas. I don't know why he bothered telling us that; well, okay, he told Matty 'cos she was gutted when they broke up, but me? Couldn't care a toss.

I noticed that Han was squishing her polystyrene Coke cup up into a tight ball when he was telling us this, and the look on her face was making me so hideously turned on, it was all I could do to swallow my garlic dough balls without choking.

Love that girl! Love it that she hates it when Ben's name's mentioned too, 'cos it makes me feel all protected and loved, even if the look on her face scares me/turns me on at the same time.

Sunday 3 February

Great Aunt May came over for her lunch today. I texted Han to see if she wanted to come over too but she was busy.

Shame. I kinda figured everyone would be too busy downstairs to see me and Han slip up to my room after dessert. Yes, I was still thinking about *that look* on her face from yesterday and thought if I didn't get it out of my system, I'd pop.

Instead I had to make do with taking Barbara out for a long walk in the woods then cleaning Uncle Buck's cage out, and I have to admit the sight of all his droppings made me forget about Han for a bit. I'd still have much preferred a duvet afternoon with Han, but I s'pose you can't have everything all your own way all the time, can you?!

Monday 4 February

Alice has got a kitten! Ems told me today during our English lesson. I felt happy for Alice, but at the same time really sad when Ems told me, 'cos I couldn't help but think that, if it'd been this time last year, Alice would have told me that herself. But she didn't. Apparently she got it last weekend, so she's had a whole week to mention it…

I'm pleased for her, though. Perhaps this means her parents are mellowing, 'cos from what I know about them, they wouldn't even let her have a goldfish before.

Texted Alice before I went to sleep tonight and said I'd heard she got a kitten and asked what its name is, but she hasn't replied yet.

Tuesday 5 February

I want to do it, I've decided. I want to tell Mum and Dad about me and

Han. They're always telling me it's better to be honest about stuff, and that I can tell them anything, aren't they?

Somehow I don't think me telling them that I'm gay and that for the last year I've been shagging the hawt Goth—sorry, EMO—who sometimes comes to our house for Sunday lunch was quite what they had in mind, though.

But I WILL do it. This weekend.

Or maybe the weekend after.

Wednesday 6 February

Or really, I don't have to tell them at all, do I? I mean, it's my business who I go out with, isn't it? Did HRBH tell them when she was seeing Ade last year, or then when she started going out with Drummer Joe after Ade dumped her? No.

Come to think of it, I never told them I was seeing Ben (yuk, yuk, yuk!) when I dated him for, oooooh, all of six weeks last year. So why should I have to tell them I'm seeing Han?

Apart from the fact that the guilt of lying to them when I come home from Han's having *done it* with her sometimes seems to eat me alive, that is.

Thursday 7 February

Suddenly realised that it's Valentine's Day next week! More importantly, IT'S MY FIRST VALENTINE'S WITH HAN!!! So I gotta make it special, which means I gotta buy her something awesome.

Looked in my wallet and saw all I had was a tatty, scrumpled-up £5 note, a used bus ticket (when was the last time I took a bus anywhere?!), and a squashed tampon. Upended the old coffee jar that I sometimes put pennies in, spread them all out on my bedroom floor, and counted them all out. I have £1.89 in pennies plus the fiver.

Hmm. Still, I have a week yet, don't I?

#optimism

Friday 8 February

I subtly reminded Han today that it's Valentine's Day next week. Well, it doesn't hurt just to give her a gentle nudge, does it? And give her time to save up.

Saturday 9 February

I found myself alone with Mum this morning 'cos Dad had gone off to get something done to his car, and HRBH had stayed the night at Joe's last night. Once Dad had left the house, I realised it would be the perfect time to speak to Mum about stuff and I kinda thought it might be an idea if I started by talking about Han, and see where the conversation led, rather than me just blurting out that I was gay.

What a disaster! I got so nervous that my voice started wobbling all over the place and all I could manage was to croak out that Han was my BFF and I thought she was awesome. Mum looked at me like I'd gone mad and just said that she thought Han was 'a nice girl too, but sometimes I wish she'd get her hair cut and wear less black because it frightens Chairman Meow'.

How could I follow that? How could I tell her that Han was my girlfriend when all my mother is worried about is how much she scares the bloody cat? I tried talking to her again, muttering about how Han was important to me, but then Dad came back grumbling about how much it had cost to get his car fixed and about how he was never going back to 'that rob-dog bastard Alfie' and then the moment was lost as Mum went off to make him a calming cup of tea.

And they wonder why some kids leave home!

Sunday 10 February

Have decided to delay telling Mum about stuff for now.

So I'm chickenshit. Bite me.

Monday 11 February

First day of half-term today, so I did what every other teenager does on the first day of half-term and stayed in bed until 2 p.m., then went into town 'cos Mum started going on to me about 'wasting my life away in bed'.

Bought Han's Valentine's card while I was in town, but struggled to find a present for her that wasn't:

a.) Going to make her puke 'cos it was so twee,
b.) Expensive.

I plumped for this soft toy bear thing that was holding a heart in one paw and a red balloon in the other. The bear was wearing a black leather jacket with chains on it, so I figured Han wouldn't find it too naff. I hope she likes it!

Tuesday 12 February

Realised with a jolt and a pang of guilt today that I haven't spoken to Alice since, like, forever, and that she didn't ever text me back about her kitten, so I got brave and rang her up and asked her if she wanted to come over. She was a bit quiet with me on the phone, which means she's still pissed off with me, but I persevered and invited her over for lunch. I know things haven't been the same between us since all that shit last year when she randomly declared her love for me, but I've tried to get things back to how they used to be, I really have!

Aaaaand I know she probably hates me, but I don't hate her, and I really do want to try and get things back to how they used to be, and so I figured I could start by inviting her over for lunch. Besides, Han had gone shopping with her mum, so I was at a loose end anyway.

She did actually agree, which surprised me, and I have to say, it was really good to see her again. She seemed a bit distracted, though, so she was no doubt wishing she was anywhere other than with me, which probably means she still hasn't forgiven me, but I've got a thick skin so I just blathered on about nothing in particular as usual and tried to forget the fact that at times it was a bit like talking to a brick wall.

Mum asked me later if I'd had a nice day with Alice, so I told her how quiet she'd been. Mum put on one of her special teacher faces and said that Alice was probably busy thinking about her exams, adding for good measure that 'It wouldn't do any harm for you to be doing the same, rather than wasting your thoughts on whatever colour you're going to dye your hair next.'

My mother would make a useless counsellor.

Wednesday 13 February

I told Han today that I'd been thinking about coming out to Mum, and she actually didn't look as horrified as I thought she would. She told me she'd been thinking about telling her parents for a while too 'cos she was sick of living a lie and that she wanted to be 'allowed to be who she was 100 percent'.

It's okay for Han. Her parents are cool, unlike mine. Her dad teaches religion, so he sees the good in, like, EVERYONE, and her mum's a nurse, so she's been there, seen it and bought the bloody T-shirt. It'll be easier for her to tell them than it will be for me to tell an uptight accountant and an English teacher whose sole aim in life seems to be pacifying the uptight accountant and bugging the hell out of me over my exams.

Life's so unfair sometimes.

Thursday 14 February

Today was Valentine's Day!! How cool is it that it falls during half-term, too??! I texted Han first thing and wished her Happy Valentine's and all that, and told her that I loved her and added, like, a thousand kisses afterwards. I lay back in bed waiting for her to text me back, but it didn't arrive until kinda mid-morning, by which time I'd got up, showered, and eaten my Corn Flakes. Never mind.

Anyway, I asked her if she wanted to come over but she said she couldn't get over until the afternoon 'cos she had some homework to do (WTF? Is she crazy?!) but that she'd be over then and 'spoil me rotten', which kinda made up for it.

She'd bought me, like, this totally amazing card with holographic red hearts all over it and had written stuff inside about how special I am (yup!) and about how much she loves me and some other stuff about how brilliant it was 'cos it was our first Valentine's together. She'd also bought me this framed picture of a wolf coming out of a wood, which was all in black and white except for the wolf's mouth, which was blood red. I thought it was WELL romantic, and kinda knocked my teddy bear clutching a heart and a balloon right into touch!

Mum and Dad had gone out for a meal tonight (oh, pur-leeeease! At their age?) so me and Han ordered ourselves a pizza and ate it up in my room 'cos HRBH was having a candlelit dinner with Joe downstairs and told me if 'I so much as stepped one foot into the lounge after 8 p.m. it wouldn't just be my pizza that had a stuffed crust'.

Sometimes I loathe my sister with a passion.

Anyway, me and Han had a totally awesome Valentine's which ended with me locking my door and showing her how totally awesome I thought she was too. I figured HRBH would pretty much be doing the same downstairs (no doubt on our bloody sofa) so, well, why the hell not, hey?

Friday 15 February

We had some new neighbours move in across the road today! Mr. and Mrs. Morris that lived at number 26 for, like, well, forever, have finally moved out and gone down to live near the coast or something, so a new family has moved in.

I stood with Mum and watched all their furniture being offloaded from this huge removals lorry and it all looked pretty decent stuff, so I think they'll be okay. Then this man and woman arrived in a car with two teenage boys and went into the house; the man and woman were arguing about something, so I guessed they were the new owners.

Mum spotted one of the teenage boys, who looked about the same age as me, and made some comment about it being nice for me 'having a boy my age just across the road' and kinda looked at me funny, at which point I turned and walked away from the window, not knowing how to answer her. And not wanting to, either.

Saturday 16 February

I was writing up Friday's stuff in my diary today about the neighbours when Han came round. She saw me writing in it and said she thought it was weird that people still wrote diaries, and asked me why I didn't just blog everything or stick it on Facebook, like everyone else does. She said, 'It's, like, soooo old fashioned, don't you think? Just get your laptop out, Clem, and write a blog. Much quicker.'

She doesn't understand. To me, there's nothing like writing my thoughts down on paper. I said, 'Besides, if I blogged it then I wouldn't be able to read it in, like, 20 years' time when I'm old and want to be all sentimental and remember how I felt when I was a teenager.'

I looked at her, kinda piously, I must admit, and said that diaries were forever. Laptops crashed, blogs got deleted, Facebook sometimes went tits up. Diaries never did. Diaries just got stuffed under beds or in wardrobes and then pulled out and read lovingly over and over again. I told her I could read the words I'd written in there and look at silly doodles I'd put alongside them and remember how I was feeling at the time when I wrote them. It was all dead profound shit and it shut her RIGHT up.

So I carried on writing in it while she fiddled with her phone, but I saw her looking at me while I was writing. She looked, I dunno, kinda irritated, and then finally she said she thought I was a kind of anachronism because sometimes it seemed like I was born in the wrong era. I took exception to that. Number one, I wasn't born in the wrong era, or else I wouldn't favour wearing T-shirts with *Smack My Bitch Up* on them, would I? Would I have got away with that in Victorian England? I think not. Number two, I am not an anachronism. Okay, so I like T-shirts with *Smack My Bitch Up* written on them, but that doesn't mean I'm an anachronism, for God's sake. I haven't got an anarchic bone in my body! The worst thing I've ever done is spray 'Up the Workers' on the underpass into town with Caroline when we were both 14 and she was going through her Libertarian phase.

Even then I couldn't sleep for a week afterwards, worrying that the council would come knocking on my door with a bucket of soapy water and a scrubbing brush—hardly the work of an anarchist, is it?

Sunday 17 February

Thought about dying my hair blue today. I don't know why. I just woke up thinking how cool it would be to have blue hair. But then I thought about Han calling me an anachronist and figured I didn't need to give her another reason to have a go at me.

Monday 18 February

I was late for school today. I forgot to set my alarm so I slept in until 8.30 a.m. and registration starts at 8.45 a.m. Of course, everyone else had got up and left the house by the time I stumbled down the stairs, bleary-eyed at 8.31 a.m. Even Mum. This would be the same Mum that's a teacher and is always banging on to me about how important my education is, and yet didn't think to wake me when she must have heard that I hadn't got up by the time she left the house at 8. If I fail my exams I'm blaming my mother for abandoning her duties to me as her daughter.

Anyway, I finally fell in through the school gates at 9.15 a.m. and got a right bollocking from Mrs. Schofield and NO sympathy from anyone when I grumbled about it at lunchtime.

Tsh.

Tuesday 19 February

Pissed off with Han today 'cos she was late meeting me AGAIN. When she finally caught up with me, all she would say was that she stayed behind to help Miss Smith clear away the oils. I just smiled and nodded, hoping she'd detect that I was pissed off, but nooooooo. She just carried on gabbling away about how much she was enjoying Art and how pleased she was that Miss Smith was her teacher 'cos she understands her as much as, if not more than, Mrs. Greene used to and she 'allows me to express my feelings and inner turmoil in my drawings'. I said I didn't know she had any inner turmoil, at which point she flashed me a look of irritation and said, 'I'm an EMO, I'm constantly struggling internally,' which made me wonder briefly if she meant her bowels were giving her gip 'cos her dad's got a spastic colon and is always struggling with it. But before I could say anything to her she said, 'Miss Smith understands tortured souls like me. She says she walks on the dark side of life sometimes too and it's only art that keeps her alive.'

I still didn't really have a clue what she was talking about but then that's nothing new—I've never really understood all this EMO stuff she goes on about. I just nod and smile and hope that I'm making a good show of at least *pretending* to know what the bugger she's on about.

Wednesday 20 February

Ugh! I heard today that Ben is now going out with Marcie's mate Sophie. That would be the same Ben that just dumped some girl called Amber, like, two weeks ago, and the same Ben that I stupidly wasted six weeks of my life on last year before I came to my senses and booted him into touch. Even now I can't walk past McDonald's without shuddering and remembering how he once tried to kiss me with lettuce on his shoes.

Thursday 21 February

Miss Smith has put a notice out asking for help with the school's production of *Grease* later in the year. Of course, I jumped at the chance, despite the fact I should be concentrating on my exams. She only wants people to help with moving the scenery and stuff during rehearsals and on the actual night, so that can't take up too much of my time, right? Anyway, any chance to see Miss Smith outside of school's gotta be a bonus, plus it means I can keep an eye on Han at the same time.

I didn't think Han looked too pleased when I told her what I was doing. She just said, 'Miss Smith's already asked me to help her, so she'll probably have enough people by now.' I noticed that Han went red when she mentioned Miss Smith's name. That was weird.

Anyway, I kinda said, 'It'll be cool, won't it, if we both do it?' but she didn't answer. Instead, she just looked at me kinda strangely, like she was pissed off with me, and I figured that was the second time in a week that she's looked like that, so I wouldn't push it for now.

Perhaps I'll mention it again in a few days.

Friday 22 February

We were talking at lunchtime today about Ben. Well, I say WE were talking, what I mean is Marcie and Caroline were telling me about how Sophie thinks she's nabbed the town's stud just 'cos he asked her out. Yeah, like I give a rat's!

I can't believe some of my friends still think I was an idiot to stop seeing Ben! FFS! It's been over a year but Marcie and Caroline still talk about him as being 'the one I allowed to get away'. The fact that they all still think I'm straight does my head in. They're so stupid! Sometimes I just want to jump up and shout, 'I wanted him to get away! I wanted him to dump me 'cos I never fancied him, and I never fancied him 'cos I fancy girls, you blind dumbasses!'

I didn't say anything, of course. Instead I watched Han carefully when they were talking about him, but she was staring off into space, deep in thought, and, unlike when we were in Pizza Hut and they were talking about Ben, this time she really didn't look like she gave a shit.

That made my stomach feel like I'd swallowed a rock.

Saturday 23 February

Met up with Han in town today. She bought me a cappuccino in

Starbucks AND a panini AND a muffin, and I felt a bit stupid for feeling so insecure yesterday.

Sunday 24 February

Han came over for lunch today. Great Aunt May was already at ours when Han turned up, and was sitting in her favourite chair by the window, talking to Mum about some bloke at Autumn Leaves who'd driven his mobility scooter too fast down the corridors of the home and had left tyre marks on the carpet.

Of course, Great Aunt May thinks Han's great ever since they had an in-depth conversation about flannelette sheets once and, unlike a lot of older ladies, she doesn't shrink into the corner when Han comes in dressed up like the living dead. When Han came in the room today, Great Aunt May's face lit up, like she was her own great niece, and Han went straight over to her, a huge smile on her face. I felt my heart bunch up in a lump just to see it, 'cos I love it when Han's like that with her, 'cos I know how much Great Aunt May thinks of her, and Han's just lovely with her.

But then, Han's just lovely, full stop.

Monday 25 February

Decided not to bother responding to Miss Smith's request for help on *Grease* 'cos Han's made it pretty clear she doesn't want me hanging around all the time, and I don't wanna do anything to piss her off, and me suggesting I'd do it seemed to majorly piss her off!

The new neighbours are weird, I've decided. I saw one of the teenage boys that lives there watching me from his front window when I came home from school today (the older one that me and Mum spotted that first day). He was wearing a hoodie with the hood up, which would have looked cool if he didn't look so gormless. I swear his knuckles drag along the floor behind him when he walks.

I'll be steering WELL clear of him, lemme tell you!

Tuesday 26 February

Got fed up of waiting for Han after school so went down to the Art studio to find her. When I got there, Han was sitting at her easel with Miss Smith leaning over her. Miss Smith was wearing a blouse which I thought was way too low-cut for a teacher, so much so that when she leaned even further forward, I swear I could see so far down that I could see what she'd had for her lunch. They didn't bat an eyelid when they saw me, Han just smiled warily at me while Miss Smith stood sharply up, evidently embarrassed that I could see practically down to her socks. Han just said, 'Am I late again? I'm sorry, Clem! Miss Smith was just showing me how I could improve my strokes to get a better result.'

I bet she fucking was!!!

Anyway, I stood there looking like a lemon while Miss Smith finished showing Han something about shading before they deigned to finally finish at which point Han sprang up from her chair, said 'C'mon then, you' to me and wandered past me, casually touching my hand as she went. I shot Smith a look that said 'She's my girlfriend, right?' but she had her back turned to us and was busy tidying things away, so she didn't see.

She turned when she heard us leaving and smiled at us both, saying 'Bye ladies. Have a good evening.' Why would she say that? What did she mean by it?? Was it her way of letting me know she thought me and Han would have an argument over her on the way home? Maybe she gets off on stuff like that. As irritated as I was, I still thought that I'd happily pay money to see Miss Smith getting off, though. Ahem.

Me and Han didn't have an argument, as it was, 'cos I decided not to say anything to her about how pissed off I was 'cos I knew it WOULD descend into a fight. So despite me being annoyed with her, and worried that something might be going on with her and Miss Smith, I decided the safest thing was to stay shtum.

Wednesday 27 February

Was thinking about Han and Miss Smith last night when I got into bed and I couldn't sleep for worrying about it all. I dunno if I'm worrying unnecessarily, but I can't help thinking Han's got the hots for Smith, 'cos she's always hanging around her and she talks about her, like, ALL the time. Okay, so I know I think Smith's hot, but I don't think I'd go so far as to say I actually fancy her. Just seems to me that Han's with her every opportunity she gets, and she gets ratty with me when I talk to her about Smith.

Something's not right, and it's starting to niggle at me.

Thursday 28 February

Had a well-cute day with Han at school today. We were walking down the corridor to our English class and there was, like, a group of people either side of us and 'cos we were hidden in amongst all these people, Han took my hand and it was just TOTALLY, AWESOMELY, BEAUTIFUL!

Okay, so she dropped my hand like a hot stone when we went into the classroom, but for those ten seconds when we were holding hands I felt like a million dollars and I wanted to tell all these girls around us that she, Hannah Harrison, was my girlfriend and that that was what girlfriends did, regardless of whether they were in school or not.

Friday 29 February

Had an argument with Han today over, yup, you guessed it—Miss Smith. Am so fed up with all this sniping and bickering. Can't even remember how it started now, but I'm sure Han'll say it was all my fault as usual.

Aaaaaaaaaaaaaaaaaaaaaaaaaaaaaaaaarghhhhhhhhhhhhhhhhh!

Why does this happen? Why do I have, like, the best time ever with Han one day, and then the next we're fighting again? Why does it always have to be so up and down? Why can't it be nice all the time? Like it used to be? So stressed right now!

Saturday 1 March

Maybe I need to talk to Han about it? Ask her outright, like. Does she fancy Smith? Is that why she's being so off with me all the time? Does she want Smith and not me any more?

Sunday 2 March

I don't want to ask Han outright, I've decided. There are three reasons for this. One, I don't want it to kick off yet another argument, two, I don't want to know the answer in case it's not what I want to hear, and three…

Okay, there's no three. But number two is a big enough reason for me to keep quiet about it all for the time being.

Monday 3 March

OMG!!! Caroline commented today on how much time Han's spending in the Art studio these days. She said to me, 'It's almost as if Han *likes*

Miss Smith, you know what I mean?' and she gave me a knowing look. I said, 'No, what do you mean?' and she said, 'Y'know, l-i-k-e. Like she's crushing on her. Why else would she spend all her time down there? She never bothered with Art too much when she had old Mrs. Greene, so it's gotta be Miss Smith's influence, don't you think?' I didn't know what to say, so I just shrugged, then she said, 'So do you think Han's gay, then, or what?' and I felt my hands go clammy. I said, 'Would it bother you if she was?' and Caroline laughed and said, 'Nah, course not! I don't give a flying whatnot what people are! S'up to them, isn't it? My Uncle Dave's gay so, like, my whole family's so cool with the whole gay thing,' and I felt my heart beating so fast I could feel it banging away in my neck. I was just about to tell her about me and Han when Ems and Matty came over and joined us and started telling us some funny story about how Mr. Troutt got his hand stuck up a Jane Austen corset which he said he was 'just putting away' during Drama class so I shut up.

I think I want to tell Caroline about things, but I don't want anyone else to know—not just yet anyway.

It was Dad's birthday today. He's 44. He looks it.

Tuesday 4 March

OMG I CAME OUT TO CAROLINE TODAY!!! I couldn't sleep last night for worrying about telling Caroline stuff but I want to tell someone about some of the shit I'm going through at the moment, so I decided to bite the bullet today and when I found myself alone with her up in the library during study break, I decided to talk to her about it. My hands went dead clammy again but I thought if I didn't do it then, I never would, so, looking around the library to make sure there was no one within earshot, I leant over to her and whispered, 'Caro, you know when we were talking yesterday about Han and Miss Smith?'

Caroline stopped writing and looked at me excitedly, probably expecting me to tell her that the pair of them were at it like rabbits or something.

Instead I just said, 'And you asked me if Han's gay?' Caroline raised her eyebrows and said 'ye-eeeeees?' very slowly, positively hanging on my every word. I said, 'Well, she is,' and smiled weakly at her.

Caroline puffed out her cheeks and leaned conspiratorially towards me, like I was telling her government secrets or something. She said, 'How'd you know that?' and I just took a deep breath and said, ''Cos I'm going out with her,' and smiled even more weakly. She said, 'Oh,' and I could see a little hamster wheel of *figuring-it-out* turning away in her head. She said, 'Oh,' again then, 'O…M…and G! So you and Han…??' and made big eyes, then said, 'And you're, y'know…?' and grinned at me. I grinned back and said, 'Yeah. Gay. As a hat. Gay as a hat,' and Caroline squealed, making it echo embarrassingly round the library, earning a stern look from Miss Bletchley-Smythe, the librarian (who looks like she'd give her own grandma a bollocking over an overdue book). Caroline said, 'So how long? And why the hell didn't I know anything about this? Do the others know?'

I said, 'Nearly a year and 'cos we wanted to keep it quiet and no, no one else knows.' I figured it was going to be tooooooo complicated to tell her that Alice knows as well, and that she only knows 'cos she came on to me in France last year. I figured one revelation at a time would be all that Caroline could probably cope with!

So she said, 'Awww, that's too cute!' So I said to her, 'So do you feel different about me now you know?' and she just said, 'Course not, silly! You're still the same short, daft, scruffy Clem that we all know and love,' and I wasn't sure if it was a compliment or not. I asked her not to tell anyone else and she squealed a bit again, pleased as punch that she was the only one who knew (or so she thought) and I specifically asked her not to tell Han that I'd told her either 'cos I figured that would be yet another thing that would piss her off.

I did, however, text Alice 'cos I needed to tell someone else, and Alice is the only other person I know I can tell right now. Yeah, I felt kinda guilty for telling Alice and not Han, but I just didn't know how Han would take me telling our friend that we were seeing each other, and I didn't want to risk it.

Anyway, I said to Alice that I'd told Caroline about me and Han (not about me and her!!) 'cos I was so stoked that I'd actually had the guts to do it in the first place. It feels like a huge step and I'm not only happy to have done it, I'm happy and relieved that Caroline didn't say it was disgusting and flounce out of the library, or something embarrassing like that. The fact she was totally chilled about the whole thing was awesome, 'cos I guess it could have gone either way. Thank goodness it went the way I hoped it would!

Alice sent me a text back that said, 'Congratulations! I think you're very brave,' and it was all I could do not to spend the rest of the day walking about with a massive grin on my face.

Wednesday 5 March

A strange thought struck me today as I was walking to school. It's, like, I just came out to Caroline, and I kinda thought I'd feel, I dunno, unburdened somehow, but I don't. I just figured that for every person I tell, there are gonna be dozens of others that still don't know, and now it feels like I'm gonna be spending my whole bloody life coming out to people.

Maybe it'd just be easier if I got a T-shirt printed or something!

Thursday 6 March

Had a bit of a panic attack in the night stressing about too much stuff. I was thinking about coming out to Caroline and how weird it had been, but how brilliant at the same time, and then I felt bad that I've told Caroline before I've told Mum and Dad, and so then the thought struck me that at some point I AM GOING TO HAVE TO TELL THEM, despite freaking out every time I so much as even think about it.

Then, as if I wasn't stressed enough about that, my brain started wandering over to Han and I realised, with a jolt (at, like 3 this morning) that me and Han haven't kissed in ages. We're always kissing! Any spare moment we've got, we're locking lips! But not lately. I wonder if that's our problem? That we just need to have a damn good session and everything will be better?

Finally got to sleep around 4 a.m. So much pressure, so young. Life's gotta get easier as I get older, hasn't it??

Friday 7 March

What a crap day. Had another tiff with Han at school today. She'd been in the Art studio, like, all morning 'cos she had some study time, so I went down there at lunchtime to find her, 'cos she hadn't bothered to come and find me, and she was, as usual, chatting away to Smith whilst the pair of them tidied away pens and stuff. I was standing in the doorway with my arms folded and a pissy look on my face and I suddenly felt like some housewife waiting for her husband to come home from the pub.

Han saw me and called over, 'Won't have time to see you, Clem, 'cos I got things to do here. See you later maybe?' and I just screwed up my face at her and stalked off. I texted her straight away and told her I was pissed off at being mucked around by her and that if she wanted Smith, she was 'welcome to her'. She texted me back after lunch and told me to 'grow up' which REALLY pissed me off, so I texted her back and told her she was the one that should grow up and stop fawning over Smith 'cos it was getting embarrassing to watch.

I was walking down the corridor later in the afternoon and she caught up with me, grabbed me by the arm and hissed, 'Don't fucking tell me what I can or can't do, all right?' She's, like, NEVER sworn at me before, so I was really shocked. All I could say back to her was, 'I'm supposed to be your girlfriend, Han, but it sure as hell doesn't feel like it at the moment,' and all she could say to that was, 'I can't talk to you when you're like this,' so I said 'Fine! Go! Go find Smith and talk to her then,' and she just snapped 'You know what? I will. At least Miss Smith understands me!'

That REALLY hurt, so I snapped back at her, 'Do what you want, I don't care any more,' and Han said, 'Get out of my face, will you? You're doing my head in, Clem,' and walked off away from me (towards the Art studio, I might add), leaving me standing there in the corridor feeling like a right prick.

We didn't see each other for the rest of the day 'cos I was so pissed off at her that I didn't bother waiting for her to walk home after school. I didn't want to text her tonight either 'cos I was worried that we'd just end up having another text argument and I can't handle it.

I don't know what to do.

Saturday 8 March

<u>SHITTIEST DAY EVER</u>

Han texted me first thing and asked if she could come over. The tone of her text was, I dunno, hard—like it didn't really sound like her at all. She came over and wouldn't look me in the eye when I answered the door to her, just smiled tightly at me and looked at her feet. We went up to my room and sat on my bed, not really speaking until suddenly she said, 'I can't do this any more, Clem.' I said, 'Do what?' and she said, 'This. Us.'

I felt like I was about to throw up, so I just said, 'Oh.'

Han was wringing her hands round and round, then she just said, 'All this bickering, all these petty fights. I'm sick of it all,' so I said, 'Sick of me?' and she said, 'I dunno…just sick of all this. Things aren't like they used to be, Clemmie. All we do is fight. Fight, make up, fight, make up. Relationships are supposed to be fun, but it's not much fun at the moment, is it?'

I had to agree with her. It's not much fun at the moment, but I'm sure that's only 'cos of all the dumb petty arguments we've been having—which have only started since Miss Smith arrived at the school. We were fine before she arrived—but I figured telling Han that would make me look stupid, so I kept shtum about her. I think we're also stressed 'cos we've got exams coming up as well. We're stressed out and busy, and that makes us bicker with each other as well. But that'll pass, won't it?

Then she hit me with it. She said, 'I think we need some breathing space, Clem. Time to think.' So I said, 'Think about what?' and she said, 'Stuff.'

Stuff? What's stuff supposed to mean anyway? I said, 'We're just up to our eyeballs in studying, thassall. We don't have time to see each other like we used to, but once the exams are over we'll have all the time in the world for one another.' I thought that would hit the right note, but instead of saying what I wanted her to say, she said, 'But it's all the other stuff too. All the jealousies and sniping and things. I hate it. I don't want to do it any more, Clem.'

I was determined not to cry, but I got that horrible feeling when your throat tightens up and it's difficult to speak, so I didn't say anything. Truth was, I didn't know what to say anyway. Instead, I just sat there like some dumbass and let Han get up from my bed and walk out of my room, out of my house, and out of my life, it would seem.

How the fuck did that just happen? Is that it? Are me and Han over? I don't know ~~what I can do~~ ~~if I can handle~~ it ~~if I can~~…

Okay, now I'm crying just writing this, so will stop for today.

Sunday 9 March

Sent Han a text telling her we had to talk about stuff, but she just replied saying she'd said everything she'd wanted to say yesterday.

Great. So she can't even be bothered to hear my side of things? She won't even let me have my say? She's happy to throw away nearly a year together without even so much as a fight??

Spent the day in bed because, to be honest, what's the point of getting up? My parents barely noticed. Great.

Monday 10 March

Scratch that. What's the point of living???

Tuesday 11 March

Saw Han in the corridor at school today. She, like, TOTALLY ignored me.

Felt like shit. Can someone please tell me how to get over a broken heart 'cos I'd sure as hell love to know?

Wednesday 12 March

Told Caroline that me and Han were finished today. She put on her sympathetic face and told me it would be a 'flash in the pan' 'cos me and Han were strong.

Then she asked me if Han had contacted me since the weekend and I told her 'No, just one text on Sunday morning.'

Caroline just pulled a face and said something like, 'Oh dear. That's not so good, is it?' which didn't exactly fill me with confidence.

I tried to avoid everyone else at school as much as I could, but Ems caught up with me just before we went in to our English lesson and asked me if I was okay 'cos I didn't 'seem right'. There's nothing right about me right now! I feel like crap, I look like crap 'cos I've been crying so much, and the last thing I want to do is come to school, but I know I've got to or people will start asking questions.

I just made up some story about having period pain so she put a sympathetic look on her face and gave me two ibuprofen from her bag. Somehow I think it's going to take more than two bloody pills to numb this pain…

Thursday 13 March

I'm trying to act normally in front of my parents 'cos I don't want to make them suspicious, but how can I be my usual self when I can't eat, I can't sleep, and all I want to do is hide away in my bedroom so I can be alone?

I had a thought today that it's at times like this I really miss Alice. I just know that if things had been okay with us, she would have been the first person I'd have told, and she would have been there for me. Instead, Caroline was the first person, but that would never have been the case a year ago.

But how can I tell Alice? How can I?! It'd be like, I dunno, rubbing a puppy's nose in its own wee. Or something.

It's been five days since Han dumped me. Five days, eight hours and thirty-three minutes, and she's only bothered to contact me once. Is she that heartless? Why hasn't she been in touch??

12.20 a.m.

Oh God, what if she's got with Smith? I'd never even considered that!! Maybe that's why she's not bothered to see if I'm okay, 'cos she's been too busy…

2 a.m.

Need to stop these thoughts 'cos there's every possibility I'll go right round the twist if I don't.

4.30 a.m.

FML.

Friday 14 March

Why does no one ever mention that when you break up with a girl (or guy, I s'pose) you not only lose your love, you also lose your best friend?

I saw something in my *Kerrang!* Magazine tonight and my first thought was to text Han and tell her about it. It was something to do with Mastodon and I knew she'd want to know about it 'cos she really likes them. But I couldn't tell her 'cos she's not my girlfriend any more, and that's crap.

We shared everything—silliness, music, clothes, laughter, kisses, and now it's all been pissed away in the wind 'cos Han says she doesn't want to share all those things with me any more, and I'm having real trouble getting my head around it all…

Mum came up to my room this evening 'cos I barely ate anything for dinner again (how can I when even the smell of food makes me feel like I'm going to throw up??) and asked me if I was okay. I told her I was stressing about my exams, but I don't think she was convinced, 'cos she said if there was anything worrying me and I wanted to talk to her about it, I only had to say. She said that was what mums were for, and she'd like to think I could tell her anything.

If only she knew!

I began to think that perhaps it might have been the ideal time to start telling Mum some stuff, but just as I'd formed the first sentence of what I was going to say to her in my head, HRBH bellowed up the stairs asking her if she'd drive her over to Joe's house. Mum left my room again, saying she'd be back in a while, and that we'd have a proper chat then. But by the time she came back (like, an hour later!), I'd decided I didn't want to talk to her and had gone to bed.

Feel so alone right now.

Saturday 15 March

Oh shit oh shit oh shit, what a weird day!

I couldn't sleep last night so I rang Alice in tears in the middle of the night and told her Han had dumped me. She talked to me for two hours, telling me that everything was going to be all right, that couples always have arguments and breakups and always get back together again, so me and Han wouldn't be any different because we loved each other. That's when I told her that I didn't think Han loved me any more, but Alice didn't say anything then that could reassure me. She just told me to come over to her house in the afternoon and I could cry on her shoulder. Just before she rang off she said to me, 'Y'know, Clem, I'll always be here for you. Whatever happens, I'll always be here for you. You know that, don't you?'

I could feel myself welling up again so I just mumbled something at her down the phone and snapped my phone shut.

Thought about texting Han this morning but didn't know what to say to her. I could hardly say, 'Hey! So are we still finished or have you changed your mind?' Besides, I thought if she'd had time to think about stuff and had a change of heart, she'd ring me, wouldn't she? Thought it best to 'let sleeping dogs lie', as Great Aunt May is fond of saying, so took Alice up on her offer of a shoulder to cry on and went over to her house after lunch. Caroline rang me on my way over there and told me she'd spoken to Han last night and had told her she knew about us. I asked her if Han had been pissed off, but she said she'd been fine about Caroline knowing everything; she said she'd told her it had been a relief for someone else to know.

Know what? There's nothing to know about now, is there??

Anyway, I spent the afternoon at Alice's pouring my heart out to her, rather than having to face 'having that chat' with Mum. Alice was very patient and listened to everything I said, butting in occasionally with some kind words, but in the end I felt like I was just going round in circles, saying the same things over and over again. Whatever I said, it wasn't going to bring Han back. Then Caroline texted me and said she'd texted Han and asked her why she'd finished with me and apparently Han had texted her back telling her that we'd 'just fizzled out and drifted apart' and that 'these things happen'.

WTF?!

I couldn't believe she could be so heartless! How could she say we'd 'drifted apart' when just, like, three months ago, on New Year's Eve, we'd stood together looking at the moon and she'd told me how much she loved me? That was just three fucking months ago! The whole reason we've been arguing lately is because of Smith! Not any drifting apart, certainly not on my part anyway. Han might have drifted in Smith's direction, but I've never drifted anywhere.

It's all Smith's fault. Bitch.

And what about 'these things happen'? How can she be so chilled about it? Maybe I didn't mean as much to her as I thought I did, if she can shake off us breaking up so casually.

Of course, I told all this to Alice, who just said, 'You know whose help you need? Jack's,' and went off downstairs before returning with a bottle of something which looked like old man's piss but which was in fact Jack Daniel's and which Alice said would 'help me get over Han'.

I've never been a great drinker, not since the incident with the cherry wine and the hula hoop at my cousin Raymond's wedding when I was 13, but to be honest, I didn't care what I did, as long as whatever I took or did numbed some of the pain that was making my heart feel like it was being scooped out with a spoon. Acting like some kinda wino, I grabbed the bottle from her and took a great swig of Jack Daniel's, felt the first gulp plop into my empty stomach like a stone into an empty well, then felt it warming my insides and began to feel better, even though it tasted a bit like cough medicine. I took another swig before Alice hastily took the bottle off me. She had a slug of it herself, then put it on the floor, well away from me.

I felt much better and began to think a bit more rationally, but as soon as Alice went out of her room and downstairs to fetch us a sandwich 'to soak up the whiskey', I began to start thinking again, and before I knew it I'd picked up the bottle and was taking walloping great gulps from it, loving the feeling of warmth and security it gave me, if not altogether loving the fact it was beginning to make my ears sing and make my tongue feel like it was wagging at both ends. By the time Alice returned with our sandwiches, I couldn't feel my feet and was having trouble focusing on my hands, no matter how hard I stared at them. Alice took one look at me, muttered something like, 'Oh for God's sake,' but all I can remember is sitting on the edge of her bed grinning at her and trying to kick my socks off so they'd land on her head.

Panicking slightly, in case her parents came home, she sat me up in her bed and listened to me ramble on about Han and how much I loved her, before then rambling on about how she (Alice, not Han) was my best friend and how she'd always been there for me and how good she was to me and how lucky I was to have her and stuff like that.

She was sitting next to me while I was saying all this (probably hoping I wasn't about to throw up on her rug) and before I knew what I was doing, I'd reached over to her and started kissing her. Now, I know I was wasted, but I still had enough faculties about me to stick my tongue in her mouth, so I s'pose I must have meant to kiss her. She pulled away from me and said, 'You're pissed, Clem,' and I said something like 'And you're cute but I'll be sober in the morning,' before thinking that I hadn't quite got that right, but what the heck anyway, and kissed her again. This time she kissed me back and made this funny little moaning noise that Han does.

Did.

Bugger.

Anyway, in the fog of my drunkenness I remember seeing Alice get up and lock her door before clambering into the bed with me and pulling my trousers off. I was still arseholed from the Jack Daniel's but sober enough to do what two hormonally pumped up gay girls like to do (and I did it quite well, even if I do say so myself) but afterwards felt like a right cow, mainly because:

> What I'd done wasn't fair on Alice,
>
> I was thinking about Han while I did it, and,
>
> The JD had made me so tired all I wanted to do was have a snooze but figured that's what boys do when they've just had their end away.

As we lay there in her bed and the whiskey gradually began to wear off, Alice propped herself up on her elbow and said, 'I know you only did that as a knee-jerk reaction to Han, but to be honest, I don't care. I've been wanting to do that with you for ages.'

I said, 'I dinnt do it as a jee-nerk naction. I wanted to do it,' and the truth was I DID want to do it, but for the life of me I don't know why I wanted to. Maybe it was out of spite to Han, maybe it was 'cos I felt lonely and Alice was there for me, I dunno. She just smiled at me and said, 'Whatever. This doesn't put you in any kind of obligation to go out with me. You know that, don't you?'

I wasn't sure what to say, but I do know I'm not the sort of girl who strings people along (well I hope I'm not) so I just said to her, 'But I want to go out with you,' and she seemed really pleased. She hugged me and told me she'd wanted me to say that for ages but thought she'd blown her chance in France last year, and she thought that me and Han were joined at the hip. I thought we were too, but Han's made it obvious we're not, so what's the harm in seeing Alice? That's what I thought in my fog of Tennessee whiskey anyway.

Anyhow, I realised it was getting late so told her that I had to go home and that I'd text her later. All the way home, all I could feel was guilt (and queasiness—but that was the JD). So much so that by the time I got in, I thought what I'd done must have been written all over my face, so I decided to have a bath and scrub any evidence of my wrong-doing with Alice away (and help me sober up before I got an earful from dad).

Texted Alice just before I went to bed and thanked her for listening to me. After I'd sent it, I realised it sounded like I was thanking her for sleeping with me and felt dirty again. Alice texted me back and her message was littered with happy smilies and loads of xxxxx's which was a bit weird, I dunno why.

No text from Han.

Sunday 16 March

OMG what the fuck have I done?????

Alice sent me a text saying, 'I'll say it again, Clem. What happened yesterday doesn't mean you have to go out with me, you know.'

WTF?

I'm so eaten up with guilt over what I did, I never even thought any further than the fact I'd had a drunken fumble with my previous best friend! I didn't know what to say, so I just wrote her one back and said, 'Okay,' which I'm sure isn't what she wanted to hear, but what else could I say?

I sat and looked at my phone for ages, then sent her another one saying, 'But I do want to go out with you.' And maybe I do. The thing is, she'd want to go out with me now, wouldn't she? I know I might be lots of things—scatty, scruffy, naïve, stupid…but the one thing I'm not is a love-rat.

Dear God, just listen to me! A love-rat! This time last year I hadn't even kissed a girl and now I'm talking about being a love-rat.

It's official. My world has gone mad.

Monday 17 March

No word from Han for over two weeks now. Oh yeah, I see her around in school, I go to classes with her, but actually speak to her? Don't be stupid!

Matty asked me today why Han hasn't been having lunch with us lately, so I just said that she's been working on the staging for *Grease*. Truth is, I don't know where Han goes to have her lunch any more. All I do know is that she's doing everything she can to avoid me, and it's making me feel like shit.

How can she switch it off just like that? How can we be texting and ringing and seeing each other, like, ALL the time, and kissing and telling each other that we love one another, and then…not?

It's like I'm missing a limb or something at the moment.

Tuesday 18 March

I mean, how can you suddenly stop loving someone when they've been in your heart and in your mind for so long? God I wish there was a switch inside me I could flick, and all this shit would go away.

Wednesday 19 March

Saw Alice in the corridor at school today and she went to link her hand in mine but I kinda pulled my hand away at the last minute so it didn't really work. Felt dead weird seeing Alice 'cos I'd managed to avoid her in person since the weekend, even though I've been texting her. I suppose I didn't really want to face her, but I can't explain why. I feel like a fraud, maybe that's why.

Caroline told me today that she'd seen Han in the Art room at lunchtime today with Smith. Caroline said Han looked really happy and she was laughing at something Smith had said, and I couldn't help but think they were probably laughing at me. I wish Caroline hadn't said anything to me 'cos I had this big, black cloud hanging over me all day which followed me home, then hung over me all evening until I gave up trying to act normal, and gave up trying to fend off questions from Mum asking me what was the matter, and went to bed.

We finished today for Easter. Thank God. Perhaps now I can just pull the duvet over my head and stay in bed for the next two weeks, and then wake up to find everything's just been a dream.

Thursday 20 March

Alice has told Caroline that me and her are going out!!! This is despite me asking her not to tell her 'cos I just KNOW she'll tell Han and I really don't want anyone knowing about it at the moment. I was seething but I didn't want to upset Alice, so I just asked her why she'd told Caroline that:

a.) She was seeing me and,
b.) That she was even gay, 'cos Caroline sure as hell didn't know that!

Alice just kinda said, ''Cos I want people to know—don't you?'

Well, no, I don't, actually. It was on the tip of my tongue to tell her that me and Han had been going out quite happily (well, till lately anyway) for nearly a year without anyone knowing because that's what both of us wanted. I wanted to add, 'So why did you have to bloody blab to Caroline??' but I didn't want to upset her.

Caroline texted me later tonight and said, 'Jeez Clem. Didn't take you long to get over H!' so I texted her back and asked her if she thought I was a floozy. Caroline texted me back again and said, 'S'all right, Al told me you got pissed on JD. Don't make you a floozy.'

Hmm. I think Caroline's got floozy mixed up with boozy.

Friday 21 March
GOOD FRIDAY

Caroline texted me again today and asked me about Alice. She said she didn't even know Alice was gay, and had been thinking about how weird it was that two of her friends had come out to her in less than a month and that it proved what her mother was always telling her—that she had a kind face.

Alice is gay. I hadn't really even considered that, to be honest, even though that's weird. A small part of me was pissed off as well, and I think that's 'cos it'd taken me years to admit to myself that I'm gay, and even longer to think about telling people, and then Alice goes and tells our best friend, like, ten seconds after she's kissed her first girl (that would be me).

Sometimes, just sometimes, I feel like my head's gonna burst with all this.

Saturday 22 March

Looks like me and Alice are proper going out with each other. She came over to my house tonight and for reasons I'll never know, we started kissing again. I dunno whether it's my way of getting Han out of my system, or my way of getting back at Han, or just my way of coping. All I know is that Alice is being there for me, and being really nice and sweet and, well, she wants me and I don't want to be on my own. And I DO like her, in my own way. I mean, she's kinda nice looking…and she does look good when she makes the effort and all, and…

Why am I such a cow???

Sunday 23 March
EASTER SUNDAY

It was Easter Sunday today. Yet again, neither HRBH or I got an egg. Okay, I know I'm not a child any more, but sometimes, just sometimes, I yearn to hear that satisfying crack when you crack open your egg and all those little chocolatey delights inside come tumbling out. And straight into your gob.

Monday 24 March
EASTER MONDAY

Woke up thinking about Han. Again. Was thinking back to this time last year when I spent Easter down at Aunty Marie and Uncle David's and I spent the whole weekend stressing 'cos I hadn't had any texts from Han. Even though we hadn't got together at that point, I knew I liked her and I remember I hated not hearing from her.

So no change twelve months on, then.

Tuesday 25 March

OMG! I saw Miss Smith in town today. I thought for one, awful, gut-wrenching moment she might have been going to meet Han or something, but she wasn't. I followed her up through town, all the time muttering swear words at her back and resisting the urge to run up and twat her, but then she walked up to some older-looking woman who looked a lot like her mother, and they both disappeared into a café.

I hate her, Miss Bloody Smith. I hate her.

She's the one that's caused all this, after all. Cow.

Wednesday 26 March

OMFG Han sent me a text today saying, 'Heard about you and Alice. Congrats.' I KNEW bloody Caroline would tell her! I texted Caroline asking her why she had to tell Han and she texted me back and said it was 'cos Han had asked her how I was and Caroline didn't want to lie to her so she told her I was okay and, like, sooo over Han. Then she told her I was seeing Alice (!!!) I wanted to text Caroline back and say, 'So it had nothing to do with you being an old gossip?' but instead I just wrote, 'Doesn't matter what she knows, I s'pose,' but inside I was upset that Han knew. I dunno why.

Thursday 27 March

Ems texted me today and told me that her Ryan got arrested last week 'cos he threatened the owner of his local shop with a box of fairy cakes just 'cos the guy serving wouldn't let him buy some beer. He said Ryan didn't look 21 and Ryan asked why he thought he didn't look 21 and the guy said it was his school uniform that gave him away.

#idiot

So now Ryan's been told he's gotta 'deal with his anger issues'. He has to go to Anger Management classes down at the church hall every Wednesday (after the WI's knitting circle has finished) until September so he can talk about 'his feelings' (and hopefully not twat anyone while he's down there).

He's also been given an ASBO restraining order by the police and has been told not to go anywhere near his corner shop for six months. Then he was told to apologise to the owner, and to pay him £50 for the distress of having fairy cakes thrust in his face, AND to pay him £1.29 for the box of cakes as they couldn't be sold on 'cos they were all squashed.

I tell you what, if I didn't think that Ryan was a total arsehole before all this, I sure as hell do now! How Ems can even think to go out with someone who's such an oaf is beyond me. One thing I know about Han is that she doesn't have an oafish bone in her body; she's just lovely and sweet, and, okay, so she had a temper, but she'd never be violent, 'cos that's not who she is.

Okay, gonna stop writing about her now 'cos feeling like I'm gonna cry.

Friday 28 March

I got my hair cut today. I got it cut, like, dead short at the back but kept it long on top 'cos I like the way it falls over my eye and I like tucking it behind my ear. Twiddling with it also gives me something to do during Mr. Pritchard's booooooring History lessons.

Han always said she liked my hair as it was and that she never wanted me to get it cut so that's why I got it cut dead short up the back, just to piss her off. I dunno why I want to piss her off, considering we're not going out with each other any more, but it pleased me anyway.

Saturday 29 March

Went to an out-of-town garden and pet store place today with Mum 'cos she wanted to buy a new coat for Barbara. Don't ask me why, though—Barbara has a coat. It's called fur.

Mum asked me if Han wanted to come too, but I just mumbled something about Han being busy today. Mum then made some comment about Han not coming round as much, and asked us if we'd had a 'falling-out', which I managed to successfully avoid answering because the phone rang at that very minute.

#timing

I texted Alice and asked her if she wanted to come with us, 'cos I kinda thought she might want to look for something for her kitten, but she didn't seem that bothered, so I didn't push it. That made me dead sad, 'cos I knew that Han would have jumped at the chance to come shopping for something for Barbara. Okay, she would have wanted to buy her a coat with 'Ain't No One's Bitch' or something like that written on the back, but the thought would have been there.

Felt really down all day. I used to love weekends, but now they just seem to drag on and on.

Sunday 30 March

Mum and Dad were invited to the new neighbours' house for coffee this morning. I think Mum was pleased 'cos she's been itching to go over there ever since they moved in. She saw antique furniture and a piano go in there when we were nosying a few weeks ago, and has got it into her head that they're 'well-to-do'.

Mum says they're very religious. Apparently they have this huge picture that you can't really miss of Madonna in their hallway the minute you walk in through their front door. That's all very nice, but I can't see what an aging pop star has to do with religion, but there y'go.

Alice rang me and asked if I wanted to go over this afternoon 'because her parents were out', but I told her I had a headache and didn't feel up to it. The truth was, I couldn't be arsed seeing her.

Can't stop thinking about Han. Wish I could, but I can't.

Monday 31 March

Back to school today. Boo! Wore my beanie to school today with my hair all kinda hanging out of it at the front. I wanted everyone to think I'd tucked my hair up under it, so I could take it off with a flourish, then wait for them all to ooh and aah about my new hair. Everyone was gathered round me running their hands over my short hair at the back and I noticed Han looking at me through narrowed eyes.

Good.

Tuesday 1 April

It's getting really awkward at school at the moment 'cos me and Han can't avoid seeing each other sometimes. Sometimes she goes off on her own to the Art room, and sometimes she goes off with Ems or Matty and I hang out with Caroline and Alice, but when Ems and Matty want to hang out with Caroline it means we all kinda hang out together 'cos we've always hung out together and to start doing things differently now is going to raise suspicion and that's the last thing I want.

What's worse is that Alice can't resist dropping little hints that me and her are going out with each other, especially when Han's around, so she'll, like, touch my hand when we're sitting next to each other or pick fluff off my jumper and stuff like that. I know Han's watching us 'cos I can feel it but it just makes me want to curl up in a ball and disappear.

To make matters worse, everyone's got dead suspicious 'cos me and Han aren't talking to each other, and I'm hanging out with Alice a lot more than I used to. Me and Han try and be civil to each other but it's obvious something's up 'cos I can see them all looking at each other with raised eyebrows all the time. I feel a bit sorry for Caroline sometimes 'cos she's stuck in the middle of it all, but she seems to be okay with it and she's being dead discreet at the moment, which is good of her.

Apart from sometimes asking me if I'm okay, no one's actually come out and asked me if me and Han have had a bust-up, so I'm gonna keep shtum about it until someone does. I mean, I guess they've figured we've had some sort of argument, yeah, but if only they knew what it was about!!!

Wednesday 2 April

Ems told me at school today that Ryan's pissed off that he had to pay the shop owner £1.29 for the cakes 'cos he found out afterwards that they're only 89p down at the supermarket. He's dead chuffed that he's got an ASBO, though, and he plans to wear it like a badge of honour. He said the best anyone had ever got in his family was a parking ticket in the supermarket a couple of years ago when his mum got gossiping with Arthur Pollinger from her Bridge group in the Feminine Hygiene aisle and forgot about the time.

I was amazed that Ems was, like, totally cool about everything when she was telling me all this, like she wasn't that bothered that her beloved boyfriend had now been labelled no more than a thug, but I s'pose love is blind, isn't it? It's like when Han tried growing dreadlocks last year, and I hated it 'cos it made her hair stink, but I turned a blind eye to it, 'cos I loved her.

I did. I loved her.

Thursday 3 April

The boy from across the road followed me home from school today. I knew it was him 'cos I could hear his knuckles dragging on the pavement behind me.

I could feel his eyes, like, just *boring* into me from behind and my first thought was that if Han had been with me, she'd have swung round and told him to bugger off, 'cos that's what she's like, and that's what I love—loved—about her. She was so feisty, so protective, so caring—she'd have done anything for me! Alice is different; she's mousy and quiet and the sort of person that would walk away from something, not confront it head-on like Han, and it's days like today that I feel like my heart could shatter into a thousand pieces when I realise that I don't have my feisty, protective, caring girlfriend around me any more.

Friday 4 April

Me and Alice were walking down the corridor at school today when we passed Han coming the opposite way. As soon as she saw her, Alice took my hand! I wanted to shake my hand away from hers but I could hardly do that, could I? I felt so embarrassed and inside I was seething at Alice but was too chicken to say anything. I thought I detected a hint of a wry smile from Han when she saw us, which made me seethe even more.

Saturday 5 April

Me and Alice went into town today 'cos it's our school prom in about three weeks' time and Alice wanted to buy a dress or something for it. I really hadn't given any thought about what to wear to it; actually I'm completely not arsed about going to the bloody thing, but everyone else is going and I'd look an idiot if I stayed at home.

Anyway, Alice bought this tight little number which, yeah, she'll look pretty fit in, I guess. I saw a wicked tight black laced-up corset thing and my first thought was that Han would like it so I didn't buy it 'cos I felt guilty for thinking about Han when I was out shopping with my girlfriend.

Ended up just buying some more socks instead 'cos all mine seem to have holes in the toes. Boy, I know how to live!

#irony

Sunday 6 April

Had a really interesting chat with Alice today about girls and being gay and a whole load of heavy stuff like that. I asked her how long she'd liked girls and she said a really strange thing. She said she didn't like girls *as such*, so I looked at her weird because we were, like, lying on her bed while we were having this conversation and she was stroking my hair and things, so I said to her she must like girls because I was one. (Well, I was when I looked at myself in the bathroom mirror this morning anyway.)

So, hmm, Alice said again that she didn't like girls in general. Now, this struck me as totally messed 'cos I know I like girls, and I know I like them A LOT. I like all girls. Tall ones, short ones, blonde ones, brunette ones. You name it. Okay, so it's taken me a while to realise it, but now I know for sure that girls are what do IT for me, I'm happy about it. And, yeah, I'm not ashamed to admit (to myself anyway) that there are loads of girls out there—on TV, in magazines, at school—that I fancy the arse off.

So then I asked Alice if she considered herself gay and she couldn't answer me. She said there must be a small part of her that's a bit gay, or else why would she like me? She said she considered herself to be 'Clemmiesexual' and then she laughed and said maybe it was because I wasn't very girly that she didn't consider me a girl as such, then I got grumpy 'cos I was insulted and we didn't speak for a bit, which was embarrassing.

Then she said she'd never looked at girls like she looks at me before, and that she'd come to the conclusion that she'd fallen for me as a PERSON—not as a GIRL. That kinda made sense to me (although I was still a bit pissed off with her for her earlier comment) because I think I'm an okay person, so why wouldn't she fall for me? Hahaha! She said sometimes in life you can't help who you find attractive, and who was to say the next person she liked wouldn't be a boy?

The strangest thing about our conversation, though, was that I felt like I should have been a bit pissed off with her again 'cos she was talking about 'the next person' which kinda smacked of her thinking ahead to a time when we wouldn't be together.

But strangely I wasn't pissed off at all.

Monday 7 April

Was still thinking about what me and Alice were talking about over at hers yesterday. It did make sense to me, that you fall for someone's personality and sparkling wit (like Alice did with me—ha, ha!) and that it's just a coincidence if that person happens to be the same sex as you. But I still can't help thinking that Alice doesn't know what she is, or what she wants. It just seems to me that she likes me because she knows me so well and I'm nice to her and I show her affection and all that. Like an infatuation, almost.

A big part of me thinks that once she's got over this infatuation, we'll go back to being friends again. The sad part is, I'd be really happy just to be friends with her again, but I s'pose that makes me a bit of a cow, doesn't it?

Tuesday 8 April

I downloaded some new music onto my iPod today. I'd bought an iTunes voucher when I was in town with Alice on Saturday and for some reason I've managed to spend it all on music that I know Han would hate.

I dunno why. Perhaps subconsciously it's my way of telling her I'm SO over her.

Yup. So over her.

Wednesday 9 April

Ems asked me today 'what was up' with me and Han. I just said we'd had words about something trivial and had upset each other and we weren't speaking. I said, 'It'll blow over,' but hated lying to her. I was on the verge of telling her everything, but I didn't. I dunno why. Instead I just said, 'Has Han said anything to you about it?' and Ems just said, 'Nah. You know what Hannah's like. She reckons she's in tune with her emotional side, but ask her about anything emotional and she shuts up like a clam. I thought EMOs were supposed to bang on about their feelings all the time, and how no one understands them, but when I ask her what's up she just tells me she's got 'issues' to deal with but she won't tell me any more than that.'

'Issues'?!!

Is that what she's calling all this???

Thursday 10 April

HRBH's boyfriend Joe is a skater! Whoa! He was over at ours this evening and we got talking and he told me he skates most weekends. I thought anyone over the age of 16 wouldn't be seen dead in a skate park, but nooooo! He's 20 and he reckons the park's full of people his age, so I told him I used to skate loads but hadn't done it for ages (I haven't since I hooked up with Han) and it'd be neat to get back skating again. Joe said I could go with him to the park on Saturday if I wanted, which was cool of him.

Friday 11 April

Mrs. Schofield asked me today for my work experience option form. I totally forgot about it!!! Mum, of course, never reminded me of it, like any normal mother would, so I'm right in the shit with school at the moment.

Mrs. Schofield got one of her looks on her face and said to me, 'The notice has been up about this for months, Clementine. Don't you ever read the notices?'

No, I don't!! Don't they realise I'm having a traumatic time at the moment? I'm too messed up over all this crap with Han to be thinking about filling out bloody forms.

Mrs. Schofield told me to 'pull my finger out and get thinking. I want the forms back by Monday.'

Whatever.

Saturday 12 April

Me and Joe went to the skate park this afternoon and it was wicked! I don't think HRBH was too chuffed about it though 'cos she had a face like a robber's dog on her all morning. Joe told me later in the park it's 'cos she wanted him to go shopping with her, but he said he'd rather stick pins in his eyes. He said this to me, of course, not HRBH, 'cos I think he's as scared of her as the rest of us are.

I was a bit rusty on the board 'cos I've not been on one for, like, nearly two years, but it's like riding a bike isn't it? Fall off and get straight back on. Who needs skin on their elbows anyway? Over-rated, if you ask me.

Anyway, I had an awesome afternoon and it was so bloody good not to be thinking about all the crap that's going on in my life at the moment, even if only for a few hours!

Sunday 13 April

Emptied out my wardrobe today and was embarrassed at all the Goth clothes I seem to have accumulated over the last year.

Got out some of my old skater clothes and was pleased to see a lot of them still fit (well, I s'pose they would do—they're baggy, h,a ha!). I put all the Goth stuff in a black bag and put it to the back of my wardrobe, all except the damn sexy corset I bought last autumn, even though it was too big for me. Maybe I'll surprise Alice in it one day.

I also deleted a load of Han's music off my iPod 'cos it just makes me too sad to listen to it. I only have to listen to the opening riffs of any Slipknot stuff and I fill up, let alone some of the other slow shizz that we used to smooch to in her bedroom.

Monday 14 April

I told Ems today that I needed to keep out of Han's way, so I'd have my lunch with Alice on my own from now on. I can't cope with seeing her all the time (Han, not Alice) and I hate the awkwardness there is between us, so I thought the best thing to do would be to take myself out of the equation. Besides, it means I can sit in our classroom and eat a packed lunch instead of having to endure Mrs. Dermott's God-awful gravy and custard (not served together, I might add—although nothing would surprise me where that woman's concerned).

Tuesday 15 April

Dug out the Take That CD that Dad gave me for my birthday last year and listened to it for the first time. It wasn't bad. Han would have hated it.

Wednesday 16 April

Ems told me that she was having a party at hers on Saturday. I said if Han was gonna be there then I didn't really want to go, but she told me Han had already told her she couldn't go, so I'm off the hook. Party here I come!!

Thursday 17 April

Caroline told me and Ems in break today that Miss Smith's getting married!!!!!!!! Caroline said she heard it from her friend Rosie who does Art with Miss Smith. She said she didn't so much as announce it, it was more that the girls got it out of her 'cos they'd noticed her wearing an engagement ring during Tuesday's lesson and they quizzed her about it. She said Miss Smith was really coy about it all, but admitted that she'd just got engaged and was hoping to get married next year during the summer holidays. Caroline got me to one side later and said that Rosie had said Han's face was a picture when Miss Smith told them all and she was, like, really grumpy for the rest of the lesson!!!

Poor Han! Ha, ha, ha!!

Friday 18 April

Han's in deep shit with Mrs. Unwin 'cos apparently she was rude to Miss Smith in Art today. Rosie told Caroline and Caroline told me that Miss Smith asked Han to help her tidy up after class and Han told her to 'go tidy it yourself' before flouncing out of the Art studio. Rosie says that Han's been dead off with Miss Smith lately, which was strange 'cos she'd always been dead friendly with her before. Now she reckons she's sullen and won't speak, and can't wait to get out of the studio after class. Ohhhh how times have changed!!!

#schadenfreude

Saturday 19 April

Me and Alice went to Ems' party tonight and I was pissed off to see Han was there, despite Ems PROMISING me she wouldn't be. She was there with some leggy EMO girl I've never seen before and it felt like someone was stabbing my heart every time I saw them together. The EMO girl did get off with one of Ryan's mates later in the evening, which made me feel a bit better because I'd kinda thought her and Han might have been an item.

I have to say, Han didn't looked too chuffed to see me there with Alice, especially as Alice clung to me like a limpet all night, almost as if to show Han that we were a proper item and she had no claims on me any more. Awkward.

I felt dead uncomfortable and didn't like it one little bit, but couldn't say anything to Alice 'cos she'd know that I was still hung up on Han. Han was looking at me with what I thought looked like total malice on her face, so she obviously thought I was a right prat for showing off with Alice in front of her. I spent most of the evening either in the kitchen or in the garden—anywhere where I knew Han wouldn't be. I can't say it was one of the best parties I've ever been to.

Sunday 20 April

Alice texted me this morning and asked if I wanted to go over to her house after lunch. I didn't really, but I thought I ought to, bearing in mind I'd spent most of the previous night thinking about Han.

We went out for a walk down by the canal and it was all right, actually. We had a laugh trying to skim pebbles across the water until the ducks started getting grumpy with us for disturbing them, and I felt pretty happy for a change. I thought how much fun Alice can be sometimes and then felt guilty 'cos sometimes I feel like I'm so horrible to her, so I made a mental note to try and be a better girlfriend to her from now on, and try and move on from Han.

Monday 21 April

Alice asked me if I'd 'take her' to our school prom 'cos she said she liked the idea of being 'escorted' by her love as it would make her feel 'so special'. I wondered for a minute if she'd been reading too much Jane Austen but told myself not to be such a cow and said, yes, I'd be happy to 'take her'.

When I got home from school all I could think about was how much better it would be if Han was to 'take me' to the prom instead. So much for me trying to be a better girlfriend to Alice and move on from Han, huh?

Tuesday 22 April

Mrs. Schofield summoned me to the staff room today about work experience. I forgot to do the bloody forms again so she's given me a list of the places that are left, along with strict instructions to get back to her by the end of tomorrow or else 'You'll be spending the rest of the term tidying this school from top to bottom.'

I suddenly had a horrid thought that I might get stuck cleaning the gym changing rooms with Pippa Goldsmith or—shudder—even worse, having to do something with Susan Divine. I had an image of tidying the Drama cupboard with Susan and having her dress me up in an elf's outfit and have me gallop round on my hands and knees 'cos that's the sort of perverted, twisted thing a nutcase like her would do. This is the girl who electrocuted her own dog and then had his initials tattooed on her fingers, after all.

Looked at the list and was dismayed to see all that was left was:

- A well-known local supermarket (can't add up so would be handing wrong change out all the time)
- The vet's (can't stand blood so would pass out at the sight of the first dog that had its bits whipped out)
- The library (can't stay quiet for more than five minutes. Would have the urge to run around screaming, just for the hell of it)
- The hospital (one whiff of sick people and I feel ill)
- The butcher's (great, so I'd go home smelling of minced beef every day)

Finally opted for the vet's 'cos I thought there might be some fit vet nurses there that could nurse me if I fainted. Even if I'm not a Yorkshire terrier, I can't be that different to revive, can I?

Wednesday 23 April

Took my form back to Mrs. Schofield today. As luck would have it, she told me that there was now some work experience going at the local newspaper 'cos Kelly Waterman was supposed to go and work in the printing press but found out last week that printing fluid brings her out in hives so they have a spare place going.

Mrs. Schofield said she thought 'the strict timescales for deadlines required in a newspaper office might be beneficial to such a tardy young lady as you, and might teach you to manage your time better'.

I think she's right. Maybe the newspaper place will be better. I've always fancied being a journalist 'cos I think tucking a pencil behind my ear makes me look more clever.

I start there in July. Can't wait. Not.

Thursday 24 April

Miss Smith's marrying Mr. Troutt. Apparently their eyes met over some scenery during rehearsals for the production of *Grease* the school's doing next month and after a whirlwind romance, they've gone and got engaged!!!

This is the funniest thing I've heard since Great Aunt May told us she went to Paris for a weekend in 1973 and ended up working at the Folies Bergère, despite the fact she's got two left feet and bunions the size of pineapples.

I would have loved to have been a fly on the wall and seen Han's face when she found out Miss Smith and Mr. Troutt are getting hitched!!!

Not that I care, of course.

Friday 25 April

It was dead hot today, so I wore my short skirt for the first time this year. If Dad pulls his finger out and actually books us a holiday this year then I'm determined not to go away anywhere with white legs, so if there's any chance to have a bit of sunshine on them, I'll take it! We were sitting on the grass by the gym at lunchtime and I was sitting next to Han and I was dying for her to touch my legs. I could see her looking at them, and I know she's always liked my legs, so maybe that's why I subconsciously wore my short skirt today, I dunno. I could feel, like, this tension between us and I got a sort of thrill from it. She kept shifting her position so her leg kept brushing against mine and she didn't move it whenever it touched me. It was like it used to be when we first got together and I began to wish that I could turn the clock back and take myself back to that time again. I was aware of Alice watching us both carefully, though, so I started talking to Ems about Ryan and his ASBO to try and deflect attention from us both, but inside I was, like, totally quivering with excitement.

God, I hope I'm not turning into some sexual deviant like you see on them late night satellite channels…

Saturday 26 April

Was lying on my bed this morning re-reading last year's diary about when me and Han first got together and it was making me dead sad. I was really grateful when Joe yelled up the stairs and asked me if I wanted to go to the skate park with him, so I shoved the diary under my mattress and tried not to think about stuff too much.

I like Joe, he makes me laugh. We had a wicked day down at the park and I only fell off eight times today. Result!!

Dad has decided to take up golf for the summer. He says it's what a lot of people in his profession do, and it'll be good for his career. I just think he fancies himself as the next Rory McIlroy or something, despite the fact that Dad is twice his age. And not Irish.

Like most dads who take up a new hobby, he's gone completely OTT and came back from some out-of-town retail park this evening with a load of clubs, balls, and bags. I heard Mum asking him in the kitchen later how much it all cost him, but I didn't hear him answer.

Great! It's bad enough that my father is a boring, old accountant, but now he's a boring, old accountant that plays golf. Sometimes the thought of leaving home is very tempting.

Sunday 27 April

Spent most of today doing revision 'cos Mum was grumbling at me 'cos she hasn't seen me 'within an inch of a book yet, young lady', so I took myself off to my room and spread all my books out, trying to muster up some enthusiasm. All I could think of was how cheated I felt not being able to revise with Han. Somehow I always saw us studying for our exams together, supporting each other, encouraging each other, just being there for each other.

Bugger.

Monday 28 April

We were a team, me and Han. A team. We used to do, like, *everything* together. We used to laugh together, cry together, encourage each other, make each other feel special, and now it's all gone. How could this have happened? She was my world.

I miss her soooo much, it's unreal.

Tuesday 29 April

OMG! OMG!!! Caroline told me today that Han texted her late last night and told her she wants me back—how cool is that??? Caroline was whispering, all conspiratorially under her breath, like she was giving me a codeword that would blow up the Science lab or something, but I was busy eating a Cornish pasty and some of the flaky pastry went down the wrong way so I was too busy choking and coughing and turning puce to reply straight away. When I'd finished dying, I asked her exactly what Han had said, so she surreptitiously got her mobile phone out and showed me Han's message. It said 'Missing Clem like mad. Dunno what to do,' then Caroline showed me her reply and then Han's reply to that, which said, 'Want her back. Should never have split up. I love her soooooo much, Caro, seeing her with Alice is killing me.' I stared at the words 'Want her back' and felt my tummy do a lurch.

Then I thought about Alice and felt a bit sick.

Wednesday 30 April

Wore my short skirt to school again today. Was thinking about what Caroline said to me yesterday about Han wanting me back and something inside me was telling me to pull out all the stops, make her realise what she's missing. I know I'm no sex goddess or anything like that, but I do know my short skirts drive Han crazy, so I have to make the best of the good bits that I DO have!

Anyway, it seemed to work 'cos I went up to the library after lunch to do some revision and Han was there, so I made sure I walked, like, dead slow past her so she could cop an eyeful. I made sure I looked her straight in the eye as well (just for good effect, like) and she kinda looked me up and down before arching an eyebrow and smiling at me and biting her bottom lip, which made me feel a bit giddy.

Tried to concentrate on revision for my Humanities exam, but all I could do was think about Han and her arched eyebrow all the time. Felt dead frustrated for the rest of the day.

Thursday 1 May

The school, in its infinite wisdom, decided to hold something called an 'Enrichment Day' today, when all we really wanted to do was just have a chance to piss about for the day 'cos we all go off on study leave as of tomorrow.

Anyway, this local poet came into school today to 'enrich' us. She stood at the front of our class and read some of her poems out, about moths flickering against light bulbs and daffodils bobbing in spring sunshine and shit like that, then asked us to go away for an hour, write a poem about something 'meaningful and important' to us, then come back and read it to the rest of the class.

I sat for ages and thought about what was meaningful and important to me and came up with this:

'Barbara'

Barbara barks at bedtime,
When she wants to go out for a wee.
But I rather think it's high time
She did it quiet-ly.

When we came back into the classroom she asked if anyone wanted to read out their poem. I was gobsmacked to see Han put her hand up and walk to the front of the class with a piece of paper with loads of scribbles all over it, then perch on the front desk and start to read out her poem.

She was looking straight at me while she was reading it, only briefly looking away for a second before looking back at me. Her poem was called 'Guilt', and this is what she'd written:

Guilt. My guilt eats at me like a maggot eats a rotting corpse

Putrid flesh peeling away under the force of your hate

Filling the maggot with your loathing.

Seeping. Your hate seeps into my veins like blood from a slaughtered lamb

Consuming my very soul, weakening me, punishing me

Filling the maggot with your loathing.

Hating. Your hate stares at me from eyes that once looked at me with desire

Eyes that were once warm with love now glassy like a taxidermists' muse

Filling this maggot with your loathing.

Longing. My longing for you courses through me like a whippet after a startled hare

Hearts pounding, loins burning, desire aflame.

When, oh when will you be mine again?

After she'd read it out, she casually screwed it up and tossed it into the bin before sauntering slowly back to her desk. Mrs. Duckworth, the teaching assistant, sat in the corner looking scared stiff, but our visitor poet, I noticed, was clutching her breast and fingering the buttons on her Afghan waistcoat in an excited manner, telling the retreating back of Han that her poem showed someone 'in tune with her inner being and demonstrated a fascinating juxtaposition of hatred and love', whatever the buggery that meant.

Anyway, when the class had finished, I made sure I hung back for a bit, waiting for everyone to go so I could get her poem back out of the bin—I was sure it was meant for me and I wanted to keep it 'cos I thought it was beautiful. I picked it out of the bin and stuffed it into my bag, and breathed a sigh of relief that Alice wasn't in the same room—she'd chosen to go and listen to some local politician spout a load of crap down in the gym—'cos she would have given me so much grief over the whole thing.

When I got home tonight I spread the screwed-up paper out on my bed and read it three times again, so that by the third time I could almost recite it by heart. I folded it up and put it inside you, dear diary, and noticed on the back Han had written 'I'm sorry', and I felt my throat tighten, so I switched on my PS3 and did a bit of snowboarding with my iPod on full blast to take my mind off stuff. I'm fed up with all this bloody crying.

Friday 2 May

It's our school prom tomorrow night. Spent all day trying to get some enthusiasm going for it, but totally couldn't be arsed, thanks to this thundering great voice that kept bellowing in my ear, reminding me that I'll be going with Alice and not Han. Like I need reminding?!

Saturday 3 May

We had our school prom tonight and it was MEGA! Everyone had been invited to bring along their dates, so me and Alice went together, and as luck would have it, managed to arrive at the same time as Kirsty Chamberlain 'cos she'd come on her own. I was secretly pleased 'cos then it didn't look like me and Alice had arrived together, despite her apparently wanting us to make a big entrance together as a 'couple'.

I was also dead pleased to see that Han wasn't there when we arrived and I kinda hoped she wouldn't bother coming, but then I couldn't see Matty either and guessed they'd probably be coming together and prepared myself for seeing her later.

Ems was there with Ryan, who kept tugging at his dickie and looking very uncomfortable; Caroline was with Rosie and Jess from her RE class 'cos this Jess girl had just been dumped the day before by her boyfriend for Amy Matthews in 13MH and wanted some moral support 'cos she knew he'd be there with her tonight…

Alice was wearing her neat little dress that she'd bought a few weeks ago, and, yeah, she looked kinda sweet in it. I would have preferred to wear my sweatshirt and jeans but thought considering this was, like, the biggest event of my social calendar I'd make an effort. I knew Han was gonna be there so wanted to make sure I knocked her sideways, so I wore my amazing tight black corset thingy but I had to stuff a pair of socks down my front to get something resembling a cleavage going on. Never mind.

There was no way I was going to wear a pretty, pretty prom frock/meringue 'cos I look like a prat in a dress and hell would freeze over before you'd get me within 3 feet of one, so I just wore a black miniskirt with it. I'd worn my biker boots too, but all undone, like, so that I shuffled and clanked like a Hell's Angel!! I'd put makeup on, of course, 'cos I didn't want to look out of place, so I'd covered my eyes in black eyeliner and loads of mascara and it looked kinda cool. I'd mussed my hair up too; when Dad saw me just before I left the house he said I looked like I'd been 'dragged through a hedge backwards', so I knew I'd got the desired effect.

Anyway, we were all standing in a group chatting away when Han did finally arrive, and it was (well for me anyway) kinda like one of those movie moments when someone walks into the room and everything seems to stop, you know what I mean?

And…OMG! She looked STUNNING!

She was Goth-ed up to the max, dressed from head to foot in black, except for these amazing purple tights, loads of black makeup on, loads of chains, studs and zips, eyebrow ring, fake nose ring, fake lip ring in, with legs up to her armpits and her hair cascading down her back. She'd put purple extensions in her hair and she looked, like, totally SMOKING HOT!!! She stood to the entrance of the hall and scanned the room (looking for me??) before grabbing herself a bottle of Coke, whipping the top off in one swift move, taking a swig from it (cool-as-fuck!), and sauntering oh, so slowly over to us! Now THAT'S what I call making an entrance!!! I felt giddy with lust for her, and my heart was pounding in my ears just standing there watching her walk towards us. I remembered I was with Alice and tried to act normal, but inside my stomach had a thousand butterflies in it.

Anyway, we all just stood around for a bit, chatting and mucking about, happy that school had finished but also scaring each other with thoughts of our exams coming up, but me and Han couldn't take our eyes off each other and there was like this simmering tension between us and I loved it. Every time I looked over to Han she was staring at me, and each time I just looked away quickly, but inside I was buzzing! Alice stuck to me like glue all evening, probably aware that Han was looking at me. She started giving me grief about how she wished Han would 'just piss off and leave us alone', and kept trying to drag me further away from her, but I kept surreptitiously heading back towards her 'cos the sight of Han in 100% Goth mode was too good to keep missing. Then Alice got a bit whiny and clingy and I was trying sooooo hard not to get narky with her.

Finally I managed to shake Alice off when I went to the loo (three Cokes and I have a bladder like a balloon!) When I came out of my cubicle, checking that my knickers weren't caught up in my skirt or anything like that, Han was standing there, leaning against the tampon machine with her hands in her pockets. She looked me up and down, from my biker boots to my sock-enhanced corset, and was grinning at me and biting at her lip, like she always used to do when she was *interested*, so I knew she was proper paying attention to me. She said quietly, 'You're looking good, Clem,' so I just said, 'So are you. Just don't spill water on your zips or you'll rust up,' then cringed at my lousy attempt at humour. Timing, Clem, timing!

Then she mouthed at me, 'I miss you,' and I felt my tummy lurch. What could I say in return? I miss her too, but I sure as hell wasn't going to tell her that! That plus the fact my girlfriend was waiting outside for me as well, of course. So I just said, 'What do you want me to say, Han? You crushed me, I don't know if I can forget that.' (Yes I can!!!!) She said, 'I don't know what I want you to say. All I want you to know is that I miss you and I'm sorry.' Just then a group of giggling girls came in so the moment was lost. I went back out to Alice, my head spinning, and tried to act normally with her, but I was feeling far from normal!

I dunno if Alice sussed anything, but when she saw me she asked me if I was okay 'cos she said I looked a bit 'flustered', so I lied and told her I'd tripped over my loose boots in the toilet. Lousy lie, I know, but I was thinking on my feet.

The rest of the night went in a kinda blur. I couldn't concentrate on anything going on, or even enjoy it really, 'cos my head was so full of Han—how she'd looked tonight, how she'd acted towards me and what she'd said to me. I was aware of her, I dunno, her *presence* all night. Every time I looked round, or went to get a drink, or whatever, Han was there, watching me, smiling at me. Secretly I loved it, but then I'd turn and see Alice next to me and get this pang of guilt…

I was glad to get home, but even then I spent half the night lying awake, turning things over in my head.

All I want is her. Han. I don't care that it's confusing me, or upsetting me. I love it! I love her. I want her.

Aaaaaaaaaaaaaaargh! Why does my life have to be so fucking confusing???

Sunday 4 May

Slept with Alice while her parents were out today. Felt wrong in soooo many ways.

Monday 5 May

Revised, thought about Han, revised, thought about Han, revised, thought about Han. I'm gonna be a nervous wreck by the end of the summer!

Tuesday 6 May

Bumped into Han in the corridor at school today on my way up to the library. I jerked my chin at her in recognition and kinda just went 'all right?' and then was just walking away when she grabbed my hand on my way past and just said quietly, 'Clem,' which gave me proper big goose bumps! She asked me how I was and how Alice was and I kinda just said, 'Fine and fine,' and then she asked me how my revision was going and I said 'Fine' (again) and then she suddenly said, 'I'm sorry, Clem.' I said, 'Sorry for what?' and she just said, 'Everything. I've been a total wanker and I'm really sorry.'

I didn't really know what to say so I just said, 'S'all right, these things happen,' then remembered with a wry smile that that was what Han had said to Caroline when we first broke up. Han said, 'All that stuff with Smith was my bad, and I'm sorry. I just got carried away, I s'pose. I lapped up the attention she was giving me, and like the complete tosser I am, thought there was more to it,' and she laughed ironically before looking hard at me and saying, 'And the worse thing of all is that I lost you over it all. I'll never get over that.'

I thought she was being a bit melodramatic but let her carry on anyway. She said, 'I love you, Clem. Always have done, even when we were going through all that crap. You're the one for me, always will be, but I s'pose that's it, isn't it? Good old Han's blown it yet again.' She carried on looking at me and I dare say if we hadn't been at school I would quite happily have jumped on her and made out with her right there, but as it was we were standing in the school corridor and I was heading off to see my supposed girlfriend, so I had to show a little restraint. All I could say to her was, 'I'm going out with Alice, Han. It's over with me and you,' and I dropped her hand and walked away from her, feeling ever so slightly like Scarlett O'Hara in *Gone With The Wind* or something. I kept saying 'It's over with me and you' in my head as I wandered off to find Alice.

I just wished I really believed that.

Wednesday 7 May

Had my first exam today. It was French speaking, so I had to sit and talk for, like, half an hour to this old person who just asked me questions about how to ask for a ham sandwich and what time the trains departed for Paris and crap like that. He also asked me loads of stuff (in French) about my family, my house, and my friends, and then he asked me to describe my life and I wondered briefly what the French for 'all fucked up' was, but held my nerve and I think I managed to answer everything he was asking me okay.

Came home to find Dad putting golf balls in the garden with an NYC baseball cap on. Mid-life crisis much?!!

Thursday 8 May

Barbara's really ill. She's off her food and off her walks and that's soooo unlike her. As if I haven't got enough crap to deal with, what with exams, revisions, Han…now the dog goes and gets ill. Someone up there REALLY doesn't like me!!

Friday 9 May

Barbara's still ill. We had to take her up to the vet's tonight and Dad was grumbling all the way there and all the way back about what the bill's gonna be 'cos the vet's just moved from being in a small house to being in this brand-spanking-new building and it's no longer calling itself a vet surgery but a vet hospital and Dad reckons that'll put an extra £50 on the bill straight away. Anyway, Barbara has to stay in for some tests so we all came home and found the house really empty and quiet without her. Mum went to give her her bedtime biscuit in her basket, then remembered she wasn't there and got all tearful. Dad was busy doing some online banking and hastily transferring funds in anticipation of a large bill. Therein lies the difference between men and women, methinks!

Saturday 10 May

Barbara still at vet's. Had some more x-rays this morning. I want to tell Han about her 'cos I knew she'd understand 'cos she loves—loved—Barbara almost as much as I do, but something keeps stopping me from picking up my phone and texting her.

Sunday 11 May

The vet rang us today to say Barbara's still not eating and that they 'found something' on the x-ray, so they're going to operate on her tomorrow morning. Mum had to go up there and sign a consent form saying she wouldn't sue the arse off the vet's if Barbara doesn't pull through…

I rang Alice and told her and she made sympathetic noises down the phone to me but didn't really say much else, to be honest. I so wanted to text Han again. I sat on my bed turning my phone over and over in my hands, not sure what to do but in the end I sent Han a text just saying 'Barbara's not well. Been at vet's for 3 days. Having op tomorrow.' A text came back from her 10 minutes later saying, 'Poor baby. Are you okay?' I wasn't sure if the 'poor baby' was directed at me or Barbara but I guessed it must have been about Barbara—she wouldn't call me baby, would she???

I sent her a text saying, 'Not really. Very worried about her,' and she rang me!! She asked what was the matter with Barbara and what had the vet said and what operation would they be doing and blah, blah, blah. It was soooooo nice to hear her voice on the end of my phone again and I really wished she'd been there with me right then. She offered to come to the vet's with us to see Barbara, which was really sweet of her but I told her we'd be okay, thanks anyway. Before she rang off, she said to me, 'If you hear anything, or if her condition changes, you'll ring me won't you? Promise me?' and I could feel my throat tighten with tears so I just mumbled 'yeah' at her and rang off.

Am now going to bed thinking about Han (yet again). Got my next exam on Tuesday but all I can think about is Hannah Harrison (and Barbara).

I'll be grey with worry by the time I'm 21.

Monday 12 May

Had a phone call from the vet's to say Barbara had her operation okay this morning and that she'd come round from the anaesthetic all right and she was looking very lively again. They found a golf ball in her stomach.

We went up to see her this evening and she looked really pleased to see us, waggling her tail and weaving her body from side to side so I could see all her stitches. Mum was soooooo happy to see her, but she soon shut up when she was given the bill 'cos she knew she'd have to go back out to the waiting room and show it to Dad and she didn't want him to cause a scene when he saw how much the cost of all this was.

Anyway, Barbara's coming home on Wednesday, so we're all really pleased. I sent Han a text and told her Barbara was okay, but she hasn't replied yet.

Tuesday 13 May

Had my Humanities exam today. It was all right except for the fact I wasn't allowed to go to the toilet on my own, in case I'd written the answers to the questions in my knickers or something, so some exam official came with me and waited outside the cubicle while I tried to go. Couldn't go 'cos I knew she was, like, less than two feet away from me so had to go back into the exam with a full bladder again. Seriously—who can piss with an audience???

Not a good start.

Didn't see Han all day. She replied to my text about Barbara late last night after I'd switched my phone off and told me she was so relieved to hear B was okay, but that was all she said. I kinda wanted her to say more. I dunno what, just…something more.

Ohhh Godddd!!! I miss her I miss her I miss her I miss her I miss her I miss her I miss her I miss her I miss her I miss her.

Wednesday 14 May

Had my Media Studies exam this morning. It was just my luck that Han was sitting at the next desk to me and I kept trying sooo hard not to look at her during the exam but it was pretty impossible. I lost track of time 'cos my head was so puddled by her being there so I had to finish the paper in double quick time. Han finished 20 minutes early so she'd gone by the time I'd got round to finishing. Shit, shit, shit!!

I still miss her.

Alice met me after the exam so we could go and study for our Chemistry exam this afternoon, but I was still so busy thinking about Han, I hardly said two words to her.

I'm such a cow.

Dad reckons he's going to sell his golf clubs to pay for Barbara's vet bill. Personally I think he's doing it out of guilt 'cos I reckon it was one of his stray golf balls from the garden that she ate, but I don't care what reason he's doing it, I'm just glad he is. At least now he'll stop fannying about in his ridiculous baseball caps out in the garden where all the neighbours can see him pretending to be some hotshot golfer. Saddo.

Thursday 15 May

Alice's parents were both out this afternoon so she texted me and asked me if I wanted to go over to do some revision. I didn't really, but I didn't want to let her down so I went.

We somehow ended up *doing it* (yes, I KNOW!) and everything was telling me it was wrong, wrong, wrong but somehow I couldn't stop myself. Got home around 6 and went straight to my room, feeling like a right selfish pig. Why am I doing this to her? Why am I leading her on? She's so sweet and lovely and all and she doesn't deserve me or what I'm doing to her.

I soooo don't want to hurt her, but surely keeping this pretence up is going to hurt her more than if I just ended things with her?

Friday 16 May

Went up the skate park with Joe again today. Was supposed to do some revision for my Maths exam on Monday, but I couldn't be arsed. I'm a teenager. I need to have fun every now and again, not bloody study all the time. That's what teenagers do. It's in our job description.

Anyway, it was dead weird up there today 'cos there was a friend of Joe's there and he said something to Joe about him 'bringing his girlfriend along', so I looked about, thinking HRBH was there or something, then realised he was talking about me!!! As I was walking to go up the triple pipe I heard this boy say to Joe, 'You get that one from the crèche, dude?' and nearly fell off my board. I dunno what was worse—the fact he thinks I'm a child or the fact he called Joe 'dude'.

So Joe was a bit funny with me for a bit until I sat him down at the top of one of the ramps and asked him if he was okay. He said he didn't think it was a good idea for me and him to go skating together again 'cos it looked weird, a boy and a girl skating together on their own all the time. I laughed and told him it was fun and that I didn't give a shit what it looked like to other people, but he just said he didn't want anyone to think I was his girlfriend 'cos he'd get grief at uni for being a 'cradle snatcher'. Then he said that he thought I was nice but he didn't want me to get any ideas and then he got all embarrassed so I told him that that there was absolutely no way I fancied him, and that there would be more chance of Tony Hawks tailsliding across his head than there ever would be of me being his girlfriend.

He cheered up a bit then and said, 'So you don't mind me saying I don't want anyone to think you're my girlfriend?' and I said, 'Well, number one, you're going out with my sister and if she even got so much as a sniff of scandal you'd be dangling from this half-pipe by your soft bits by nightfall, and number two, you're sooooo not my type, so quit worrying!'

So then he said, 'So what is your type?' which somehow I just KNEW he was gonna say, so I didn't answer, I just hopped up and skated off the top of the ramp, up the other side, sat down on the opposite ledge and blew a raspberry at him. He skated over to me and said, 'Y'know, I don't know anything about you. You're, like, my girlfriend's sister and I've never really spoken to you. All we do is skate and piss about, but we never talk.' I said, 'Doesn't my sister talk about me?' but he just laughed and said, 'All she says is how much you irritate her.' Typical!

I picked at my trainers and just told him there was nothing to tell. I kinda wanted to tell him everything but I don't want him to blab to HRBH and I don't know him well enough to trust him with something so secret and personal as my sexuality and all my sodding girlfriend problems!!!

Saturday 17 May

Great Aunt May came up for her tea tonight. I was telling Mum and Dad at teatime about Ryan's ASBO that he's got until September and I had to explain to Great Aunt May what an ASBO was 'cos she thought I'd said UFO, and for a minute she whitened, thinking that Ryan had been beamed up by little green men. Great Aunt May is convinced 'we are not alone', ever since Great Uncle Roy saw a white light in the sky in 1952 on his way home from the pub late one winter's night. She went out, so the story goes, and borrowed a load of books from the library on UFOs and all that alien shizz, and took to sitting in their outside toilet for a week with a piece of foil on her head and a copy of the New Testament clutched to her bosom.

When I explained to her that Ryan had only been beamed up by policemen, not little green men, she pulled her lips thin, adjusted her wig, and said that Ryan deserved all he got cos he's 'a rumm'un—just like his grandfather'. I never even knew that Great Aunt May knew Ryan, let alone his grandfather, so she's either got herself confused (more than likely) or there's some history between her and the grandfather!

Her eyes went all watery then, and she took to staring out of the window and dabbing at her nose, so I didn't bother pushing it. Not for the first time since we split up, I reaaaaaaaally wished Han had been here with us as well. She'd have sat with Great Aunt May and said soothing words to her. Great Aunt May likes that.

She's not the only one.

#TryingNotToCry

Sunday 18 May

Hahaha! HRBH has taken to reading a left-wing broadsheet newspaper on Sundays, much to Dad's dismay 'cos he thinks Joe is a communist anyway and he's worried that his daughter is turning into a 'loony lefty' (his words not mine).

I don't think he needs to worry much, though; for as much as my sister says she reads it for all the 'intelligent, in-depth discussions' on the economy and politics and the like, I still notice every time I pick it up that the problem page is *well* dog-eared.

Monday 19 May

Had my Maths exam this afternoon. Han was in the same exam hall as me and I was desperate to leave the room with her after it, but there was such a crush to get out that I lost her along the way.

Walked home alone feeling so depressed I could have cried.

Tuesday 20 May

OMG strange day. So, I had my English Literature exam this afternoon. It was okay. We had questions about *Macbeth*, such as did I think Lady Macbeth was 'a villainess or just misunderstood'? (I wanted to write that the whole bloody book was misunderstood—by me, anyway—but I figured that'd get me a big, fat zero, so refrained). We also had some poem to dissect, which was easy enough.

Anyway, 'cos it was English and we were all sitting it, the whole gang was there and, as luck would have it, Alice got talking to Caroline and Matty after the exam so I hung back a bit 'cos I knew that Han hadn't left the exam hall yet, and I was determined to walk out with her 'cos I felt like I'd missed out yesterday. I was dead casual, of course, just slowly packing my pens and stuff up, but keeping a sneaky eye out for her, and it worked 'cos she came over to me on her way out!!!!

And if that wasn't brilliant enough, she gave me a friendship bracelet!!!!

She said, 'I got you this, right, and, yeah, I know we're not seeing each other any more but that doesn't mean we can't be friends, and I sorta want you to wear it and remember what we used to have, 'cos it was awesome while it lasted. For me, anyway.'

It was, like, THE coolest bracelet ever! It was leather and cloth, and in all the colours of the rainbow and it looked totally amazing on my wrist 'cos my skin's gone a bit brown in the sun lately. I put it on and stared at it, then saw she had one on too, and felt my insides do this weird flipping thing.

She said, 'And then every time I'll look at mine I'll think of you and remember what I've lost,' and then just sort of walked slowly past me, leaving me standing by my table clutching my pencil case and lucky puppy beanie toy that I always take to exams 'cos it reminds me of Barbara even though she's not a puppy any more.

Wednesday 21 May

I've decided to only wear my friendship bracelet at home 'cos I don't want Alice to see it and then get questioned to death over it. Can't stop looking at it. Keep getting it out from the box where I keep it safe next to my bed and holding it, and thinking of Han…

Thursday 22 May

I lay in bed last night looking at my bracelet and thinking about Han again. I should be mad with her for thinking she can give me gifts and come on to me again, after everything she's done to me, and for her to think she can get me back, just like that—but I'm not.

I should be pissed off with her for thinking it's okay to do this to me now she knows I'm with Alice—but I'm not.

I should be pissed off with her for making me confused all over again—but I'm not.

I'm just hopelessly, totally, beautifully, and completely overwhelmingly in love with her.

Shit.

Friday 23 May

I had a Business Studies exam with Alice and Ems today.

As I was heading into the exam hall, I saw Han coming towards me on her way in as well, so I kinda hung back a bit and told Alice and Ems I'd catch them up. I knew Han had her first Philosophy exam today, so I wanted to wish her luck, and it's weird, but I felt so damn happy that I managed to see her and speak to her before our exams. Crazy, huh?

She's had her nose pierced!! She told me she had it done on Tuesday after our English exam and after she'd given me the bracelet and she said she did it as a spur-of-the-moment thing 'cos she felt so shit about everything she'd done to me, and saw having another piercing as 'a punishment, to let me have some pain to make me realise what an idiot I've been'.

I have to say, I thought that was a bit extreme, but there y'go. Personally if I was looking for some sort of punishment I'd deny myself chocolate for a week, or whatever, but I know Han always has to take it one stage further. I was secretly pleased, to be honest, 'cos I thought her piercing made her look even hotter than she normally does, even if she did have to keep putting her hand over her nose to hide it from the teachers today.

Anyway, I tried to put all thoughts of Han and her sexy nose ring out of my head for my exam, and I think I did okay. Me and Alice walked home from school together afterwards, and Alice kept holding my hand, and although I held it for a bit, any chance I got, I let it drop 'cos I didn't want anyone to see. I feel such a cow, and a fraud, and so totally messed up right now. Sometimes I wish I could run away from all this—from Alice, from Han, from the thoughts in my head, from these stupid, bloody exams.

But I can't, can I?

Saturday 24 May

My mother has apparently developed a fixation on Simon Cowell but it's beyond me how anyone can find a man who chooses to tuck his nipples into his waistband anything other than revolting.

Sunday 25 May

Had a filthy dream last night, which involved Simon Cowell, and piercings. Let's just say it wasn't his nose that was pierced.

Woke up feeling sick and only managed four slices of toast and butter for breakfast today.

#queasy

Monday 26 May

It was a Bank Holiday today, so Mum graciously allowed me to come out with her and Dad for the day, rather than staying at home to revise, 'cos she said she thought it would be good for me to have a change of scene (and probably thought it would make me more willing to study once we came home again. Yeah, right!)

We went to the beach! How awesome was that?! We took Barbara with us and she went a bit nuts running up and down on the sand, which was so cute. I had thought I might ask Alice to come with us, but frankly, it was good to have a day away from everything and I came home with a clearer head and a more positive attitude than I'd had when we left this morning.

Tuesday 27 May

The woman from across the road came over today and asked if she could use our phone 'cos apparently the phone people have made some mistake and cut them off.

Mum said afterwards that the phone company only cut people off when they haven't paid their bills, so she went over to see if the woman had got everything sorted. When Mum came back, she looked a bit white and said that the woman had got so cross over it all that she'd gone home and torn down her picture of Madonna off her hallway wall in a fit of temper.

WTF?!

Mum said, 'You know the one? Hangs in her hallway. Gives her inspiration when she comes in through the door, apparently?'

I nodded, but I didn't have a flipping clue what she was talking about. Why would I? Most things my mother says are a mystery to me.

Personally, I thought that was quite harsh, as well. Okay, so no one can forgive Madonna for divorcing Guy Ritchie, and there are some that say her cowboy stage was a bit weird, but isn't it a bit extreme to tear her down from the wall for it? Especially when she apparently gives our neighbour so much inspiration (I didn't know the neighbour was a singer, but there y'go).

Actually, come to think of it, why would a woman her age even have a poster of a pop star on her hall wall in the first place? I knew they were weird, but that's taking the piss, isn't it?

I texted Alice and told her all this and she texted me back saying that was the funniest thing she'd heard in ages, and that I was 'so hilarious it was painful.' I'm glad she finds me funny (I think).

Han always thought I was witty, so at least through all my heartache I've not lost it.

#ThinkingPositively

Wednesday 28 May

Han sent me a text late last night telling me she misses me again and that she'd been an 'arse' and could I ever forgive her? I sent her one back saying that it could take time but maybe one day I'd find it in my heart to forgive her. I didn't mean it, of course. Let's face it, Han's the love of my life and I'd forgive her just about anything (within reason!) but I didn't want her to know that. A bit of grovelling won't hurt her one little bit.

Thursday 29 May

I'm thinking about buying a guitar to help me over Han. After all, it seems to work for folk singers, doesn't it? As long as I don't have to sing about my dog dying, 'cos Barbara being ill earlier this month still makes me upset to think about it.

Better grow my thumbnail first, though. And learn to play the guitar.

Friday 30 May

I want her. I miss her.

Saturday 31 May

FML.

No, actually, FML and everything in it 'cos it's lousy and crap without Han in it.

Sunday 1 June

Great Aunt May came over for lunch today. After wading her way through her own body weight in roast potatoes (who said old people don't have appetites?) she started telling us about this man who's moved in to the room next door to her and who has apparently 'caught her eye'.

She told us his name is Elvis and after I'd finished choking on my sprouts with laughter, she went on to tell us he was '83, bald as a coot but had all his own teeth'. She said they sit next to each other at meal times so he can pick all the things out of her tea which give her wind, and that they've taken to walking round the grounds with each other every afternoon. Bearing in mind Great Aunt May has a plastic hip and walks with a Zimmer frame, I should say their walks would be more like shuffles, but never mind.

I heard her telling Mum later in the kitchen that Elvis had 'quite stolen her heart,' but then started talking about her bowels again, so I left them both to it.

Monday 2 June

Revised for History exam tomorrow. Quite frankly if I never pick up another yellowing book telling me about another suffragette chaining herself to some railings somewhere, I'll be happy!

Am growing my thumbnail ready to start learning the guitar soon. Why do nails have to grow so bloody slowly?!

Tuesday 3 June

English exam this morning was a piece of piss. We were asked to write a creative story on something 'close to our hearts' so I just let my imagination run riot. I've got enough worry and angst built up inside me to write a whole volume of hardbacks, lemme tell you!

History this afternoon. Loads of questions on suffragettes so v.v. glad for all those yellowing books after all! Up the suffragettes!!!

French tomorrow. Am knackered.

Wednesday 4 June

My birthday!!! But instead of celebrating today, I had a bloody French listening exam! What's fair about that?!

Anyway, my French exam was helped greatly by the fact that the person speaking was no more French than I am and spoke dead slowly, 'cos my head was full of thoughts of Han and how when I'm with Alice I wish I was with Han.

Why is my life so fucking confusing???

Felt a right cow for thinking about Han when Alice said to me after the exam that she wanted to take me into town to buy me lunch for my birthday 'cos she wanted to have me all to herself for a change.

She'd bought me a present and a really nice card too, which said, 'Happy Birthday to the girl that's made me the happiest girl in the world. You're one in a million, all my love forever and ever, Al xxx'

Mum and Dad had bought me some new games for my PS3, and HRBH had bought me a wicked new black beanie and some sweatbands. I think maybe she's finally getting some fashion sense where I'm concerned! Even Joe had got me some drumsticks, which was cool of him (even if I don't have a drum kit and, erm, can't play the drums). Ever since we had our chat up at the skate park a coupla weeks ago he's been really sweet to me, kinda like an older brother.

Mum had cooked me a really nice tea but to be honest, I spent the whole evening thinking about Han, wondering if she was thinking about me at all.

Hoped Han would text me but had to wait until late tonight before she sent me one which just said, 'Happy Birthday, Clem.' Sat and looked at my phone for ages, hoping she'd send me another one, but she didn't, and I felt so disappointed it pretty much ruined my birthday.

Thursday 5 June

I love Han. I don't love Alice. Writing it down doesn't make it any easier, though.

Friday 6 June

I like Alice, and I s'pose in a way I DO love her—just not in the way I love Han. I'm IN LOVE with Han, I just love Alice. Therein lies the huuuuuuuuuuuge difference!

But Alice is in love with me. And she hates Han.

Bugger.

Saturday 7 June

Mum and Dad went to see Great Aunt May today. When they came home they told me she's still smitten with Elvis and about how when she talks about him, her eyes go all rheumy and she has to have a dab at them with her Kleenex.

I'm so pleased that a pair of wrinkly, half-dead octogenarians are having more luck than I am in the romance stakes.

#sarcasm

Sunday 8 June

Went out for a walk with Barbara this morning to have a think about stuff, 'cos I do all my best thinking when I'm up in the fields on my own. When I got home Joe was sitting in our lounge watching the news with Dad. Joe told me that he was supposed to be going out with HRBH today but she'd got a headache so he was at a loose end, and did I want to go up the park with him? Then he asked Dad if he wanted to come with us, and I was almost weak with relief when Dad said he had to bleed the radiators or something. Can you imagine how much my street cred would plummet if my bloody dad came to the skate park with us???

Anyway, I dunno whether it was 'cos I got exam exhaustion or emotional exhaustion or both, but I was crap on the ramps today and kept falling off and swearing, and then kept getting pissy with Joe 'cos he kept laughing at me. He asked me what was up with me so I decided to tell him what's been going on. I said to him, 'If I tell you something, will you promise—PROMISE—not to tell my sister?' and he laughed and said, 'Depends what it is!' so I swore at him and he said, 'I'm a big lad, Clem. If you ask me not to tell someone something I won't.'

So then I told him about me and about me and Han, and about me and Alice and how screwed up I was over everything and wished it would all just go away. He said, 'I'm no genius, but I figured there was something going on with you and Han 'cos of the way you are—were—with each other. I guess the fact she doesn't come round any more kinda makes sense now. I'm surprised your mum and dad haven't said anything to you about it, though, 'cos Han was, like, round at yours all the time, wasn't she?'

I said, 'They did ask a while back but I just told them we were both busy with revision and stuff and they didn't ask any more. I guess they think we've had a falling-out. Over a boy or something, probably!'

Joe said, 'They don't know you're gay, then?' and I laughed. I said, 'Nah, there's only you and a friend at school that knows—plus Han and Alice, of course! I don't want it broadcast all over the place.'

So then he said, 'Does your sister know?' and I nearly coughed up a lung laughing. I can't imagine telling Mum and Dad about me, let alone HRBH! Yeah, like SHE'D understand!

Joe said, 'And you're cool with being gay?' which I kinda thought was a strange question 'cos I'm very cool with it inside my own head—I just don't want anyone else to know just yet! I told him that, yeah, I was okay about it and he looked at me and said, 'You poor kid' (I AM NOT A KID!!!) and then asked me what I was going to do about Han and Alice. I said, 'What can I do? She tells me she's sorry, and that she loves me and misses me, and she's told a mate she wants to get back with me…but I'm going out with Alice now, aren't I?'

Joe said, 'Would you get back with her if she asked you outright?' and my head was saying 'Yes, yes, yes!!' but instead I said to him, 'I don't wanna hurt Alice.' Joe just said, 'Yeah, but you gotta do what you think's right. If you really want to be with Han, then staying with Alice isn't fair on her, is it? And the longer you stay with Alice, the deeper she's gonna get with you and the more hurt she's gonna be if you and Han do eventually hook up again. You gotta think it through, Clem.'

When I got home I thought loads about what Joe had said to me, and I started to feel a bit better about the whole thing. You know, for a scruffy, bleary-eyed, lazy student, Joe talks a lot of sense sometimes (except when he's stoned).

Monday 9 June

Went into school today to do some revision 'cos HRBH was home and doing my bloody head in. I was sitting up in the library when Han walked in and, I swear to God, I think my heart stopped at least three times.

She sat about two desks away from me, but every time I looked up from my books, she was looking at me, and then every time she saw me looking, she smiled and my heart just seemed to melt that little bit more.

Fuck! Why has she got to be so damn hot? Why can't she be a minger that I wouldn't look twice at?

Anyway, she just sat there watching me, while I did my best to ignore her and concentrate on my revision, then the next time I looked up she'd gone and the crushing disappointment I felt at seeing her empty chair was so huge it felt like a bloody rock in my stomach.

Tuesday 10 June

Is it possible for a heart to physically ache for someone? 'Cos every time I think of Han, my heart feels like someone's squeezing it.

Wednesday 11 June

Woke up this morning with this thought: as if I haven't got enough shit going on in my life at the moment, even my great aunt decides to get jiggy with some old boy who's named himself after a dead rocker.

Where's the justice in that?!

Thursday 12 June

Had TWO exams today! WTF? Isn't there a law against that sort of thing? 'Cos if there isn't, there sure as hell should be! Anyway, I had a French reading exam in the morning (which was a total pièce de pisse) and then my Geography one in the afternoon (which, er, wasn't!)

Friday 13 June

Have grown my left thumbnail when I should have grown my right one.

FFS! Can't I do ANYTHING right??

Saturday 14 June

HOLY SHIT WHAT A DAY!!!!

So, like, Han texted me this afternoon totally out of the blue and asked me if I wanted to go for a walk with her. She said she 'wanted to talk to me' and that she 'missed the silly conversations we used to have when we walked our dogs together'.

I was so totally stoked at getting a text from her, and everything inside me was telling me not to meet her, but OMG I soooo wanted to see her and wanted to talk to her, and if I'm honest, I s'pose part of me was kinda hoping that if she DID still want to get back with me then she might perhaps tell me face-to-face? I was at a loose end anyway, 'cos Mum and Dad had gone shopping to some out-of-town retail park, and I wasn't in the mood to see Alice today so I texted Han back and said, 'Sure.'

Anyway, we met up and walked up through the fields, into the woods and down through the valley, just like we always used to, and it was really nice to spend some time with her again. It was like how it used to be when we first got together, feeling happy in each other's company, just laughing and joking with none of the silly, petty arguments that we were having towards the end.

So, like, it started raining and we had to start walking quicker, but the quicker we walked, the harder the rain came down until in the end Han shouted to me, 'This is useless! We're gonna get soaked before we get home! We better go shelter in the woods, wait for the rain to pass. Whatcha think?'

The rain was coming down so hard by now that it was beginning to run down my back and I thought Han was probably right that we should wait for the downpour to go over before we set off for home. We ran into the woods, whistling frantically for Barbara and Toffee to follow us, and stood, panting and laughing, under a big oak tree. I leaned back against the tree and wiped the rain from my hair, flicking water at her from the end of my fingers before brushing my soaking-wet trousers down and muttering to myself 'cos I'd got my Vans soaked.

When I looked up, Han was standing right in front of me, with a look on her face I hadn't seen for yonks. Her hair was plastered to her face and she had rain running down her cheeks making her look so cute I could feel my heart thumping away like a drum in my ribcage. Without saying a word, she took both my hands in hers and started kissing my wet neck, making my tummy go to mush. Not really meaning it, but thinking I ought to say it, I said, 'Don't, Han,' but she just said, 'Do you really mean that?' and I shook my head. She said, 'Tell me to stop, Clem,' and I felt my legs go wobbly. I knew I couldn't tell her to stop 'cos I didn't want her to stop, so instead I just leant further back against the tree and let her carry on kissing my neck, under my jaw, and over my throat before kissing me full-on. I remembered how nice she tasted, and wondered why she tasted nicer—better—than Alice does but then felt bad for thinking about Alice at a time like this.

I had horns up to my eyebrows so I started unzipping her top, but she grabbed my hand and said, 'No, Clemmykins. Not here, not like this. I want to take you home and show you how much you mean to me properly.' Personally I would have been happy for a quick shag up against that tree, but didn't want to spoil the moment so carried on kissing her and had to contend with just a handful up inside her top for the time being.

Finally the rain eased off so we walked in silence back to my house 'cos I knew that Mum and Dad wouldn't be back for hours yet. When we got home, I led her by the hand up to my room and started to make some feeble joke about taking her wet clothes off before she caught her death of cold but before I could finish she had unzipped my fleece and was busy tugging on the button on my jeans so I kinda just let her get on with it.

The next bit was amaaaaaaazing! She pinned me to my bed and hopped on top of me, leaning over me so that her wet hair was dangling over my face and tickling my nose. She said to me, 'You want this as much as I do, don't you?' and I nodded and she unzipped her top, flung it on the floor, and started kissing me, like, dead hard, just like she used to when we were first going out with each other. Alice never kisses me like that. Then she buried her head in my neck and started nuzzling at it, saying to me over and over, 'You're mine, Clemmykins. Always have been, always will be. Mine.' It was on the tip of my tongue to say to her that, technically, I was still Alice's too, but by that point she'd started to head south, kissing her way down my body and drawing circles on my tummy with her tongue, which made my teeth go all tingly. I wanted her to keep heading south and thought that if I so much as mentioned Alice's name, she'd start to head north again, which would have been toooo frustrating!

Afterwards, after Han had clambered back up to me, she grinned that lazy grin of hers and said, 'I bet Alice never does that to you.' I said, 'Don't mention her name, Han!' but she carried on, 'She'd have to look it up in a book, find out what to do,' and flopped herself down next to me. I said again, 'Please don't talk about her, Han. I don't like it,' but Han just kissed my forehead and giggled to herself, which I didn't really like either.

We lay in each other's arms for a bit and she kept telling me how much she loved me and how sorry she was for being such a cow to me and how sorry she was that she'd dumped me and that she would 'never let me go again'. I wanted to say I kinda hoped she WOULD let me go soon 'cos I was really hungry and could have murdered a sandwich but I didn't want to say anything to spoil the mood 'cos I was hoping if we lay there long enough together she might repeat what she'd just done…

Then she said all of a sudden, 'You'll tell Alice that we're back on, of course?' and I nodded miserably, and she just said, all casual, 'And you'll do it today, won't you?' Despite dreading having to tell Alice, I found myself saying, 'Of course I will. Today.'

I'm so weak, but then again I so love it when Han's forceful.

Sunday 15 June

Gotta figure out a way to let Alice down gently but am dreading it. She rang me today and asked me if I wanted to go to town with her but I told her I had a headache and was just going to stay home all day. I didn't want to add that I'd just been having a filthy texty conversation with Han which had got me in a right old state.

Why am I such a rat??

Monday 16 June

WHAT A CRAP DAY!!

Couldn't sleep last night for thinking about this shit I've managed to get myself into. Lay in bed turning stuff over and over in my head and eventually decided that I had to go see Alice today to finish with her. I know I'm gonna lose her as a friend, but I can't go on two-timing her—it's not fair to Han and it sure as hell isn't fair to Alice. Texted Alice and asked if I could go over later. She replied with a load of happy smileys and I felt a rotten, stinking cow.

Anyway, I went over to hers this morning 'cos I figured it would be better just to get it all out of the way. We went out for a walk 'cos I didn't want there to be any scenes in front of her mum and dad, so we went down to the old disused railway line behind her house and I started to think about what I was gonna say to her. She asked me if I was all right 'cos I was kinda quiet and stupidly I said 'yeah,' and we carried on walking a bit further before I suddenly said, 'No actually, I'm not all right.' She put on a concerned face, which tugged at my heart and made me feel an even bigger rat than I already felt, but I kinda thought 'it's now or never' so took a deep breath and started telling her that me and Han had been talking a lot lately, had been getting on dead well again and that, well, we wanted to give it another go.

She stopped walking and just stared at me, her face kinda all drained of colour, then said something like, 'You're kidding me? Tell me you're fucking kidding me,' but I didn't really hear exactly what she said 'cos I was so intent on getting out what I knew I had to say.

She just said, 'I had a feeling this might happen,' and started chewing on her fingers.

I told her that I felt horrible for doing what I was doing but that I wanted to try again with Han and that I wanted to let her (Alice) down gently because I thought I'd already messed her around enough, but no matter what words I used, or how gentle I tried to make them sound, the truth was I was being a complete wanker towards her and I hated myself for doing it. Alice just said, 'She'll let you down again. She's that type,' and I didn't know what to say, so I just shut up and bit on my lip a bit, and wished that I could go home.

Then she suddenly turned to me and said, 'Haven't you got anything to say?' and I shook my head miserably. She said, 'How about sorry?? How about sorry for leading me on, using me, then dropping me like a stone the second SHE comes back on the scene? Do you have any idea how that makes me feel?' and all I could do was shake my head miserably again.

She breathed out dead deeply and sat down on a rock, inspecting her fingers closely. I sat down next to her and she said quietly, 'How could you do this to me, Clem? Do you have any idea how much I love you?' I said, 'You don't love me, Al. You just think you do,' and she turned to me and spat, 'How the fuck do you know how or what I'm feeling? Do you ever stop to think about anyone other than yourself?' and I just mumbled 'No,' quietly at her.

She went on, 'Do you know how many sleepless nights I've had over you when you were with her last year? How many times I've cried myself to sleep thinking about you and Han? Wishing you were mine but knowing you were someone else's?' and like a prat I just mumbled 'No,' again at her, then as an afterthought, 'Sorry.' She started picking up stones and throwing them hard down on the ground; then she said, 'I knew it was too good to be true. I knew the second Han came sniffing round you again you'd drop me. Story of my life.'

I said, 'I don't know what to say that'll make this better,' but she just turned to me, looked at me with total hatred and said, 'Piss off, Clem.' I said, 'I'm not leaving you here,' and she just said, 'Just piss off. Leave me alone.' So I said, 'I can't just go! I can't just leave you like this!' and she just turned to me and shouted, 'For fuck's sake will you just please PISS OFF AND LEAVE ME ALONE!!!' so I just got up and walked away from her and hoped to God that I didn't get a phone call later that night telling me she'd jumped under a train or something.

11 p.m.

Remembered that it was a disused railway line, so there wouldn't be any trains coming through. Still feel like crap, though.

Tuesday 17 June

Sent Alice a text when I got home last night, but she didn't reply. Texted Han and told her I'd done it. Feel like the worst person in the world right now.

Wednesday 18 June

Sent Alice another text first thing but still no reply, so I rang her mobile but it was switched off. Thought about ringing her house but was too chicken.

Then Han came over this morning and asked me about it all. She tried to look concerned but I knew she didn't give a toss, really. She just asked me if it was 'awful', and I nodded miserably and told her I'd felt a shit doing it to her. She hugged me and said it was for the best 'cos I couldn't keep stringing Alice along when it was her I really wanted to be with, and it wasn't fair on Alice and Alice deserved better and blah, blah, blah.

We were sitting on my bed and Han started kissing me and telling me not to feel bad about it, that me and her were meant to be, and Alice was just a rebound and not really my type and that me and Han were soul-mates. I could feel my head spinning the harder she kissed me and wondered why my head never really spun with Alice. I mean, I liked Alice a lot, but I never got that giddy feeling that I get with Han, those butterflies, that rush of excitement inside.

I tried really hard not to think about Alice, but it's like the guilt's eating me up. I hope to God she gets in touch with me soon, lets me know she's okay.

Thursday 19 June

I rang up Caroline this morning and told her what had happened. She offered to meet me in town and buy me a coffee so we could talk about it 'if I wanted to', and I said, yeah, I really wanted to.

We went down to Starbucks and she bought me a cappuccino AND a chocolate muffin 'cos she said I looked like I 'needed the sugar'. I didn't decline her offer!

I told her I was feeling like the biggest rat in the whole world over what I'd done to Alice and I really thought she might have a right go at me over it all, but instead she just said, 'I s'pose you did what you thought was the right thing to do at the time,' and I just nodded at her, kinda meekly.

I said, 'I do like Alice, but I love Han. It wouldn't have been fair on Alice to keep stringing her along like that,' and Caroline agreed. She said, 'The thing is, Clem, there are some people in this world that are meant for each other, and the thing that I've noticed about you and Han, since you told me you were dating each other, is that you are two of those people.'

I just said, 'We are, we are,' and bit sadly into my muffin.

Caroline said, 'And when the dynamics and the attraction and the fireworks and all that shizz are there, there isn't a whole lot you can do to ignore them, is there?'

I wiped chocolatey crumbs from my front and shook my head miserably. I said, 'So you don't think I'm a total cow for doing what I did to Alice, then?' and she said, 'You're both my friends, Clem. I won't side with either of you, but Alice was always going to be the rebound shag, wasn't she? And I s'pose I would have thought you a total cow only if you'd carried on stringing her along, knowing it wasn't her you wanted, 'cos, let's face it, if Han hadn't kissed you, you'd still be with Alice now, wouldn't you?'

I had to agree. I said, 'It's always been Han and I s'pose it always will be. I just wish I'd had enough about me to not get Alice mixed up in it all, thassall.' Caroline smiled dead kindly at me and said, 'Alice will be fine, I'm sure. I'll text her and go and see her—she's got all her mates ready to help her if she needs it, hasn't she? So quit beating yourself up over it.'

I felt sad when she said that, 'cos I knew that I'd never be able to be friends with Alice again, but I felt better for talking to Caroline about it all. A problem shared is supposed to a problem halved, isn't it? I figured my heart-to-heart with Caro barely scratched the surface of all my problems, but at least it was a start…

Friday 20 June

Alice was sick in her exam today! It was sooooo embarrassing! Well, she wasn't exactly sick in the room itself, but she had to leave really quickly and I saw her running to the toilets down the corridor, clutching her mouth.

One of the exam invigilators followed her down there but she didn't come back into the exam room again. We were only about 20 minutes into the exam as well, so I really hope they'll let her re-take it.

Poor Alice! I texted her tonight when I got home from school and made some joke about the inferior school canteen sausages, but she didn't reply. Why would she? She hates me!

I feel totally eaten up with guilt. What if it was all because of me that Alice was sick? What if I'm responsible for her screwing up her exam? I just wish she'd talk to me, let me know what's going on.

I said to Han that I was worried about Alice. She didn't seem that bothered that Alice was ill, but I suppose I shouldn't be that surprised considering everything. I said I was worried that Alice had been sick, but all Han could say was 'So the little mouse ate some cheese that was off. It won't kill her!' I thought that was well harsh, to be honest.

I really hope Alice doesn't die. If she does, the EMO with an apparent heart of stone will have a LOT of explaining to do.

Saturday 21 June

Han told me today she wants to buy me a present 'cos she didn't get me anything on my birthday 'cos she was worried I'd throw it back at her. We went down to Goths and Cloths this afternoon and she told me to choose whatever I wanted!

I'd sent Caroline a text last night before I went to sleep and asked her if she'd heard from Alice, but she hadn't, so I woke up stressing over stuff and asking myself if I was the nastiest person in the world right now. So I figured a day out in town would probably help to take my mind off things, and it did a bit…

I chose this dead wicked pair of black wristbands and then I told Han I'd started skating again since we'd broken up. I was well pleased that she didn't laugh, and even more pleased when she took me along to a skate shop and bought me some grip tape for my board AND a black T-shirt with 'Anti-Hero' written on it. As if that wasn't awesome enough, then she took me to Pizza Hut and we had a stuffed crust—EACH! Result!!

When we got home we found a note from her parents saying they'd taken Joe to his karate class so the house was empty. I seized the opportunity and took her up to her bedroom to thank her for everything she'd bought me. She insisted I wore my beanie for some strange reason, but who was I to deny my extremely horny, extremely fit girlfriend? It seemed to have the desired effect, and I for one was particularly glad the house was empty 'cos things got, erm, a little noisy, shall we say…

Sunday 22 June

Great Aunt May came down to our house for her lunch today. She's still hung up on this Elvis bloke and was telling us that all the other old girls at Autumn Leaves were quite jealous about her burgeoning relationship with him 'cos he's seen as quite a catch in the home.

She said that Ariadne Dawkins from down the corridor had been 'fluttering her false eyelashes at him but he'd seen right through her'. This wouldn't be difficult. Ariadne Dawkins is about 4 foot 3 and about 6 stone in her wrinkled stockings. Even if he couldn't see through her, he'd sure as hell be able to see over her.

Texted Han and told her Great Aunt May has found herself a man. Han texted me back to say 'I love your Aunt May. And I love you!' and I felt dead loved up. It was a nice feeling. I've missed it.

Monday 23 June

Went over to Han's to do some revision for our dreaded Maths exam tomorrow 'cos Dad's got it into his head he's some DIY expert and he's decided to sand down our banisters, which means the house is not only going to be noisy, but filled with bloody wood dust.

My dad taking a week off to do some DIY would be okay if:

a.) He'd keep the noise down,
b.) I wasn't trying to revise,
c.) He was any bloody good at it.

Anyway, everyone was out at Han's house so we ended up *doing it* on her bedroom floor.

I'm only human! Revision can wait!!!

Tuesday 24 June

Had my last exam today (Maths). Thank God for that!!! No more revision, no more worrying, no more stress.

Well, until the results come out in two months' time, anyway.

Wednesday 25 June

Han and I had a real heart-to-heart today. We talked about all the shit we'd been through and both made a vow that we'd never be like that with each other again. She told me that the time we'd been apart had been 'the worst of her life' and that she'd regretted finishing with me but thought she'd lost me to Alice so she was damn sure she wouldn't mess up with me second time round. She said to me, 'You're my soulmate, Clemmykins. I spent every day we were apart wishing we were together. I missed you soooooo much you wouldn't believe.' She was holding my hand while she was telling me this and I felt dead romantic and soppy. Then she said she'd never let me down again and would spend the rest of her life trying to make it up to me for what she'd done.

I asked her about Smith and she at least had the grace to blush. She said she'd been 'swept along in a tide of longing for someone she knew was out of reach', which I thought was a bit too Emily Brontë for Han, but never mind. I said, 'So you did fancy her then, or what?' and she started spouting all this deep shizz about 'wanting to reach out to her emotionally and spiritually' and about how 'She got into my head, my heart, my soul. I couldn't seem to rid myself of her, no matter how hard I tried.'

I couldn't really comment 'cos I'm the first to agree that Miss Smith is as fit as the proverbial, despite the fact I once loathed her for splitting me and Han up, but I can't say I really understood all this 'reaching out' business. The only reason I would have ever wanted to 'reach out' to Miss Smith would have been to grab her, throw her on a bed, and ravish her senseless, but I don't really think that's what Han was trying to tell me.

Thursday 26 June

Tried texting Alice today 'cos I realised, with a pang of horrible guilt, that I haven't contacted her since she left the exam room that day to be sick. I just kinda sent her a message saying 'Hope you're okay' which, yeah, was wishy-washy and a bit of a cop-out, but I seriously didn't know what else to say.

She hasn't replied. Why would she? She truly hates me, doesn't she?

Friday 27 June

Dad has been well and truly bitten by the DIY bug. Not content with sanding down the banisters in our hallway, he's now decided to REMOVE them and replace them with some spirally ones he found down the DIY store. Our house has so much sawdust in it at the moment, it's starting to resemble the Sahara Desert.

Even Barbara seems pissed off with him; I found her sitting out in the garden behind the shed with a long face on her (and sawdust in her fur).

Saturday 28 June

Han told me again today that we were soul-mates and meant for each other and all that. I was slightly worried that she might try and make us cut ourselves, press our bleeding flesh to each other's or something revolting like that, but instead she just kissed me and put her hand up my top, so I was mightily relieved.

Sunday 29 June

Mum asked me today what I wanted to do with my life now that my exams are over!!! This is just typical of my mother. She can't let me bask in the warmth of finally having no exams! Noooooo, she has to spoil everything by talking about probably yet more school in September.

I told her I had NO idea what subjects I want to take, and that I'd decide once my exam results came in and then she got all dead ratty with me, probably 'cos she has to stay at school until the end of July and I don't! Hahahahahahaaaa!!

Monday 30 June

Dad has booked for us to go on holiday to Scotland in August. Why he's left it until the end of June to book, heaven only knows (although Mum said to me in the kitchen he was hoping to get one of these last-minute deals where you get some draughty cottage for half-price 'cos everyone else is too sensible to book it).

Why Scotland? What is there to do in Scotland? If my father buys a kilt I'm disowning him. End of.

Tuesday 1 July

Texted Han last night and told her we're going to Scotland for our holidays. She said they drink whisky like water up there. Things are looking up already. If I'm bored shitless I can buy myself a bottle and drink myself stupid. It'll warm me up as well, 'cos I'm thinking it ain't gonna be tropical weather up there.

Wednesday 2 July

I got a text from Alice today! Like, totally out of the blue. It just said, 'I'm okay.' Nothing else, but at least I know she's still alive. The relief I felt when I saw her name flashing at me on my phone was so overwhelming I could have cried—even if she could only manage to say two words to me.

Thursday 3 July

Went over to Han's today and we had this, like, dead deep conversation about love and desire and confusion and stuff like that. She was telling me how much she loved me and how sorry she was for everything she'd put me through and how embarrassed she was about how much she'd let herself get confused over Miss Smith and how she now more or less hated Smith for 'the way she sucked me in with her animal magnetism' and how much she regretted what it had done to us and how she would never, like, EVER let it happen again.

I have to say I'm kinda over all the Smith stuff now, so I just laughed and said something about how crap unrequited love is, 'cos as far as I know, Smith never even looked twice at Han and never gave her any reason to think she could be interested (she was her teacher, for heaven's sake! Why would she?!) and Han just said to me, 'Don't tell me you've never been a victim of unrequited love?' and so I thought I might as well tell her about J, 'cos I've never told a soul about it but I figured Han could know about it 'cos, after all, it was all such a long time ago, and we've left school and everything now, so there's no danger of it ever getting back to J (or at least I hope not!!!)

After taking, like, five minutes trying to explain who J actually was, I told Han about how I'd really fancied J and about how she'd been the one who'd made me realise I was gay because as far as I'd been concerned at the time, she'd been more than just a crush. It'd been real love, or so I'd thought. Han said she'd had no idea I'd been into anyone else at school, but then of course when Han joined our school I became really into her instead and started to forget all about J, so I suppose she'd have no reason to know, would she?

Han asked me if I still thought about J, but I honestly don't. I thought I saw a flash of the old, jealous Han, the one that would threaten to rip the head off anyone who so much as looked at me, but she managed to hide it well. Maybe she's mellowing with age? It's true that there was a time when my head was full of J and she occupied my every thought, my every move, and I thought I'd die if I couldn't be with her, but then Han came along and replaced her and, like the old cliché says, time's a great healer. I'd still sometimes see J around school, but she'd be with different friends and we didn't have many of the same classes so it was easy for me to forget about her, especially as soon as Han came on the scene.

We both agreed how shit it is to fancy someone and not be fancied back, and how much it messes up your head, and then we both thought we'd had enough of this deep, meaningful conversation for one day so had, like, this marathon kissing session which only ended when we heard Han's mum coming up the stairs with the vacuum cleaner muttering something about having to clean under the beds.

Friday 4 July

Went to bed last night thinking about J and Han and being gay and a whole heap of other things that just refused to leave my head. I was thinking about what I'd said to Han about J being the person who made me realise I was gay, and that got me thinking about coming out to Mum and Dad again.

Mum's convinced the boy across the road likes me 'cos he's always staring at me. I try and ignore it, but Mum made some comment about it the other day and was kinda suggesting it might not be a bad idea for me to get to know him, 'cos, as she put it, 'You don't have a boyfriend, do you?'

No, Mum. I don't have a boyfriend, but I do have the hottest girlfriend on the planet, and I wouldn't look twice at the bozo over the road, even if he was a girl. Which he's not. So there's, like, NO chance I'll ever be interested in him.

I sent Han a text this afternoon telling her I was stressing a bit about telling Mum and Dad about me and her, and she just texted me back and told me that I shouldn't stress, and that when the time was right, I'd know it, and I shouldn't put pressure on myself to tell anyone anything. Not until I was ready to, anyway. I reckon Han's right. I'm not gonna think about stuff too much, and just kinda take each day as it comes.

There's no hurry, right? I'll still be gay in the morning.

Saturday 5 July

Han told me today that she was thinking about our text conversation last night and nearly told her parents about me and her but chickened out at the last minute. She said to me, 'It's not right, talking sex with your parents, Clem. I mean, I know they know all about it and all, but I don't want them to know that I know they know all about it.'

I can see her point. I don't think I'd like to have to talk about sex with her parents either. Not that I imagine they do it that much, mind you, not the size her mother is. I mean, she's not THAT big (well, nothing that a few walks past the pie shop and straight into the salad shop wouldn't fix) but I imagine it would be a bit like riding an inflatable tractor tyre down the water slide at a theme park for her father.

So neither me nor Han can tell our parents. It's official. We are both chickenshit.

#madeforeachother

Sunday 6 July

Dug out all my Goth clothes from the back of the wardrobe this morning. I've decided to start wearing them again 'cos, as much as I like my skater hoodies and things, I miss wearing all my black gear. Hoodies and cargo pants are cool enough, but there are days where I yearn to wear mesh slash tops and ribboned corsets and scare the living shite out of the kids down the end of our road.

Monday 7 July

Went to the skate park with Joe today. I asked Han if she wanted to come but she said an EMO being seen in a skate park was as bad as pork chops being served up at a Bar Mitzvah, so I took it that she didn't want to come.

I told Joe that me and Han were back on and he was really pleased for me! I made him swear not to say anything to HRBH and he promised (on his board's life) that he would never say a word to her unless I wanted him to.

I like Joe. He's cool. Why he chooses to go out with my sister is a mystery to me!

Tuesday 8 July

Mum and Dad went up to Autumn Leaves to meet Elvis tonight. So it must be serious between him and Great Aunt May!!!

When they came home they told me he was very nice but he had a tendency to break out into 'Heartbreak Hotel' at inappropriate moments and they got all embarrassed. I think Elvis sounds cool! You go for it, Great Aunt May!!

Wednesday 9 July

My sister warned me off Joe tonight!!! If this weren't so pathetic it would be funny. She said to me, 'It's your tough luck you don't have a boyfriend but just quit sniffing round mine, will you?'

I was absolutely speechless so all I could splutter was, 'Are you kidding me??' which she took offence at, for some reason, and just spat at me, 'Stop going skateboarding with him, okay? He's not interested in you, he already told me, so you're wasting your time.'

I said to her, 'I go to the skate park with him 'cos I like skateboarding and so does he, thassall. Seriously, I'm not in the LEAST bit interested,' and looked at her, hoping she might pick up on some hidden meaning, but instead she just got all huffy and told me to 'butt out and quit pestering him', so I just told her to ask Joe if I'd ever shown the remotest bit of interest in him, adding for good measure, 'Joe sooooooo isn't my type! Ask him,' and she said she would.

Dear God, has the world gone mad???

Thursday 10 July

Han came round today with Toffee, so we took a walk up to the woods with her and Barbara. We took a picnic with us, 'cos it was dead hot, and I wore my shorts so I could show off my legs. She wore her skinny jeans, despite the fact it was about 100 degrees in the shade, and I thought for a minute her legs would get so hot they'd drop off. They didn't.

Anyway, we set up our picnic in this clearing in the woods and it was sooooo lovely! While the dogs went off snuffling around in the undergrowth, we spread out a rug under the shade of the trees and just kinda lay there, staring up at the sky, touching each other, and just stroking one another's leg or arm. It reminded me of when we had our first kiss, all that time ago, when we took a picnic down by the reservoir and both admitted that we liked each other. I got all soppy then, just remembering, and, I dunno, it felt like everything that had happened in between had meant to be, just so we could get back to this point.

We started kissing, and I felt so totally loved up it was unreal, and I dare say I would have happily stayed all afternoon up there in the woods, kissing the face off Han if it hadn't have been for Barbara returning with a half-dead rabbit dangling from her chops, being chased by Toffee, and running right over our picnic rug.

11 p.m.

Han's just sent me a text telling me she loves me to the moon and back a thousand times. Awesome doesn't even begin to describe her!

Friday 11 July

Dad has finally paid for the Scotland holiday in August. So we're definitely going. This is just typical. Other people go to France, Spain—the wilds of America, even—but we have to go places which doesn't involve any flying 'cos Dad 'doesn't trust a hundred-ton Coke can that flies 50,000 feet in the air' because 'it's not natural'. So we all have to suffer! I heard Mum saying to him once that flying was the safest form of travel and he replied, 'Yeah, if you're a bird.'

Sometimes I wish my dad would grow some, I really do! Then we could at least go to bloody Disneyland like Matty does each year, AND her dad's a librarian. He's not scared of flying like my bloody father is!

Saturday 12 July

HRBH told me today that she'd 'had a word' with Joe about me and that he'd told her everything was cool. When she says 'had a word', of course what she means is she gave him earache about me for an hour until he probably told her to shut up.

Anyway, she said to me, 'Just so's you know, I've told Joe it's okay for you two to go skating together, if that's what you like doing.' I was bowled over by her generosity (#sarcasm) and repeated what I'd said to her the other day, that Joe, like, sooooo wasn't my type and even if he was the last man on earth I still wouldn't want to get with him.

HRBH said, 'It's cool, I told you. Anyway Joe said the same thing about you, so I'm cool with it all.'

I felt like bowing to her in gratitude but didn't really want to push it with her. HRBH being civil to me for five minutes doesn't happen very often, so I didn't really want to spoil the moment.

Sunday 13 July

Start two weeks' work experience at the *Gazette* local newspaper offices tomorrow. Am surprisingly nervous about it, not helped by Mum asking me what I was going to wear!!! How the bugger do I know??? I'm not bloody 40!!!

I mean, why do we have to do work experience in the middle of the summer anyway? Why couldn't we have done it during the school term so that we could have had time off school? I'm not officially at school any more anyway, so why do I have to do it?? Had a grumble to Mum about it this evening but all she said to me was 'This is meant to be educational, so quit griping on about it, will you?'

Does she have to be so blunt all the time?! Anyway, Han starts her two weeks at a photographer's tomorrow as well. I hope he doesn't get her posing for nude pictures or anything smutty like that.

Monday 14 July

Had my first day at the *Gazette* today. It was all right, actually. I was met in reception by a girl called Felicity who wore pebble glasses and was cross-eyed, and she took me up to the offices where I met this bloke called David—but insisted I called him Dave—who gave me a sweaty handshake and a weak smile.

I spent the morning having a tour of the offices, then Call Me Dave got me doing some filing, so by 5 o'clock this afternoon I was nearly pulling my hair out with boredom. Sent Han a text and told her I was bored shitless and she replied telling me she was too!!!

Hope tomorrow's better.

Tuesday 15 July

Took a notepad and pen with me to work today in the hope that they would notice and see that I was keen to learn some of the journalism side of things at the *Gazette*, but nooooooo! Today they had me clearing out the stationery cupboard and putting things into alphabetical order, so I spent a mind-numbingly boring day putting biros on the top shelf, through to Tippex on the bottom shelf.

I think I may have opened a vein by Friday.

Met Han straight from 'work' tonight and went into town for a coffee and muffin. She told me that she's working in a studio above a sandwich shop and that the guy she's working with bought her lunch both today and yesterday. When I asked if he'd taken her out to lunch (keeping the jealousy from my voice very well, I thought) she said (kinda airily, I thought) 'No, he's just bought me sandwiches from downstairs.'

Felt a bit better at that. The thought of some strange bloke taking Han out to a pub makes me want to punch a wall.

Wednesday 16 July

Got taken round the Classifieds section today and introduced to everyone. I was asked to sort some e-mails out and forward them on to various people, then type up some classified adverts ready to be seen by the deputy editor later today. I typed dead carefully, worried in case I got the births and deaths mixed up or wrote that someone's dear Aunty Elsie had died rather than had just celebrated her 80th birthday.

Then they got me working with some boy called Ed who's in charge of the obituaries. He was weird looking and kept telling me he enjoyed sifting through the death announcements because they were all 'so beautiful' and that 'death was a beautiful thing'. He was certainly in the right job 'cos he looked very funereal to me, with dark sunken eyes. I'm sure I got a whiff of formaldehyde off him as well, but that was probably just my imagination running riot.

Went over to Han's house straight from the paper's offices tonight and we had a right laugh comparing our placements. She said the closest she's been allowed to a camera so far has been fetching one from a cupboard for the bloke she's working for! Poor Han!!!

Thursday 17 July

Had lunch with Felicity and Call Me Dave in town today. Felicity said she knew of a wine bar in town that did great quesadillas and asked me if I wanted to go. I had no idea what a quesadilla was and kinda hoped it wasn't some sort of drug, but then figured Felicity isn't a drug-taking kind of girl 'cos she wears cashmere cardigans, so accepted their invitation and went along.

I've never been in a wine bar before 'cos:

> They're not really the sort of place a gay skater girl and her Goth—sorry, EMO—girlfriend would frequent, and
>
> I don't like wine.

I have to say it was a bit of an eye-opener, though! They were playing the sort of naff twinkling music that Dad favours and they had these really polished wooden floors which made my shoes squeak like a frightened mouse when I walked across them, and the place was packed to the roof with people on their lunch break. Awesome!

We found ourselves some seats at the bar and I had a bit of trouble getting up on the stool, but once I was up there I felt quite at home. Felicity ordered something called a spritzer and Call Me Dave had a glass of lager, which looked like weak dogs' piss, while I had a Coke. They ordered some Tapas, which was basically some square plates with slices of omelettes and some dips on them, with a few olives thrown onto another plate for good measure. We had these quesadilla things too, which were, like, dead messy to eat so I was careful not to get anything down my front 'cos I would get grief from Mum about it when I got home if I did.

After my second Coke I was bursting for a wee, but figured it would be just too much hassle trying to get down off the stool again so just held on then went when we got back to the office. Plus, I didn't want to look a complete bozo for needing the loo after just two drinks. I figured I had a sophisticated front to keep up, after all, 'cos I was out with office-working types, not silly kids that can't hold on to their wee for more than a bloody hour.

Texted Han in the afternoon and told her I'd been to a wine bar for lunch. She texted me back and said, 'Oooh, how very Friends!' and I texted her back and said that they weren't my friends, just some people I work with. I don't consider them friends—after all, I'll never see them again after next week, will I?

Friday 18 July

Was busy sifting through a pile of e-mails and stuff this morning when Call Me Dave asked me if I wanted to go out for lunch again. Mum had packed me some chicken sandwiches and a packet of crisps, which I was really looking forward to, so I politely declined his invitation, but then he asked me if I fancied meeting him in town tomorrow instead!!!!!

I told him I had already made plans tomorrow (this is true—me and Han want to go to Goths and Cloths to get her a new dog collar 'cos the one she's got at the moment is showing signs of leather fatigue) and he looked a bit disappointed, then asked me if I had a boyfriend and was it him that I was going out with tomorrow??!

I was just about to tell him that I didn't when I suddenly heard my voice telling him that, yes, I had a boyfriend and yes, I was going out with him tomorrow. I thought he'd be satisfied with this and leave me alone, but noooooooo! He asked me what his name was and how long we'd been going out and blah, blah, blah so I just bluffed my way through his questions and told him my boyfriend was called Hal and that we'd been going out for, like, ages. Just for fun I told him that 'Hal' was a rugby player and was currently under an ASBO for GBH, and I saw Call Me Dave visibly pale so that obviously did the trick.

Thought about texting Han and telling her that Call Me Dave had asked me out, but then thought better of it, bearing in mind she's not the most tolerant of people. Okay, so she might have mellowed with age, but not that much! If Han got so much of a whiff of me being asked out by a boy, it'll be Call Me Dave's obituary I'll be sifting through next week.

Saturday 19 July

Had a lie-in this morning and it was bliss! I made the mistake of saying to Dad while I was eating my breakfast at 11.30 a.m. that I was tired after my week at the *Gazette* and grateful for a lie-in, then got 10 minutes' worth of nagging from him about how I 'would have something to complain about after 20 years' of working, but not after one week so stop feeling sorry for yourself and eat your Corn Flakes'.

Fascist.

Met Han in town at 2 and we went to Goths and Cloths for her new dog collar. Saw a wicked black, kinda burlesque, vest top with 'Bitch' written on it in sequins and shizz, and wondered if the *Gazette* would mind me turning up to work in it on Monday, but then figured Felicity would get a fit of the shakes if she saw it, and would have to lie down in the photocopying room for an hour to recover. She's not exactly what I'd call a 'Woman of the World'.

While me and Han were in town, Han was talking a lot about the photographer's studio where she's working, and about how much she's enjoying being there. Then, she casually told me that the guy she works with is called Will, and that she thought he was a really nice bloke, and then added that she thought he worked out ' 'cos he's really buff'.

Buff?!

She also told me that Will reckons she'd make a good model, 'cos according to Han, he told her she had good bone structure and would be a 'photographer's dream,' but all I could think of when she was telling me this was that I'd like to meet this Will prat, rip his lens cap off and shove it up his aperture. I mean, WTF??

Okay, I know Han's stunning, and I'm not just saying that 'cos she's my girlfriend, but I don't want some bloke, who's probably this ancient, sweaty greaseball, telling MY girlfriend that he thinks she'd make a good model!

I didn't let on to Han that I was unhappy with what she'd told me, though, 'cos all I have to do is remember what happened when I got jealous of her and Smith, and that stops me. I don't want a repeat of all that, so I just bit my tongue and nodded in all the right places, but inside I was hating it all.

Sunday 20 July

Woke up thinking about what Han had told me yesterday, and dreading the fact I've got to go back to that boring shithole *Gazette* tomorrow. Work experience is supposed to do just that—give you experience of a potential workplace, but all it's done for me is make me determined to do well at school and find somewhere better to work than the bloody local newspaper.

Let's hope I haven't buggered up my exams, then!

Monday 21 July

Back to the *Gazette*, worse luck! I was hoping for a slightly more exciting week than last week but I was to be disappointed (surprise, surprise!) 'cos today they got me doing a pile of photocopying that I later heard Ed say to some ditzy blonde called Tina he 'couldn't be arsed to do so I'll get the work experience weirdo to do it'. Realised after the 560th copy that he meant me and was sorely tempted to photocopy my arse and slip it in with the copies but then thought about how embarrassing it would be if I was crouched on the photocopier and someone walked in…

Had a moan to Han tonight about how boring it is there. She told me to say something about it to someone but I daren't 'cos they'll probably end up making me clean the Gents with a toothbrush or something as punishment.

Tuesday 22 July

Mrs. Schofield came into the *Gazette* offices today to see how I was getting on!!! I seized the opportunity and told her I didn't really think I was learning anything useful but I don't think she was listening to me 'cos she just looked at a list on a clipboard and muttered something about not really having time to discuss it in depth 'cos she had to get through a visit to a florist's, the hospital, and some solicitor's office in town by 5 'cos she had to be home by half past 'to lay out nibbles for my weekly poker evening', so I figured my comments had fallen on deaf ears!

Roll on Friday.

Wednesday 23 July

Han finished up early at the photographers today so she came and met me after work and walked home with me. I loved it. She didn't mention anything about what she'd told me at the weekend about Will, so I guessed he hadn't said anything to her about it again. That made me feel pathetically relieved!

While we were walking back I imagined what it would be like if me and Han weren't at school any more, but working full-time, and, like, living together. I imagined Han coming to pick me up from work each night, and us going back to our own home, where we'd cook tea together and do housework together and stuff like that. And have lots of sex, of course.

My bubble of domestic bliss was popped like an overinflated balloon, though, the second I stepped in through the front door and I saw HRBH's miserable face looking at me from the lounge, and my mother crashing pots and pans about it the kitchen, obviously in a bad mood about something. Again.

Thursday 24 July

Dad asked me today if I wanted to ask Alice along to Scotland with us 'cos he's booked a four-berth caravan and 'might as well get his money's worth.' Yet again HRBH has chosen not to come with us, but that's only 'cos she'd rather have a week of drunken debauchery with Drummer Joe while the house is empty. Can't say I blame her (not that I'd want to do anything drunken with Joe—he's bad enough when he's sober!)

Dad has obviously not cottoned on to the fact that I haven't spoken to Alice in, like, over two months, but I suppose men aren't the most observant creatures in the world, are they? Instead I asked him if Han could come with us and, after what I thought was a brief flash of panic on his face, he said he'd talk to Mum and ask her if it was okay.

So that's settled, then. Mum's bound to say yes and what Mum says goes in our house.

Friday 25 July

Last day of work experience, thank goodness! Felicity, Call Me Dave, and Ed took me back to that strange wine bar place for lunch to say goodbye, which was nice of them, I suppose. Even if it's not really my type of place, they do a cracking omelette and fries there, and it's only £4.99!!!

Ed made an embarrassing speech about how much they'd enjoyed having me for the last two weeks, and how valuable my help had been. It was on the tip of my tongue to say to him that all they'd had me doing for the last two weeks was photocopying and filing, but instead I smiled demurely and said it had been nice working with them too. It hadn't.

Call Me Dave cornered me by the coffee machine in the afternoon and said that he'd 'miss me' and then pressed a piece of paper into my hand with his phone number on it!!!!!!!! I wondered for a second if he was going to try it on with me, but I was holding a hot cappuccino in my hand and he probably thought I'd chuck it over his head if he did!

Saturday 26 July

Han's coming to Scotland with us and I can't wait! I rang her up this morning and asked her if she wanted to come, and had to hold the phone away from my ear 'cos she screamed so loudly with delight! She said she'd love to come, adding that it would be our 'first holiday away together' and that it would be 'dead romantic.' I fail to see what could possibly be romantic about spending a week in a draughty caravan in the middle of Scotland with my parents less than three feet away from us all day and night, but there you go.

Then she started making jokes about letting me have a feel of her sporran and stuff like that, and then our conversation just descended into pure filth. I'm in love. Sue me.

Went downstairs after I'd finished talking to Han and told my parents that she'd be coming with us. I thought I saw Dad pale a little, but Mum just smiled and said it was good she was coming because I'd be 'less likely to get bored and up to mischief if I had a friend with me'.

It was on the tip of my tongue to tell her I wasn't 8 years old any more, but then I thought if I gave her cheek she might change her mind about letting Han come with us, so I just smiled serenely and kept it zipped.

Sunday 27 July

Went through my dirty washing and found Call Me Dave's phone number in my pocket. Looked at it briefly before screwing it up and throwing it in the bin. Felt a bit bad about being so dismissive, but then figured hell would freeze over before I ever called him! He's a nice enough bloke, I suppose, but he has dangly bits, and of course dangly bits aren't my scene.

Monday 28 July

Was woken up (on my first morning off in, like, weeks, I might add!) this morning by the sound of Mum nagging Dad to do our banisters before summer's out or, as she told him, she'll 'get a man in and get you to pay him'.

No! The banisters still haven't been finished, diary! Oh, he started doing them, like, weeks ago, but Dad being Dad, his enthusiasm faded the second he realised he wouldn't be able to do it in a few hours.

Anyway, just before I pulled the duvet back over my head and tried to get back to sleep, I heard him telling her that he didn't have money to waste and so he'll do them himself and, as he put it, 'save us a bob or two'. He reckons he'll have it done by the weekend.

Just before I went back to sleep, I texted Han to tell her what I'd just heard. I told her Dad reckons he'll be done and dusted by Saturday and Han texted me back to say, 'A tenner says he isn't.'

Han knows my dad tooooooo well!

Tuesday 29 July

So, I was woken up this morning, not by the sound of Mum and Dad arguing this time, but by the sound of Dad hammering and crashing about on the landing outside my room.

I came out of my room and glared at him, but one look at the look on his face told me not to complain, so I just went downstairs, got myself some breakfast, and took it back up to my room. It appears that he's taken the whole week off work to fix the dumb banisters so that he doesn't have to have any more earache from Mum about it, but I don't think he's doing it with much grace, if the furious look on his face this morning was anything to go by!

Went into town with Han this afternoon to buy some new clothes for Scotland, but somehow managed to come home with a dodgy-looking lesbian DVD that we found for £2.99 and a new sticker for my skateboard. Oops.

Wednesday 30 July

Was getting all my clothes out of the wardrobe this morning, looking to see what I could take on holiday with me, when I heard swearing coming from the landing that a sailor would be proud of.

Why the hell does Dad think he can fix these bloody banisters all on his own? The only other bit of DIY I've ever seen him do in my lifetime was when he painted the upstairs toilet and left the tray of paint on the floor which Chairman Meow then stepped in and walked blue paw prints all down the stairs.

My father is an accountant. He's not Bob the Builder. That much is obvious.

Han came over after lunch and even she was surprised to see Dad with a screwdriver in his hand. Me and Han went to my room and I locked the door (habit), but knowing Dad was literally right outside my door hammering on bits of wood put paid to any naughtiness with Han.

I wish he'd bloody hurry up and finish the job!

Thursday 31 July

Met up with Han, Ems, Matty, Marcie, and Caroline in town this morning. All the drilling and hammering at home is beginning to wear me down, so I figured a day pissing about in town with the gang was just what I needed.

I asked Caroline today if she'd heard from Alice and she said she'd been over at her house at the weekend. I asked her how she was and Caroline was, like, really vague answering me, which probably means that Alice has told her not to talk to me about her. I asked Caroline to tell Alice I said hello next time she spoke to her, and she said she would, but I'm not sure whether she meant it.

I miss Alice. I miss our friendship. We were friends for years before everything went tits up last year and then again this year. Why did she have to fancy me? Why did I have to be so weak and get with her?

10 p.m.

Why has my bloody father STILL not finished the sodding banisters?!

Friday 1 August

Spent most of this morning in A&E. Mum has broken her wrist. And how do you s'pose she did this, dear diary? By falling through the stupid banisters that my stupid father didn't fix properly. And now she's broken her wrist and has to wear a cast for, like, the next God knows how long.

I tell you what, you could cut the atmosphere with a knife in this house at the moment. I wonder if Han would ever let me come and move in with her?

Saturday 2 August

Saw Dad packing the car up with sanders, drills, unused wood, and some packets of screws. Apparently some bloke called Ron's coming round to finish the banisters tomorrow. Ha, ha, ha!!!

I asked Mum if I could write on her cast, but she looked at me witheringly and told me it was so painful that if I even came within an inch of her, she'd grab the one hammer that Dad hasn't taken back to the DIY store and bash me over the head with it.

Mum's on strong painkillers. I think they've weirded her out.

A strange thing happened this afternoon, too. Han came over, and while we were *having a moment* on my bed, her phone beeped, and after she'd read the text that had come through, she said (casually), 'I'll have to scoot in a while, Clemmykins. I'm out tonight.'

I felt this plunging disappointment, 'cos I'd hoped she'd stay for the evening, but I didn't say anything. Instead, I just asked her where she was going, and assumed she was meeting one of the gang, and did kinda wonder why I hadn't been invited too. She told me she was meeting Will.

WTF?

So I said (dead calmly) 'Will that you worked with?' and she just said, 'Yeah,' like it was the most ordinary thing in the world. So I just said, 'Oh,' 'cos I didn't know what else to say, and she said, 'You don't mind, do you?'

Hmm.

Did I mind that she was going out with some bloke that:

a.) Thought she was fit enough to be a model, and
b.) That Han thinks is 'buff'?

Noooooooooooooooooooo. Of course I didn't mind! #sarcasm

But again, I thought back to Smith and how weird Han went with me over that and so, despite wanting to ask her, like, a million questions (the first one being, why the fuck are you going out with a man?) I stayed shtum.

Then Han did that thing that she does which she knows I like, and which always reassures me; she pulled me into a tight hug, kissed my hair, told me she loved me, and that she thought it would be cool to see him, just to say hi and see how he was.

She said, 'I'd invite you too, but, well, you don't really know him, do you?' and it was on the tip of my tongue to tell her that I'd never get to know him if I never got the chance to meet him, but I didn't say anything.

<u>11 p.m.</u>

Lying in bed waiting for Han to text me to tell me she's home and not kissing the face off Will.

<u>11.30 p.m.</u>

Han home. Phew. Asked her how her night was, and she said 'Okay.' This doesn't make me feel any better.

<u>1.15 a.m.</u>

I can't sleep 'cos I'm too cross with Han. I mean, Call Me Dave was obviously interested in me 'cos he gave me his phone number, and I was so scared of Han finding out, I threw his number away and never gave him a second thought. Okay, so Call Me Dave revolted me to my core, but that's not the point, is it?

Why is it okay for Han to swap numbers with the bloke SHE worked with, without thinking it would upset me? Worse still, what part of her thinks it's all right to go out with him??

Sometimes I feel like it's one rule for her, and another for me.

Sunday 3 August

Had a BBQ at home tonight because it was dead hot out. Han came over, dressed more like she was about to bury her grandmother than snaffle a few burgers, but never mind.

I asked her why she was picking all the burnt bits off the sausage that Dad had chargrilled to within an inch of its life and she told me that burnt sausages are carcinogenic and that she didn't want to die from eating one.

I have to say I never knew burnt sausages were carcinogenic. I thought magic mushrooms were, yeah, and if you lick a toad's back and shit like that, but burnt sausages? Never! No wonder Mum always gets a bit giddy at family BBQs. And there was me thinking it was always the wine…

I asked Han about her 'date' with Will (I didn't use the word 'date', of course) and she said it had been fine, and that they'd just been out for drinks and a catch-up. Part of me thinks that because Han's being so up front about it, and because she still wants to come round to my house and eat my dad's burnt offerings, she can't be cheating on me, can she? This comforts me slightly, but I still want to do evil things to Will's shutter.

Monday 4 August

This bloke Ron that Mum got in to finish the banisters managed to do it in one day. Dad's face was a picture, but I'm sure I heard him say to Ron as he was paying him that he'd done all the hard work and all Ron had to do was 'top and tail it'.

My father is priceless sometimes.

Me and Han took Toffee and Barbara for a walk into the woods this afternoon and had this, like, epic ten-minute kissing session deep in the woods where we knew no one would be able to see us. Came home and tried to act normal in front of Mum and Dad, but I've gotta say, sometimes it's hard to do that!

Tuesday 5 August

I texted Alice today and told her I was going to Scotland next week. I dunno why I told her that; I guess I just wanted to. Perhaps I thought it would kick-start a texty conversation, but she didn't reply, and it's now gone midnight and she still hasn't replied, so I guess she's not going to, is she?

Wednesday 6 August

Dad took me to one side tonight and asked me quietly if I would ask

Han not to pack her full-length distressed leather coat for going to Scotland 'cos the thought of being stuck in a car with the stink of old leather for over eight hours was making him feel ill already.

Honest to God, my father is a wimp! This is what happens when you're brought up by your mother and grandmother. *No cojones, papá!*

Rang Caroline tonight after tea and asked her advice about what she thought about Han going out with Will the other day. Caroline said to me exactly what I'd been thinking at our BBQ on Sunday: if Han WAS seeing Will behind my back, she wouldn't have told me about going out for drinks with him, would she?

Caroline said, 'Is she off with you? I mean, like she was when she got confused over Miss Smith?' and I told her she was acting normally, and that she was still coming over to mine, and we were still hanging out all the time together. Then Caroline lowered her voice (not sure why) and asked me if she was being tactile with me, and I told her that I didn't think Han had used much tact, to be honest, 'cos she'd just sat on my bed and told me straight she was going out with him, rather than kinda softening the blow.

Caroline sighed down the phone at me and said, 'Noooooo, are you and Han still, y'know? *Intimate* with each other?' and I told her that me and Han had been kissing up in the woods the other day, and that Han had put her hand up under my hoodie while she was kissing me, so I kinda thought that must mean we were still okay. Caroline went, 'Awww!' and told me she thought we were 'cute' (WTF?) and that if Han was still wanting 'to cop a feel of your soft bits then that has to mean she's not copping a feel of someone else's soft bits, so quit worrying'.

Blimey! Don't ever become a relationship counsellor, Caro!!

Thursday 7 August

Great Aunt May brought Elvis down to our house tonight. Well, I say she *brought* him, but what I meant was Dad went and fetched them 'cos Great Aunt May can't walk more than three steps without wheezing.

He's a funny bloke, is Elvis, and full of bullshit stories, which were making us hoot. He was telling us this tale of how he went to Memphis in 1953 and met a young man with a guitar wearing blue suede shoes sitting at the side of the road on a hill looking sad. Elvis said he asked this man what the problem was and the man told him he was a singer and wanted a stage name but couldn't think of one. Elvis apparently asked the man what his name was and he told him, 'Trevor Presley,' so Elvis suggested *his* name, Elvis, and, in Elvis's words, 'Hey presto! A legend was born, all thanks to me.'

We sat listening to this, looking at each other, not really sure if he was serious or not but then he started going on about how this singer wrote to him years later and told him he'd named one of his songs, 'Blueberry Hill,' after him 'cos Great Aunt May's Elvis was eating a blueberry muffin when he met him. And he was sitting on a hill.

I asked Mum later in the kitchen whether Elvis had been spinning us a yarn and she snorted, 'Course he was! I asked the nurses at the home if Elvis was his real name and they told me his real name's Ernest, so the only similarity between him and his Elvis story is that they share the initial E!'

I don't care whether he was telling the truth or not. He seems like a decent bloke, and he makes Great Aunt May happy, so I s'pose that's all that counts really, isn't it? I texted Han just before I went to bed and told her that Elvis had come to dinner tonight, and that Great Aunt May was still totally smitten with him, and that I thought it was kinda sweet. She texted me back and said, 'If the old girl marries him, Clemmykins, you'll have a Great Uncle Elvis. How cool would that be?? How many people can say they have a Great Uncle Elvis?!'

Han has a point. Caroline has a Great Uncle Derek, and I think Matty has an Uncle Kenneth, but does anyone else have a Great Uncle Elvis? Noooooo!

I hope Great Aunt May hurries up and marries him now. After all, it's not like she can hang about at her age, is it? Every day when she wakes up, stretches her toes and they don't touch wood has got to be a bonus, hasn't it? Hahaha!

Friday 8 August

There was a programme on the telly tonight about transgender teenagers. It was really interesting but I felt dead uncomfortable watching it with Mum and Dad, and I wish I hadn't felt so uncomfortable, because, really, there wasn't anything TO feel uncomfortable about, if that makes sense.

I was watching their faces while it was on, and had this real urge to try and talk to them about stuff, but couldn't for the life of me think how I would even begin to start talking about it. How could I? How do I bring the conversation up? How do I start to even try and explain stuff to them? It does my head in sometimes.

I also figured we were off on our holidays on Monday and I didn't want anything to spoil it, so I stayed shtum. What if it caused a huge argument? What if they wouldn't speak to me? What if—even worse—they then said Han couldn't come with us once they knew me and her were together, or even worse, banned me from seeing her?

Okay, I know I'm old enough to technically be able to do what I want, but the thought of being with Han 24/7 for a whole week is the only thing I can think about at the moment, and there was no way I was going to risk that going tits up.

Saturday 9 August

OMG I was walking into town to meet Han today and the boy across the road caught up with me and asked me if he could walk in with me!!

I mean, WTF? He's never even spoken to me before, just leered at me from behind, or watched me from his lounge window, and now he wants to walk with me?

Anyway, I kinda just said, 'Yeah, s'pose,' and we walked in near silence for about a minute before he told me his name was Daryl and that he went to St Andrews school and then kinda asked me my name and what school I went to, so I told him. He said, 'St Bartholomew's is for posh girls, isn't it?' and I was about to tell him it's about as posh as picking your nose and flicking it at the dog, but something stopped me. I figured if he thought I was posh he might leave me alone, so I told him it was a really exclusive school and that we all played lacrosse and wore straw boaters.

I dunno whether that put him off at all, but when we finally got into town and he saw Han waiting for me, dressed from head to toe in black leather and chains, and looking as hot as hell, I thought I saw him practically wither up on the spot with shyness. At least it made him leave me alone, anyway, 'cos he just kinda mumbled a goodbye to me and wandered off in the direction of a gaming store.

When I got over to Han, she had an eyebrow arched in a kinda 'Who the hell was that?' way, which only managed to un-arch itself when I took her to the nearest Pret A Manger and bought her a Flat White and a Gingerbread Man. Her obvious suspicion at seeing me walk into town with Daryl got me thinking about Will the Photographer again, and I asked her if she'd heard from him lately. She told me she hadn't spoken to him since she met up with him last week, and kinda said, 'Why would I?' and looked at me funny.

Then she asked me if I was jealous of him!!! What could I say? I told her I found it 'unsettling', and as she was pulling the head off her Gingerbread Man she gave me the sort of look that makes my insides go gooey, and told me there was nothing 'unsettling' about it, and I had nothing to be 'unsettled' about, and mouthed 'I love you' to me. Then she gazed at me all seductively while she licked the iced buttons off the front of her gingerbread and I felt like I was going to slide off my chair and melt into a pool of lust on the floor, and have to be carried out of Pret feet first.

Sunday 10 August

Off to Scotland tomorrow!!! Packed my bag up tonight but wasn't sure what the weather's going to be like, so I packed for every eventuality, which means I've put in everything from a swimming costume to a pair of wellington boots. If Dad moans at me then I'm not coming; I'll just spend the week at home on my own with Han.

11.33 p.m.

Hang on, why AM I coming to Scotland when I could have just said no and had the week at home with Han instead? You're such a dumbass sometimes, Clem!!

Monday 11 August

Packed up the car with enough supplies to last five months in the Andes, let alone a week in a caravan in Scotland! Han arrived at our house at 8 looking like it was Halloween or something 'cos she was dressed from head to foot in black with all her 'accessories' jangling from various parts of her body. She told me in the car later that she wanted to 'show those Scotties that us English girls know how to rock', and I briefly thought that the 'Scotties' will take one look at her and think all English girls are nutters.

She told me while Dad was putting the last of the things in the car that she'd packed some underwear, which, as she put it, 'Shows all my bits and pieces off to their full advantage.' I told her as awesome as it was that she'd packed some nice undies, there was no way I'd be indulging in any bedroom aerobics while I was under the same corrugated-iron roof as my parents. She thought about that for a bit, and eventually had to agree with me, but not before she made me promise to at least have a peek at them while they were on her, otherwise it would all be for nothing. I agreed.

Anyway, HRBH is staying in the house with Drummer Joe while we're away so she's been left with a list of instructions as long as your arm, and Mum's pinned reminders up all over the house telling her not to forget to feed the dog, cat, or rabbit 'cos if she comes home and find HRBH has starved them, she'll get the authorities on to her. And she means it. Now I know that HRBH is gonna be home all week I'm soooooo glad I decided to come along after all!!

Arrived in Scotland around 4. Journey up okay, but by the time we'd arrived at the Scottish border my bum was so numb from sitting still for so long that I could barely feel it! The caravan is, well, basic, and I told Han that she can DEFINITELY forget about any hanky panky for the next week now, 'cos the walls between our bedroom and Mum and Dad's are so paper thin they'll be able to hear us fart, let alone anything else.

Tuesday 12 August

We all went for a walk round this loch that's near the caravan park today. I got bitten to death by bloody midges! Dad had told me Scotland gets, like, loads of midges in August and he's brought this net to go over his head, and a sort of zapper thing that looks like a small tennis racquet and which he can splat them with. He looks a right twat! I told him there was no way I was wearing a bag over my head, or swishing a tennis racquet round and round and he got all pious and said something like, 'On your head be it, then.'

So we got to this loch, right, and the midges must have smelt me coming 'cos they all started buzzing round my head and getting in my hair and shit like that. They didn't touch Han! Oh no! I would have thought that Goths—sorry, EMOs—would have liked getting bitten, as they're all into blood and death and stuff, but they wouldn't go near her! They're obviously as scared of her as Dad is!

Mum got bitten a bit, but nowhere near as bad as me! So now my face is all red and blotchy and I look like some 15-year-old boy who's just shaved for the first time in his life. Mum dabbed some cream on it just before I went to bed, but Han keeps complaining that I smell like I've been preserved or something, so looks like if I'm to have any hope of going out at all this week, I'm gonna have to give in and wear one of Dad's bloody stupid nets over my head!

Wednesday 13 August

We went to some draughty castle today that was owned by some Scottish clan, like, 800 years ago. It was full of tourists oohing and aahing at the swords and knives and shields and shit like that, so me and Han left them all to it and went on this boat that takes you out onto the castle's loch to see some seals bobbing about in the water.

Of course, the second we got out on the water the midges descended on me again, like something out of a horror movie, so I had to pull my hood up over my head and look like a right idiot for the 40 minutes it took the boat to go round the little islands.

I want to go home.

Thursday 14 August

Saw a man in a kilt today!! We went to this outdoor museum thingy and there was a man walking around in a kilt! I thought he was part of the exhibit, even though he didn't have any bagpipes with him, but it turned out he was a tourist. And French. I mean, WTF?! Can't he be done on the trades' description act or something?

Now I feel stupid for taking so many photos of him when he's no more Scottish than I bloody well am!

Friday 15 August

Dad has been banging on about wanting to go and visit a whisky distillery all week, so Mum finally gave in to him and they went to one today. He only wants to go 'cos they give you a free sample of the whisky, apparently, but I didn't care 'cos it meant I could have an afternoon with Han all by myself. The distillery was next to another loch (Scotland's full of 'em!) so while Mum and Dad disappeared inside, me and Han found a neat little café where we had lunch, then went for a dead romantic walk around the banks of the loch. Afterwards we found this gift shop overlooking the water, which had a bloke standing outside playing his bagpipes to all the tourists. The shop sold bagpipes and soft toys with kilts on and stuff like that, and Han bought me this totally awesome leather necklace that I saw and liked. I kinda stood outside the shop with the sound of the water lapping behind me, and the strains of that lone bagpiper, and let her put it round my neck, and I swear to God it was one of the most tender and loving moments of my life!

It was all sooooo romantic and lovely, and I thought for a minute that I could happily spend the rest of my life there, next to that loch, with Han by my side, but then I started to feel the midges biting at my neck again, evidently attracted by the scent of the blood from freshly bitten skin last night, and figured if I ever did decide to move to Scotland, I'd have to move back to England each August or risk getting bitten to bloody death.

Saturday 16 August

Han crept into my bed in the middle of the night last night 'cos she said she couldn't sleep. Of course, once I felt her hot body pressed up against mine, I got all horny, especially when she pulled the covers over our heads and started kissing me under the duvet.

I whispered to her that we couldn't do anything while Mum and Dad were just next door, but she just kept on kissing me and saying to me, 'Why not? They're asleep, won't hear a thing,' so I told her as long as she promised to be quiet, we could *do it.*

I felt hideously guilty *doing it* in such close proximity to my parents, and I was petrified they'd come in, but I have to admit it added a dead romantic frisson and I got this thrill from doing it. Is that twisted? I'm so gonna fry in Hades for this, you mark my words.

Sunday 17 August

Mum said me and Han looked tired this morning and asked me if we'd not slept very well. I couldn't look at Han and tried really hard not to squirm, but Han just chewed on her toast nonchalantly and said that it 'had taken her a while to get off, but once she did it was great', and I nearly spat my Corn Flakes out across the table at her.

Monday 18 August

Back from Scotland today. I can't say I'm sorry. I looked at my skin in the mirror when we got back to the safety of our house in the English suburbs, far, far away from midges and water, and thought that my face resembled a pizza. They've bitten me to death!! How am I supposed to go out and see my friends when my face looks like someone's taken a sander to it?!

Next year I'm going to Australia. Do they have bugs in Australia?

Tuesday 19 August

Exam results are out on Thursday. Am crapping myself.

Wednesday 20 August

Oh shit, oh shit, oh shit!!!!!!!!!! This time tomorrow!!

Han told me that Will had sent her a message this morning wishing her good luck for her results tomorrow, and that if she'd failed them spectacularly, there would always be a job for her with him at the studio. I asked her if she'd ever take him up on the offer and she gave me a withering look and said, 'Like I'd ever fail my exams?'

I don't like the fact he still texts her, even though I don't really know *why* I don't like it, if that makes sense. I mean, she's known him for about a month now, and she's very open about texting him and talking to him, and she doesn't act all suspicious like she did around Smith…

But…aaaargh! I still don't like it, and there doesn't seem to be a thing I can do about feeling jealous over it.

Thursday 21 August
EXAM RESULTS DAY

Went round to Han's first thing and we walked to school together to get our results. It felt dead weird being back after nearly three months away but I was well pleased to see everyone again after such a long time. We had to go see the school secretary, who had a load of envelopes with our names on, and when she handed me mine, my hands were shaking so much I could hardly hold the paper still! Anyway, I was pretty pleased with my results. This is what I got:

Maths	C
English Lang	A* (gettinnnnnn)

English Lit	A
Geography	C
History	A
Media Studies	B
Humanities	C
French	C
Biology	B
Chemistry	C
Physics	D

I heard Han whooping when she opened her envelope 'cos she got, like, five A*s, four As, a B for Economics and a C for Geography. I briefly wondered how it was she managed to get such good results bearing in mind all the shit that was going on when we took our exams but then figured Han's not the sort to let things mess with her mojo or anything like that. Wish I could say the same for me.

Just as we were leaving, Matty and Caroline turned up, so we waited with them to see what they got, and they got pretty much the same as I did—bit of a mixture really. On our way home Ems texted me and asked me what I got so I told her. She told me she got four Cs, two Bs, and a G (!!!!), so she's really pissed off. Didn't hear what Alice got, though.

When I got home Mum was just coming back from checking all her pupils' results. She was dead pleased with what I'd got but then started banging on about me having to choose what I want to do now and I wanted to tell her to shut up and let me bask in the glory of my success, but instead I just nodded and told her I'd have a think about it!!

Friday 22 August

OMG, such a weird day. So, like, the doorbell rang this morning and I heard Mum answer it and then call me to the door and Alice's mum was standing there looking upset and asked if she could talk to me and

I REALLY thought for a minute she'd found out about me and Alice. Mum asked her in for a cup of coffee and took her into the lounge and I started praying that it wasn't all going to kick off.

But instead of accusing me of defiling her daughter, Alice's mum just asked me if Alice had told me about her exam results. I said I hadn't had a chance to speak to her yet (great big fat lie) and her mum said that Alice had done a lot worse than she'd been predicted and did I know if there was anything up with her? Alice obviously hasn't told her mum that we haven't really spoken since we split up so I just sat there, crimson with embarrassment and said I really didn't know.

I asked her mum what she'd got and she told me she'd got, like, random Cs and Ds when she'd been predicted all As, and then she said that she and Alice's dad were at a loss to understand why Alice had done badly when she'd spent the last two years working really hard for them. They said that she'd seemed 'distracted' since about Easter time and that they'd tried to talk to her but Alice has been 'shutting them out lately and won't talk to them' and they were sick with worry over her.

Then her mum asked me if I'd go over and have a word with Alice and I kinda meekly said I would, but then decided I'd ring her on her mobile and talk to her (there was NO way I was going to her house!)

When Alice's mum had gone I went to my room and started crying. Crying 'cos I know Alice doing badly her exams is all down to me and that's unforgiveable of me. I texted Alice but guess what? No reply. I don't know what to do about it all…

Saturday 23 August

Rang Caroline late last night and told her about Alice. Caroline said I wasn't to blame myself, but I think she was just being kind, and she said she'd try and get hold of Alice and talk to her and let me know what she said. Felt a bit better.

Han went over to the photographer's studio to say hi to Will this afternoon. I hated her going, especially as she's off on holiday tomorrow and I won't see her for a week, but I couldn't really tell her that, could I?

Sunday 24 August

Han went to Turkey for a week with her mum, dad, and her brother, little Joe, today. I soooo wished I could have gone with them, but instead I'm staying here, being bored as usual.

I went over to see her in the morning to say goodbye to her. When I got there, her house was in total chaos 'cos her mum had thought Turkey was in Europe and used euros and had packed a load of euros until her dad pointed out they weren't, and they didn't, so her mum had dashed off to get them changed into Turkish Lira and her dad was crashing about in the bedroom muttering something about 'bloody women'.

I helped Han pack her clothes and was pleased to see she hadn't packed any skimpy underwear or anything too revealing. I asked her if it was wise to take so many black clothes, bearing in mind it was gonna be, like, 100 degrees in the shade over there, but she just said black would reflect the blackness she would have in her heart 'cos I wouldn't be there, which I thought wasn't a very holiday-like thing to say. She told me she wished I was going with them and I hugged her and told her it was only for a week and that I'd think of her every minute of every day until she came home again, and she hugged me even tighter and said she'd do her best to get a good tan 'cos she knew how much I love it when she's all tanned and sexy and all.

Her flight was at 3.30 p.m. so I tracked it on this Flightplanner thing online until I saw that it'd landed safely and then logged off, feeling really down. She's only been gone a few hours and I miss her already.

Monday 25 August

Caroline texted me this afternoon and told me she'd spoken to Alice and that Alice had seemed okay and not as bad as she thought she'd be. I texted Caroline back and asked her to text Alice again and tell her I wanted to talk to her. Alice is obviously ignoring my messages (can't say I blame her) but if I could just talk to her then I think I might not feel as guilty as I do right now. Okay, that sounds selfish, but what I mean is, if I could just talk to her and see how she is for myself, I wouldn't feel like such a shit about everything. Maybe.

Tuesday 26 August

A text! From Alice! It said, 'Everything's great, no need to worry. Caro said you wanted to talk but no need. Nothing to talk about.' I texted her back straight away and asked her if I could see her 'cos I said everyone was dead worried about her and I really wanted to see her, but she said no. I texted her back again and more or less pleaded with her and she finally gave in and said she'd meet me in town for coffee on Thursday 'cos she had some stuff to sort out today and tomorrow. I'm relieved. Perhaps if I can talk to her face-to-face I can go some way to apologising for everything. Am dead nervous though.

Went over to school this afternoon to sign up for school again, now I've had my results back. I've chosen to do four subjects next year—English Literature, English Language, History, and Psychology.

Wednesday 27 August

Mum's been asked if she'll help out at this year's WI Autumn Fayre. Mum has been promoted within the WI ever since Beryl Nevis was diagnosed with Tourette's Syndrome last spring and has taken to spitting and swearing at the vicar. I overheard Mum telling Dad in the kitchen that Beryl was 'blackballed' (whatever that means) by the committee and 'politely asked to leave' 'cos they couldn't run the risk of her calling the vicar a 'titwank' like she did when he was presenting her with an award for Most Fragrant Clematis at the WI Summer Garden Show.

All this, of course, means that Mum has now stepped up to the plate in Beryl's enforced absence and is now a bona fide member of the committee. This is a joke in itself 'cos I always thought WI ladies had to be homely and bake nice cakes (neither of which Mum is or does) and had to be kind to children (ditto).

The Autumn Fayre is being held at the vicarage on the first Sunday in October and is a chance for all the old dears to show off their cakes and for all the old men to show off what produce they've grown over the summer, which means there will no doubt be a chance for me and Han to come along and crack loads of smutty jokes about tarts and the size of cucumbers. Can't wait! Thought about texting Han and telling her but figured she'd be too busy sunning herself (and probably texting Will) on some Turkish beach to be bothered with it.

Thursday 28 August

Met Alice in town today. I don't really know how I thought she'd look, but she looked okay actually. I thought hugging her probably wasn't the best idea so I just smiled when I met her, and she smiled tightly back at me. We went to Starbucks for coffee and I asked her how she was and she said she was all right, and then I told her that her mum had been to our house and told me about Alice's exam results and that her mum had asked me to speak to her 'cos she was dead worried about her.

Alice laughed dryly and said to me that I wasn't asking her 'cos I wanted to know, but because her mum had asked me to ask her, and that it made a change for her parents to give a toss about her, or something like that. Then she said that she was 'sorting stuff out on her own', adding 'as usual', and I felt a stab of guilt and didn't know where to look so I just stared down hard at my cappuccino and tried not to blush. Alice said that she'd 'pissed her exams into the air' so she was signing up at college to retake them, and hoped she'd do better next summer. She said she'd been to the college yesterday and it looked really cool there and she was quite looking forward to 'starting afresh', which I took to mean trying to forget about everything that had happened at school and with me.

I made some feeble comment about being pleased for her and said that I felt guilty about her doing badly, but she just raised her eyebrow and told me that it wasn't my fault, it was her fault for 'getting involved with me in the first place' 'cos she'd been so in love with me that she couldn't concentrate on anything but me. She said she shouldn't have been so weak, and she shouldn't have let me get under her skin so much, but perhaps in hindsight it had all been for the best 'cos at least she could leave school and move on. She said the exams she'd really messed up were the ones she took after 16th June 'cos after then nothing really mattered any more. I looked at her, confused, and she told me to 'go figure', and I guessed 16th June was the date I finished with her.

I told her I was sorry. It sounded feeble and pathetic and unconvincing, but I just didn't know what else to say to her. To be honest, I was pretty pleased when she said she had to go 'cos I'd run out of things to say. Everything I'd said had just sounded pathetic and I was cringing inside, just dying to go home again.

Right now I really hate myself.

Friday 29 August

HRBH got her summer exam results yesterday, and oh boy, were they crap!! I know she's not the sharpest tool in the box, but I did at least think she'd do better than the two Cs and two Ds that she scraped.

She went off to the Higher Education advice place in town today with a face as black as thunder 'cos she was planning to go to Joe's uni but they won't let thickos in, apparently, so that's her out the door. I bet Joe's relieved!!

Wish Han would hurry up and come home. I miss her.

Saturday 30 August

Great Aunt May asked me at tea tonight when Han would be coming round again 'cos she wanted to talk to her about leather. After Mum had picked up the pile of cutlery she'd dropped in astonishment, Great Aunt May said that Elvis had said he wanted to 'take her for a spin on his Harley', so she wanted to invest in a pair of leather trousers 'cos the skin on her inner thighs was so thin 'it'd rip like muslin within 10 minutes of straddling'.

I told her that Han was in Turkey but that I knew of a shop in town called Goths and Cloths that sold that sort of thing and I'd take a look for her next time I was down there. She thanked me and called me 'a pet', but later in the kitchen Mum told me under no circumstances was I to encourage Great Aunt May's stupid idea, hissing at me, 'If I so much as get one whiff of cow hide round Great Aunt May, I'll know who to come looking for.'

Sunday 31 August

Han came back from Turkey today. At bloody last! She texted me at 11 tonight and told me to come over first thing tomorrow morning to see her tan. Can't wait!!

Monday 1 September

Went over to Han's first thing this morning. I was sooooo pleased to see her! She looked, OMG, stunning 'cos she has a cracking tan and she'd bought herself some more leather bracelets which looked wicked against her brown skin. She bought me one too, and said that we should both wear them all the time, like we do our friendship bracelets, and whenever we're apart we can look at them and think of each other. For a sometimes-grumpy Goth—sorry, EMO—she can be dead romantic! I've already put the bracelet on my wrist, right next to the friendship bracelet, and which I never, like, EVER take off. Not even in the shower.

Her mum was busy unpacking clothes in the bedroom and her dad was slumped in front of the TV catching up with a week's worth of programmes on his hard drive so we couldn't really do much more than sit in her room. She showed me her tan marks and I felt a brief stirring which disappeared as quickly as it came when I heard her mum walk past her room on the landing muttering about having to 'give the loos a quick once over before lunch'.

Tuesday 2 September

Han told me today that she's decided to go to college rather than go back to school next week!! She came over this afternoon and we took Toffee and Barbara up to the woods and she just, like, casually mentioned that she'd registered with the college that morning!!!

I was a bit pissed off, to be honest. I said to her that I thought she was coming back to St Bart's like I am but she said she'd talked it over with her parents when they were on holiday and that she'd changed her mind. She said she thought college was a better idea than 'going back to school' 'cos it was more mature, and it did the exact course that she wanted to do. That, plus the fact it has longer holidays.

She said she originally wanted to do English, History, Geography, and Sociology, but she'd been speaking to Miss Smith at the end of last term and she'd suggested doing a course in Photography 'cos she'd shown such a talent for it in her Art classes, and then working with Will and talking to him about it had made her decision easier.

Han looked embarrassed when she said Smith's name as if it was, like, forbidden to ever mention her near me again, but all I gotta do when Smith's name is mentioned is think of her having to sleep with Mr.

Troutt and I giggle. That, and the pleasure I'll get knowing I can call her Troutt from next year, of course. Preferably putting the word 'Old' before it too.

#easilypleased

Anyway, Han's now going to do Photography, Film Studies, English, and History 'cos our crappy school doesn't do such exciting subjects as Film Studies, but the college does. I feel, I dunno, a bit sad about this and, if I'm honest, I'm majorly put out that Han hadn't discussed any of this with me.

I've signed up for another two years at school now, and we go back next week so it's too late for me to change it. But I don't really want to go back there if Han won't be there too…

Wednesday 3 September

Was thinking in bed last night about Han going to college and everything and I felt really strange about it all 'cos I suddenly realised that Alice is going to one college, Han's going to another college, Caroline is going to a different school 'cos she said she was sick of St Bart's, and Ems is leaving altogether to go work at some out-of-town superstore! There won't be anyone left! I'm the only idiot out of all of us (apart from Matty) who's decided to stay on at school. It's gonna be dead weird 'cos it's like the whole gang's broken up now.

I suddenly wish I was going to college too, but it's too bloody late now! Why the hell did I ever listen to my parents? This is all their fault.

Thursday 4 September

HRBH is still trying to get into a university somewhere, preferably some place where she can get a decent degree and not one that does degrees in flower arranging and road sweeping and shit like that.

She wants to do Psychology for some reason, so she's got to go through something called 'clearing' which will find her a university that'll take her with her crap results. I think she's gonna end up pretty much anywhere in the UK, which will piss her off 'cos she wants to stay near to Joe.

Scotland would be good by me, though!

I finally plucked up the courage to speak to Han about Will tonight. I'd been chewing over a whole heap of things that had been going round and round in my head for what seems like forever; about him, about Han's decision to go to college rather than come back to school with me, and felt so fed up with it all, I thought the best thing would be just to ask her outright about everything.

I'm glad I did! I said to her, 'remember a while ago I told you I felt uneasy about you and Will?' and Han just kinda went, 'Uh-huh?' so I said, 'Well I still feel unsettled about him, and I can't seem to stop myself from feeling like that about him.'

Han was fab! She held her arms out to me and told me to come to her, which I did, and she told me to tell her everything that was bothering me. I said to her that I knew I couldn't tell her who she could or couldn't speak to, or see, 'cos that would be just too weird, but that I didn't really like it when she met up with him, or when they texted each other. But I also told her that wasn't fair of me, 'cos she was free to go out with whoever she liked, but that a part of me was worried that she'd leave me for him.

Han thought for a minute, then told me I was 'silly' to think she'd ever have eyes for anyone other than me, and when I muttered about her telling me she thought he was buff, she just pulled me closer to me and said, 'But that doesn't mean I fancy him, does it? I just think he's a good-looking bloke, like I think—I dunno—David Beckham's a good-looking bloke, but that doesn't mean I fancy them, does it?'

I mumbled a 's'pose' into her shoulder and she kinda took my face in her hands and looked at me all soppy and told me she fancied me, and no one else, and that there wasn't one part of her that fancied Will remotely. She said, 'I love you, Clemmie Atkins. I thought I'd lost you forever earlier this year 'cos I was so stupid. Do you think I'd do anything like that to you ever again?'

I mumbled another 's'pose,' 'cos I was beginning to feel a bit daft now, and Han said, 'I like girls, remember? Not boys. And when I say I like girls, I mean I like ONE girl—you. No one else. You,' and then she kissed me dead slowly, which made the backs of my knees go a bit wobbly.

She told me she'd stop texting him if I didn't want her to do it, but I thought that just made me sound all possessive, so I told her she didn't have to do that. Then she told me she hadn't heard from him in ages anyway, 'cos she thought he was hitting on the girl who worked in the florist's below the studio where he works, and that made me feel REALLY stupid.

Then we had, like, this epic kissing session up on my bed, which only ended when her mum rang her and asked her when she was coming home.

Went to bed feeling totally loved up (and hideously horny).

Friday 5 September

Woke up to a text from Han telling me that 'I never had to worry about her with anyone' and 'If ever anything was bothering me, I had to talk to her about it rather than keeping it all to myself.' She'd sent me another 'I love you to the moon and back' text as well, and then another one with hearts all over it. Feel much better about everything now, and wish I'd had the guts to talk to her about it all before now, rather than letting it chew away at me like it has over the last few months.

HRBH has been in a foul mood all day 'cos she's been stuck on the phone trying to get her university place, but by the language coming from her room, I guessed she wasn't having much luck.

I took myself off over to Han's house after lunch and had a nice, long chat with her mum. I like Han's mum. She's the sort of person you feel like you could tell anything to, and I did have a brief moment of wondering if I could start telling her about me and Han, but then Han came into the room waggling a DVD of *The Texas Chainsaw Massacre* in her hand and told me to come up to her room. She had one of *those looks* on her face, which meant she didn't really mean for us to be watching a slasher DVD, and when Han summons me to her room, I go.

I'm so weak sometimes. I love it!

Saturday 6 September

I told Han today that Alice was going to college too, but all she could say was, 'Oh Christ, I hope she's not going to my bloody college. Imagine if I got stuck sitting next to her in English? One week of that irritating little mouse and I'll have stabbed her with my biro,' which I thought was a bit OTT.

I didn't like Han talking about Alice like that. I know I did the dirty on her, but I do still care about her and I hate the way Han bitches about her sometimes.

Sunday 7 September

Back to school tomorrow. Spent the whole day feeling like there was a black cloud hanging over my head, which wasn't helped every time I remembered that I wouldn't be able to walk to and from school with Han any more. I used to love doing that, especially when we used to take a diversion on the way home and have a sneaky kiss and feel of each other under the underpass that leads out from town.

Life seems to be shifting away from me and there's nothing I can do about it!

Monday 8 September

Back to school! Aaaaaaargh! Where did the summer go??? Han had her first day at college today too, and it was dead weird not having her around school with me.

I got given my new form details but there was hardly anyone there that I knew from last year, only Rosie Brown who I've barely even ever spoken to and Kirsty Chamberlain, and no one really speaks to her either. I went and found Matty at lunchtime and we both said how weird it was being back at school when the others weren't here.

I don't like it.

Tuesday 9 September

Got given my timetable today and it's sooooo bloody busy! The school does know there are only about 7 hours in the school day, don't they??

Han was telling me tonight about how she's already made loads of new friends at college. I'm pleased for her, 'cos it's not everyone that can feel comfortable in the company of someone who favours wearing bolts and chains on a daily basis.

She told me there's another EMO in her Film Studies class, so they sit next to each other. She said she's pleased she's found a 'kindred spirit', 'cos she always felt like she stood out a bit at St Bart's and never really liked the way all the little year 7s used to press themselves against the corridor walls and look scared whenever she swept past them, 'cos even if outwardly she was dark and mysterious, inwardly she thought the year 7s were all little sweeties and didn't much care for scaring them.

Wednesday 10 September

We've got boys in the sixth form with us!!! Ew, ew, ewwwwwwww! It's a new thing for this year, apparently. Who knew?!

Made mental note to make sure I choose who I sit next to carefully, so I'm not lumped with sitting next to some boy with a twatting baseball cap on back to front and who spends the whole lesson with his hands in his pockets playing trouser snooker. 'Cos they all do it. Caroline told me, so it must be true.

Mum's cast came off her wrist today. She managed to keep it on for 6 weeks without letting me even so much as write my bloody initials on it! Where's the fun in that?!

Thursday 11 September

OMG Dad announced at the dinner table tonight that two women he works with are getting married on Saturday!

I thought this was amazing, but I'm sure I could sense a smirk on his face when he was telling us, which made me think that perhaps he didn't think it was as amazing as I did. He said they were having this ceremony down at the town hall and that a few people from his work were going, and had been talking about it all day. I asked him if he was going but he said he hadn't been invited (that's no surprise—I doubt he's got any friends at work anyway) but that he wouldn't have gone anyway because he didn't think it was 'right'.

That made Mum get one of her looks on her face. She put her knife and fork down slowly (and that's always a bad sign) and asked Dad what exactly wasn't 'right' with it, and would he care to elaborate? I think they must have had an argument after I'd left for school this morning 'cos I was definitely sensing an 'atmosphere', as Great Aunt May would call it. Dad went red a bit, like he always does when Mum tackles him over something, and said he was of the 'old school' and thought marriage should just be between men and women.

He said he didn't hold much truck with 'the gays' (FFS!!!) marrying, and kinda said he didn't understand why they couldn't just live with one another quietly without having to make a show about it all.

That seemed to get Mum's back up. She asked him if Great Aunt May wanted to marry Elvis one day, would he feel the same way, and he told her that was a ridiculous thing to say, and Mum said 'why?' and Dad couldn't answer her.

Mum said that just because someone happens to fall in love with someone of the same sex, it shouldn't mean they're not entitled to the same marriage rights as someone who falls in love with someone of the opposite sex, and that, anyway, why the hell should straight couples be put up on a pedestal as something special?

Mum said, 'People can't help who they fall in love with, Chris, and happiness isn't just reserved for straight people, you know.'

(Yay! Go Mum!!!)

And, 'Gay people have just as much right to happiness as anyone else. Marriage is a sign of commitment and love, so why should it just be reserved for straight people? If you love someone, then you want to shout it from the rooftops, don't you? Gay, straight, whatever. You want to commit to that person for the rest of your life and there's absolutely nothing wrong with that.'

I watched all this unfold, from my position between the pair of them, swivelling my eyes from one to the other, a bit like when you watch a tennis match, and couldn't help but think of me and Han while she was saying all this, and had a kinda *Hell, yeah!* moment in my head.

Dad shuffled uncomfortably in his chair and kinda pushed his peas round his plate like a five-year-old who's just been shouted at for showing off and mumbled something about wishing he'd never brought the bloody subject up in the first place.

But was Mum going to let go? Ohhhh no! She was 40–0 up and going for the love game here.

She said, 'Just because we don't know many gay people doesn't mean to say we have to make sweeping statements about them, does it?'

I stared down hard at my plate when she said that bit, wishing now that the pair of them would just shut up, but she just kept on and on and on, like a dog with a bone, putting her point across (and putting it across very well, as it was) and telling Dad some gay people had enough of a hard time in life without some bigot—and she prodded her fork at him when she said that—coming up with the sort of guff he was coming up with.

That shut him right up, but then she ended her lecture by telling him he was—and I quote—'an old fart' and that it was about time he 'dragged himself kicking and screaming into the real world, bucko'. Game, set, and match to Mother, I think.

Now I'm so bloody glad I've been too chicken to talk to either of them about me and Han. Can you imagine anything more embarrassing than having to sit through him spouting all that bollocks with both of them knowing I'm gay?? It's clear that Dad isn't going to understand it at all, is he? Okay, I think Mum's going to be all right about it, but how can I tell just her and not him? They've both got to know 'cos it's not fair on Mum if it's her that knows, but lemme tell you, after tonight's little display there's no way in hell I'm telling either of them anything right now. Decision made. End of.

Friday 12 September

Had my first English lesson today, and guess who's in the same group as me?

J!!!!!!!!!!!!

I don't think she even remembered me (not surprising—I've barely seen or spoken to her for well over a year) 'cos she came and sat next to me and smiled at me like she didn't have a clue who I was.

Jeez, it felt soooooooo weird!

I mean, I'm, like, TOTALLY over her, but it's still freaky sitting next to someone who you used to fancy the arse off but who you haven't given a single thought to in nearly 18 months, but you can still remember really strongly about how you used to feel about that person…and they have no idea!!

Anyway, she didn't really speak much to me but I'll be real interested to see if she sits next to me again in our next lesson.

We got given *Pride and Prejudice* to read by next Tuesday. I have the attention span of a fruit fly so it's gonna be tough going.

Saturday 13 September

Woke up this morning thinking about what Dad had said about the two women from his work getting married, and had this warm, fuzzy feeling in my tummy knowing that they'd have both woken up feeling so happy because today was going to be their very own totally, awesomely special day.

I know my decision to wait to tell Mum and Dad things is the right one, but that's not to say I won't tell them in the future—of course not.

It's just that…perhaps now isn't such a good idea, bearing in mind the argument Dad saying what he'd said on Thursday night caused. It's moments like that when I think timing really is everything…

But I've been thinking a lot about what Mum had said, about love being special and all that, and I want to get Han a commitment ring now, just to show her how much she means to me. I know she bought me the friendship bracelet back in the summer, but we weren't together then. And the leather bracelet from Turkey too. But a ring says so much more than a tatty bit of cloth round your wrist, doesn't it?

I'll nip on eBay tomorrow and see what I can get.

Sunday 14 September

Went over to Han's house for lunch today. After we'd eaten and helped her mum to wash up, we went for a walk with Toffee along the canal towpath, and while we were walking I told Han all about the women that Dad works with getting married yesterday. She said she thought it was dead sweet, and we both agreed how brilliant it was that they could do it, when even just, like, 10 years ago it would have been unheard of.

We sat on a bench for a bit, just watching the barges going up and down in the locks and I felt dead happy. I felt really loved up, so I told Han I wanted to get her a ring as a sign of my love and commitment to her, and she kinda squealed a bit and grabbed my hand and told me she loved me, which made me a bit embarrassed 'cos there were so many people walking past.

She said if I got her one, then she'd get me one as well and I had a brief moment of wondering if anywhere did a 'Buy One, Get One Free' but then thought that wasn't very romantic of me. Anyway, we're gonna go looking for rings on Thursday after school/college and I can't flipping wait!!

Monday 15 September

Great Aunt May and Elvis are coming to stay with us for a few days 'cos apparently Autumn Leaves has a cockroach infestation in the kitchens and they have to get the pest controllers in and they're worried the fumes from the chemicals they're gonna use might see all the old folk off, so Mum said to be on the safe side they'd better come and stay here until the chemicals have had a chance to disperse.

I asked Mum where exactly they were gonna stay 'cos our house only has three bedrooms and if Great Aunt May and Elvis are gonna be sleeping on an inflatable bed in the lounge I'd want to know 'cos if I come home late one night I might step on them if I didn't know they were there.

Mum said to me, 'They're both going to stay in your room and you're going in with your sister for a few days.' When I complained, Mum snapped at me, 'They're 82 and 83, for God's sake. Where do you want me to put them? In the shed?' I thought about this for a while but figured even when you take the lawn mower and garden chairs out of the shed, it would still be a bit of a squeeze for the pair of them, so wondered why Mum had said it.

I grumbled for a bit about it but stopped when I saw the look on her face. However, this will be nothing compared to the look on HRBH's face when she finds out…

Tuesday 16 September

Mr. Harman told us very excitedly today that we'll all be going to see a production of *Hamlet* that the Royal Shakespeare Company is doing in November. We're doing *Hamlet* as part of our English Literature course and he told us we're all very lucky to get tickets for it 'cos they're like gold dust apparently. Frankly, I couldn't give a shit, but Mr. Harman obviously could 'cos he totally went off on one, wandering up and down the classroom, flinging his arms around and fingering his tie excitedly saying 'Ahh girls, the Royal Shakespeare Company is unrivalled in its productions of the great Shakespearean plays. We should all feel honoured that we've been offered the chance to see one of the Bard's masterpieces performed by the greatest company in the world.'

Whatever.

He then started blathering on about how marvellous it'll be for us to watch a live performance of what was undoubtedly the greatest English writer who has ever lived and how we'll be able to appreciate first-hand Shakespeare's mastery of the English language and the beauty of his iambic pentameters.

I was trying to feel all honoured about iambic pentameters (WTF?) when Matty leant over and whispered 'And Jude Law's in it, and he's as fit as a butcher's dog.'

I'm sure Shakespeare would be cock-a-hoop to learn that his mastery of the English language means jack-all to the likes of Matty Hardacre.

#sarcasm

Wednesday 17 September

I'm sooooo snowed under with work at school at the moment, it's un-bloody-real. I keep thinking back to the good old days when all I had to worry about was Mrs. Howell's French vocabulary tests and learning how to be a tree in Drama. Things have changed big-style and I'm a bit scared. I'm only young, for God's sake! I can't cope with all of this! Come back when I'm in my 30s and too old and past it to care!

Thursday 18 September

J sat next to me in English Language again today but it didn't feel as weird, thank God. We had to do this, like, group task, analysing some advert and picking key words out of it or something, so at least I got to say more than three words to her today. Had a good look at her too and was pleased (and relieved) that I didn't feel any stirrings for her, 'cos I realised that even though she's well fit, she still isn't a patch on my Han in the looks department.

Came out of school at 4 and Han was waiting for me at the gates. We went down to McDonald's for a burger and held hands under the table. It was sooooo romantic! Afterwards, we went and had a look in some jewellers' windows for rings. How much?! Who knew rings were so bloody expensive?! I could see Han frowning and looking worried, so I suggested we had a weekend trawling the Internet and that seemed to cheer her up a bit.

Friday 19 September

HRBH found out tonight that she's gotta share a room with me for three nights. She cornered me in the bathroom before bed and hissed at me, 'As if it's not bad enough two old wrinklies sharing a bed and getting up to God knows what, I've got to share a room with you and your stinking feet. The sooner I move out of this place, the better.'

When I got to bed I thought about what she'd said to me. I hadn't actually appreciated that Great Aunt May and Elvis would be sharing a bed—and not just any bed. My bed! Yuk, yuk, yuk! Had horrible thoughts about them being in my bed, but tried not to think about it 'cos it was making me feel queasy. If there's one thing that knocks me sick it's the thought of old people *getting jiggy*. It's bad enough that Mum and Dad sometimes 'have an early night' every third Friday and every birthday without thinking that Great Aunt May and Elvis might be rubbing bones too. And in my bloody bed!!!!!!!!!!

Saturday 20 September

All that thinking about *doing it* yesterday reminded me that I hadn't *done it* for ages. Mum and Dad were going food shopping this morning so I knew they'd be gone for ages, HRBH was over at Joe's, so texted Han and asked her if she 'wanted to come over for a bit of *you know what*'.

She texted me back and said, 'Can't I come over all day, not just for a bit?' so I realised I needed to be a bit more…explicit. So I texted her back again and said, 'Noooo I meant, come over for A BIT,' and she texted me back and said 'A bit of what?'

Sheesh! This doesn't happen in those funny old erotica stories that you can read on the Internet (allegedly). I texted her back and said 'Get your arse over here for sex. Now.' And she texted me back and said, 'Ohhhh! Why didn't you say?'

Within an hour she'd been to mine, flung various items of clothing off onto my bedroom floor, and had me twice, pulling her fleece back over her head just in time to see Mum and Dad getting out of the car with numerous bags (Mum) and a grumpy face (Dad). By the time they'd stepped in through the front door, me and Han were slumped in front of the TV watching MTV like butter wouldn't melt!

Who said romance was dead?

Sunday 21 September

Remembered in a blind panic that I haven't read ANY of *Pride and Sodding Prejudice* and we gotta do this résumé thing by Tuesday.

Spent, like, ALL day reading it, but by the sixth chapter I was sick to the back teeth of all these preening Regency ladies and their twee manners. Why can't school give us something juicy to read, like a rollocking Jackie Collins or something??

Monday 22 September

Finished reading *Pride and Prejudice* at 7 this evening, then wrote a half-page résumé of it, which was something along the lines of dainty little country girl with ringlets has love-hate relationship with some grumpy bloke called Darcy.

Big fat hairy deal.

(I didn't write that in my résumé though).

Great Aunt May and Elvis came to stay tonight, so I've gotta spend the next three nights in the same room as HRBH! I shan't sleep a wink.

Tuesday 23 September

Went and had coffee with J and Matty after English today. J was still laughing at my all-too-brief summary of P&P, much to my indignation, then Matty started telling us about this boy that's in her class who she says really loves himself 'cos apparently he carries a mirror in his bag and he's always checking his hair!!! She said, 'He's, like, soooooo metrosexual! He's such a joke!'

I laughed 'cos J was laughing, but I couldn't help but wonder what the hell was funny about a boy who likes having sex in underground stations.

#weirdo

Mum and Dad went out for a meal tonight so that Great Aunt May and Elvis could have their weekly Bridge night in our front room. Apparently they have one each Tuesday between 8 and 10 p.m. at Autumn Leaves, and Elvis didn't want to risk losing his winning streak which, apparently, stretches back over four months. I overheard him telling Dad in the kitchen that he 'owned Arnold Merryweather's arse where card games were concerned', but Dad told me later he thinks Elvis has been watching too many of his *Godfather* box sets in between meals at the home.

8:10 p.m.

Ariadne Dawkins has just arrived at our house with a party pack of Guinness, three tubs of Pringles, and a bag of poker chips. I've taken to my room and brought Barbara up with me. It's going to be a long night.

Wednesday 24 September

OMG what a night last night!!! Let's just say that was the last time Mum and Dad go out and leave Great Aunt May and Elvis here on their own, and I can't say I blame them.

The evening turned out to be nothing more than a cover for Elvis's weakness for gambling because rather than playing a refined game of Bridge, they all ended up getting wasted on sherry and playing strip poker. In our front room. Even Great Aunt May got involved, which surprised me, to be honest, but then I heard her telling Mum this morning (after everything had calmed down) that she didn't want to lose face in front of 'that strumpet Dawkins' who, according to Great Aunt May, is 'hell-bent on leading Elvis astray'.

Anyway, the evening had started off relatively quietly, apart from a bit of light-hearted banter, which I listened to from the safety of my bedroom. At my last count there were around eight of them, all sitting round Mum and Dad's dining room table, which Elvis had covered with a green felt cloth, playing cards very nicely, but then it all started getting a bit boisterous when, again according to Great Aunt May, Ariadne spiked their drinks with some cooking sherry which she'd stolen from the Autumn Leaves kitchen a few days before.

Within the hour they'd raided Dad's record collection and were belting out songs by some old singer called Johnny Cash who, I heard Elvis telling anyone who would listen, he once knew 'like his own brother'. I rang Han at this point and asked her if she'd come over to help me, but all she said was, 'Average age 85, Clemmie. What harm can a group of old people do?' and then (kinda unhelpfully, I thought in the circumstances) started telling me about some assignment she had to do for college.

When I'd finally finished talking to Han and felt brave enough to poke my head through the banisters to see what was going on, all I could see was Arnold Merryweather stripped down to his underwear, Ariadne Dawkins out cold in the corner surrounded by empty Guinness cans, and playing cards scattered across the carpet. I have to say when I heard someone calling for Elvis to perform his Ring of Fire, I decided it was time to retreat back to my room, lock the door, and phone Mum.

By the time Mum and Dad finally came home around half an hour later, two neighbours had already knocked on our front door threatening to call the police because of all the noise, there were Pringles squashed into the carpet from one end of the front room to the other, empty bottles and cans strewn around the house, and some old bloke (I've NO idea who!) asleep behind the sofa, still clutching his hand of cards, but without any socks on.

I've told Mum and Dad that under no circumstances will I ever, EVER allow myself to be left alone with Great Aunt May and Elvis again. They both agreed.

Thursday 25 September

Was woken by Barbara jumping on my bed with a pair of men's white Y-fronts in her mouth, slightly damp. Not a great start to the day.

Came down to get myself some breakfast only to find Great Aunt May and Elvis getting a dressing down from Mum in the kitchen. I have to say, it was weird seeing two adults standing, heads bowed, being given another right royal bollocking by a fiery (menopausal) woman in a pink, fluffy dressing gown. Weird but funny.

Went shopping for Han's birthday present after school today. I got her this wicked black top from Goths and Cloths and some dead cool purple laces for her Vans. Thought about getting her another Funeral for a Friend CD but she hardly ever listens to the one she's got, so I thought I'd save myself a tenner and got her a pair of dog tags on a chain instead.

Great Aunt May and Elvis went back to Autumn Leaves tonight. I can't say I'm sorry.

Friday 26 September

I've been dragged into attending the WI Autumn Fayre next week 'cos both Dad and HRBH have copped out, and Mum said she didn't want to have to face it alone. She said I could 'bring a friend' with me, adding that if it was Han 'please tell her to dress down, darling. It's an Autumn Fayre, not a séance. We're trying to raise money, not raise the dead.' I told Mum that Han was a free spirit and I couldn't really tell her what to wear and what not to wear, but Mum just smoothed down her skirt, got one of those looks on her face, and reminded me that the Autumn Fayre would be 'full of elderly ladies who don't see Goths every day' and that 'Han scared the life out of Mrs. Goodman last time she saw her. Apparently she had to sleep with the light on for a full week after she met her.'

I shall have a word with Han and ask her to hold back on the chains, studs, and scary black boots. It won't be easy for her, though.

Saturday 27 September

HRBH got a phone call today offering her a place at university!! Miracle of miracles, she's got herself a place doing Psychology, and it's at a university that's only an hour from Joe's, so she's dead pleased. She's gotta be there for Monday, so it was all chaos in our house for a few hours as Mum shot off into town to buy her bedding and stuff like that, while Dad crashed around in the kitchen trying to find some pans that weren't burnt to within an inch of their lives.

So that's it! She's off! The very second the car's left the drive, I'm moving my stuff into her room, I'm telling you!

Sunday 28 September

Mum and Dad took HRBH over to her new university today. They left at 9 with the car piled high with everything from tin openers to toilet rolls and Dad moaning something about 'Why not go the whole hog and pack the bloody kitchen sink as well?' earning a stern look from Mum. They asked me if I wanted to go too, but there was no way I was going to miss the opportunity of having the house to myself AND on Han's birthday too!

I wished HRBH luck (although it's the university that needs the luck having her as a student—ha, ha, ha!) and waved them off with one hand while texting Han with the other, telling her I had the house to myself and did she want to come over so I could give her her present personally?

When she got to mine, I asked her if her parents had minded her not being there for her birthday, but she just gave me a pitying look and said, 'I'm not 12, Clem,' then kissed me when she saw the hurt look on my face. She was wearing this shit-hot tight black T-shirt and black skinny jeans which I thought she'd poured herself into, they were so tight, so I instantly forgave her for her sarcasm. I fetched the T-shirt I'd bought her and hoped she'd like it; when I gave it to her she whipped off her own T-shirt and plonked mine over her head and I have to say it looked verrrrrry nice on her!

I gave her the purple laces too, and the dog tags, and she was dead pleased with them, squealing with delight and throwing her arms round me, nearly knocking me off my feet. I think she liked them! Then we went down into town and I took her into Pizza Hut and bought her a Super Supreme while I had something called a Sizzler which had jalapeno peppers in it which made my eyes water and my lips sting, but I don't think Han noticed too much.

Han asked me how long I thought Mum and Dad would be, so I told her I didn't think they'd be back until late afternoon, so she asked me to take her back to mine so I could give her another present. I panicked a bit, worried 'cos I'd only bought her three presents, but then I saw the look on her face and the penny dropped.

Took her back to mine and gave her another present. Twice.

Monday 29 September

Mrs. Schofield told us in morning registration today that the school wants to publish its own magazine for sixth formers, and is looking for volunteers to write articles and stuff like that. I think I might talk to Mrs. Schofield about getting involved, 'cos despite my boring two weeks at the *Gazette*, I still wouldn't mind being a journalist when I leave school 'cos I figure it's got to be a good career, especially if I get to interview lots of fit girls, right?

Tuesday 30 September

Spoke to Mrs. Schofield about the school magazine at break today. I went to the staff room and Mr. Harman answered. While he went to find Mrs. Schofield, I noticed old Miss Robinson the PE teacher having a snooze on the chair and figured it was time for her to retire 'cos if she can't even cope with standing at the side of a hockey pitch blowing her whistle every 5 minutes without needing an afternoon nap, then it's time to go, don't you think??

Anyway, Mrs. Schofield came to the door (wiping cake crumbs from her mouth, I noticed) and I told her I wanted to get involved with the school magazine. She said 'as long as you don't start writing articles on whips, nails, and self-harm, and scare everyone half to death, I don't mind what you do,' and stood there looking at me before adding 'go and have a think about how you'd like to contribute to it, okay? Now if that's all, there's a Danish pastry in here waiting for my attention,' and shut the door on me.

Charming! After having evil thoughts and thinking about writing an article on 'The Inefficiency of Teachers at St Bartholomew's Grammar School for Girls', I decided I'd talk to Han and see if she's got any ideas.

Wednesday 1 October

Me and J swapped phone numbers today, which felt a bit weird. I was worried for a bit that I might go a bit bonkers and start texting her declaring that I used to fancy the arse off her, but then told myself to get a grip and stop being such a prat.

I've stored her name under Justine Button, her real name, 'cos then at least if Han ever looks at my phone she won't (hopefully) know who she is.

Thursday 2 October

Wow, I just read yesterday's entry in my diary again and realised I'd written J's name out in full for, like, the first time ever. I sat and looked at it, and remembered how she used to make me feel, and about the power she used to have over me. I began to feel a bit sad then, so I snapped my diary shut and rang Han instead. Felt a LOT better then, especially when Han started talking dirty to me.

Friday 3 October

Went over to Han's house tonight. She was telling me all about college and how cool it was there and how wicked her Photography course is and how she hopes she does well, 'cos her brother Dan has already told her his university does a good Photography course, and she'd think about going there and get a degree in it if she does okay at college. This all made my head spin! She was racing far too far ahead for my liking, with all this talk of uni and degrees and shit, and I came home feeling like a little schoolgirl, and just a little bit depressed.

Saturday 4 October

Was worrying about what Han was saying to me last night about uni and everything so when I went over to her house today I had a kinda heart-to-heart about it with her. Ever since what happened between us in the summer, I've thought it better to talk to her rationally about things rather than bottling them up, and anyway, I figured she couldn't get narky with me for talking about our future, could she?

Anyway, I told her I was scared about university and everything 'cos I didn't want it to mean the end of us, 'cos I'd read stuff in magazines about people drifting apart when they go away to study. She was sooooo sweet! She gathered me up in her arms and planted kisses all over my face, telling me I was a 'silly sausage' because it had never crossed her mind that we'd go to different universities!

She said, 'I thought it would be wicked if we went to the same place, Clem. Just imagine it—we could share a house together and everything! It would be perfect. We'd be like a proper couple, no creeping around worrying that our parents would find out. It'd be soooo grown up, don't you think? Just you and me.'

I briefly wondered if we'd be able to afford to rent a house big enough to take all her clothes and boots and things, but then thought about living with Han 24/7 and, more importantly, having sex on tap 24/7 and the worries left my head as quickly as they'd entered it…

Sunday 5 October

It was the long-awaited WI Autumn Fayre today and it was totally awesome!

I dragged Han along 'cos she promised to dress down, and I figured it would be better to have her with me rather than go alone (even if she might scare some of them half to death). Anyway, we had a right hoot at the vegetable judging, with some old bloke called George Somethingorother winning pretty much all of the prizes, and being complemented by the WI ladies on the size and smoothness of his plums, which made Han nearly fall over the trestle table, she was laughing so much.

The only sour moment came when there was nearly a fistfight in the marquee over the size of someone's courgette, which made Han lean over to me and whisper 'and they say size doesn't matter' and then get the fit of the giggles again so I had to take her outside to calm down.

We managed a sneaky kiss and cuddle behind the cake marquee, which felt *really* naughty, but *really* exciting, and only stopped when we heard Mum calling for us, asking us to help her come and count the day's takings. The grand total of our glorious day in the Autumn sunshine was £750, enough to pay Jones the plumber for a new toilet in the Church Hall.

Success all round, then.

Found out tonight when we got home that Great Aunt May and Elvis are getting married!!!! If this wasn't so funny, it would be romantic. I hope I get an invitation to the wedding—I'm dying to see how they cope walking up and down the aisle, Great Aunt May with her Zimmer frame and Elvis's knee popping out of its socket if he walks any further than three steps at a time.

Texted Han just before bed and told her about the wedding and she replied with a message that said, 'Woohoo! So you get to have a Great Uncle Elvis after all!'

I have a Great Uncle Elvis! That's so cool it hurts.

Monday 6 October

I've decided to be the sixth form magazine's Agony Aunt. Han said to me that she thought I'd be an ideal Agony Aunt 'cos I'm 'empathetic', which I thought was dead nice of her, then she added, 'And besides, I can read all the letters you get in. I'm dying to read about girls' sex problems.'

I went and saw Mrs. Schofield again today and said that I wanted to be in charge of the magazine's problem page. After what I thought was a snigger from her, she agreed and said she'd ask the IT department to allocate me an e-mail address and then put a message out on the school noticeboard asking for students to submit any problems they might have to that address. I was a bit disappointed that Mrs. Schofield said that anyone writing in would remain completely anonymous, but cheered up a bit when I realised I'd be able to suss out all the ones writing in about sex 'cos:

> the ones that are getting it will be walking funny, and
>
> the ones who aren't getting it will be the grumpy ones.

Tuesday 7 October

Great Aunt May and Elvis are getting married on Saturday, and I mean, like, THIS SATURDAY! I asked Dad what the rush was, 'cos it's not like it's gonna be a shotgun wedding or anything and Dad just said, 'At their age, if they leave it too long one of them might be dead by the time they get up the aisle,' and started laughing so hard he made his eyes water, which I thought was a bit ageist of him.

Anyway, they're having a small wedding in the register office in town then a little 'do' at Autumn Leaves afterwards. I'm confident I'll be able to bring Han as my guest 'cos Great Aunt May thinks the sun shines out of Han's whatnot, and it's her day, so there'll be no arguments on that score!

Wednesday 8 October

I finished school early today 'cos Mr. Pritchard, our History teacher, was ill. We were told to go up to the library and use the time to study, so I did what every other sensible schoolgirl does and buggered off home early.

I went over to Han's college rather than going straight home, and kinda just hung around outside for about half an hour until finally a load of people started coming out. Han came out about five minutes later, with some Goth boy who I guessed was the same boy from her Film Studies group that she was telling me about. He looked okay (apart from the fact he looked like he needed a good, square meal inside him) and was dressed just kinda like Han dresses, really—like he was about to go dig a grave and hop in it.

When Han spotted me waiting for her by the wall, she said something to this boy and left him to come over and join me, and I was pleased to see how happy she looked to see me.

#insecure

Anyway, we ducked into McD's for an hour and shared some fries and I asked Han if she'd like to come to Great Aunt May's wedding on Saturday.

She said she'd love to come (yay!), and that she'd dig out something 'fitting for the occasion', but you can bet your life whatever she wears, the good people of the Autumn Leaves Retirement Home will never have seen anything like it!

Thursday 9 October

IT has finally allocated us an e-mail address and has put out a message that I've written to all students on the school's intranet bulletin board which says:

> Fellow sixth formers. We all know being a teenager is hard sometimes. Don't carry that burden around with you like a backpack full of misery. Tell your resident Agony Aunt all your woes and we will do our best to give you sound, honest, and, most importantly, *wise* advice about anything that is bothering you.
>
> E-mail any problems to the sixth form magazine, whether they are emotional, parental, school-related, or friend-related and we will publish some of your problems (all anonymously) along with our reply in the next issue of YOUR school magazine!

Now I've just got to sit back and wait for them to all come flooding in. Can't wait!

Friday 10 October

We got told today that anyone bringing anything to be signed by Jude Law (photos, books, breasts, ha, ha!) when we got to see *Hamlet* in Stratford on Avon next month will have it confiscated. Matty leant over to me and whispered 'Fascists. I was hoping to get a photo signed. I'm buggered if I want any Shakespeare crap signed, so I'll have to smuggle it into the theatre in my knickers now.'

I went down to town after school and bought a new top for Great Aunt May's wedding tomorrow. I chose something suitably demure, even though I'd seen an awesome pair of ripped lowride jeans on my way to the demure shop, that I thought would look amazing to wear next time I'm at the skate park. I had to use every ounce of restraint I had in my body not to go in there and spend the £20 Mum gave me this morning on them rather than a smart new top that I'll wear tomorrow and probs never wear again!

Saturday 11 October

Went to Great Aunt May and Great Uncle Elvis's (snigger) wedding reception today and it was a blast! They had a small ceremony down at the register office in town, with just Mum, Dad, and Elvis's daughter there. Dad told me later she was called Hyacinth, and had blue hair and a dress covered in such bright flowers he wished he'd worn his sunglasses.

Then we were all invited to their reception up at Autumn Leaves which only went on until 10 p.m. 'cos Great Aunt May said Elvis liked to be in bed by half past ten. The chef at the home had baked them a cake and the staff had moved all the chairs to the side of the dining room and put some of what Great Aunt May called 'Old Tyme Music' on which was, like, dead slow so all the old dears and old boys could have a dance. We were all given a sherry on arrival, then later we all had a glass of celebratory champagne, except for Ariadne Dawkins who said champagne gave her wind, so she had a pint of celebratory Guinness instead.

I took Han with me, of course, and I think Mum and Dad were relieved that she'd done as promised, and had slightly toned down her dress, which pretty much meant she just didn't have any studded collars or chains or anything, and had left some of her piercings out. I still noticed a few of the old girls surreptitiously genuflecting when Han came into the room, though, whilst Matron made sure she didn't stray too far all evening from the cupboard in the kitchen where all the knives were kept, which I thought was a bit unnecessary. Han didn't look that scary…but maybe I'm just used to her? I suppose it's not every day that an old folks' home sees a sight like my sexy, gorgeous, EMO-to-the-core Hannah!

Anyway, me and Han danced with some of the more able ones amongst them, then found ourselves dancing to some old song together until I realised that the chef was watching us from the kitchen through his serving hatch with his hands buried deep in his pockets and I got all embarrassed. Then Elvis started yawning so loudly I could hear his jaw click so we all figured it was time to wrap things up, and we all clapped and threw confetti over the newlyweds as they both hobbled off down the corridor to their room and Matron grumbled about the mess from the confetti on the floor.

So that's it! Great Aunt May is a married woman, and I have to say, she looks absolutely chuffed to bits to be one, but then I guess anything at her age has to be a bonus, doesn't it?

Sunday 12 October

I asked Mum this morning if Great Aunt May and Great Uncle Elvis would be having a honeymoon and she said, 'Of course! A week white-water rafting in the Gambia and then a week chasing the powder on the slopes of the French Alps.'

I figured she was joking ('cos I'm astute like that) and gave her a withering look while she laughed at her joke. People should never laugh at their own jokes. Especially when they're not funny.

She told me later that May and Elvis (I wonder if I can start calling them Melvis?) were being taken out for the day by Hyacinth to a garden centre, then back to Autumn Leaves for afternoon tea to finish off the wedding cake, 'cos Elvis apparently can't bear anything to be wasted, even though Mum says Great Aunt May reckons that candied peel makes him constipated.

Monday 13 October

Matty's having a party at her house this Saturday so she asked me and J if we wanted to go. I asked her if she'd asked anyone else and she said she'd texted Caroline, Ems, and Han, so I was relieved that I didn't have to ask if I could bring Han 'cos that would take, like, just tooooo much explaining, 'cos Matty and Ems still don't know about me and Han yet, and of course J has no idea, and I kinda want to keep it that way. Life sure as hell doesn't seem to get any simpler as I get older!

Tuesday 14 October

Reading *Wuthering Heights* for English. Am sick of reading about straight shenanigans. Why can't the school give us a filthy, throbbing lesbian novel to read instead??

Wednesday 15 October

Think I might be in love with Cathy from *Wuthering Heights*. Is that wrong of me?

Went into town after school 'cos it's Mum's birthday this Saturday. I had NO idea what to buy her, and when I still hadn't bought her anything by 5.30 p.m., just as the shops were all starting to close, I practically ran round the nearest shop I could get to, in a blind panic, and did an impulse buy.

Mum is getting vacuum cleaner bags, a chopping board, and a glass vase this year. She should count herself lucky I even bother at her age (44).

Thursday 16 October

I had a first e-mail as Agony Aunt today!! At bloody last!!! It was from

'Anon' asking me how he could make his dick bigger. Spoke to IT at lunchtime and asked them to filter out any e-mails with rude words in them. Not a good start.

Friday 17 October

Han told me today that she's told a few people at college that she's gay and that everyone's really cool about it. She reckons people at college are, like, so much cooler than people were at school and that 'no one takes a blind bit of notice of anyone that comes out 'cos half the college is gay'. She said there were loads of EMOs there too so she felt really at home—much more so than when she was at school.

I dunno, it seems to me that Han's really matured since she went to college, and certainly doesn't seem as frightened about people finding out she's gay. I wish I was as brave as her. I still don't feel anywhere near ready telling more people that I'm a lesbian yet, 'cos it was hard enough just telling Caroline all those months ago, and every time I think about telling someone else—regardless of whether it's Mum, Ems, Matty, or whoever—I start to shake.

I suppose I'm worried that people will act differently towards me, and I guess I don't want to be the one everyone points at and whispers about in the school corridors. Maybe if I'd gone to bloody college with Han rather than staying on at school then I'd be out and proud by now, but I guess I'll never know, will I?

I just said to Han that if anyone asked if she had a girlfriend to tell them that she did, but just don't mention my name. I don't want people to think she's available, but I also don't want my name bandied around college either in case it gets back to people I go to school with.

Saturday 18 October

It was Mum's birthday today, so me and Dad took her out for lunch in town. I gave her the chopping board, cleaner bags, and vase that I'd bought her and she looked a bit unimpressed, so I've decided that next year she's getting a gift voucher and then she can buy what she bloody well wants!!

Went to Matty's party tonight. It was wicked! I think Mum was pleased to have the evening to just herself and Dad, it being her birthday and all (yuk, yuk, YUK!), so I didn't feel so bad about going out rather than celebrating her 'big day' with her.

Anyway, Matty's dad had left loads of lemonade and Coke and crisps and stuff out for us, which was very nice of him, I suppose, but we put it all back in the fridge and instead drank some cheap, fiery Croatian alcopops that Matty had smuggled into the house earlier in the day. Much nicer than lemonade!!

Me and Han turned up in matching black corsets, but she wore a ripped skirt with hers, while I wore black skinny jeans with mine, so at least we didn't look like twins. J turned up with some boy called Ethan so I guess she's not seeing the ghastly Garrrrrrreth any more, hey? Alice wasn't there, 'cos Matty said she'd told her if I was going to be there with Han she didn't want to come. I should have been gutted, I guess, but, to be honest, I was quite glad 'cos at least it meant I didn't have to spend the whole evening trying to avoid her.

Anyhow, the party was awesome, apart from when Matty decided to put some Beyoncé on, with Beyoncé urging someone to 'put a ring on it', whatever the hell that meant, so me and Han disappeared into the garden 'cos Han always says that R&B music makes her want to beat herself with twigs. I have to say, I agree with her. It was dead dark out in Matty's garden, and everyone was still inside, shaking their booties, or whatever it is people do when they're listening to R&B, so me and Han had a quick snog underneath Matty's dad's magnolia tree 'cos it was so dark and we were far enough away from the house that nobody could see us. It was dead romantic and we didn't even notice how cold it was, we were so into it!

When we came back into the kitchen, Caroline was sitting at the table, pissed as a fart, and lurched towards us slurring, 'I know what yoooo twoooo have been up to,' and grinning manically at us, so we walked her round the garden a few times to try and sober her up. And shut her up.

Got home around 1 a.m., and Han sent me an 'I love you' text at 1:15 a.m., so I went to sleep with a smile on my face.

Sunday 19 October

Mum and Dad were still in bed when I got up this morning (having a lie-in after her birthday—excuse me while I throw up!) so I got myself some breakfast and watched *Scuzz* on the TV downstairs until Dad banged on the bedroom floor and told me to 'belt up'.

Texted Han and asked her if she wanted to hang out, but she said she had work to do for college next week, so after suddenly thinking how cool it would have been if I'd been able to call on Alice and then getting a bit sad, I finally (and reluctantly) started doing some essay on Freud that's gotta be handed in by Friday, then cleaned out Uncle Buck's cage while he had a run round the garden, and that was my Sunday.

#boring

Monday 20 October

Han met me outside the gates again after school. I love it when I come out of school and see her there waiting for me, sitting on the wall looking shit hot and cool, and knowing that she's mine.

She was talking to some girls that she used to do RE with but when she spotted me she hopped down from the wall and I heard her say to these girls, 'Gotta go, ladies. My date's arrived,' and I saw her wink at them, which made me go all gooey inside, even if what she'd said wasn't exactly subtle.

God, I love that girl!!!!!

Tuesday 21 October

OMG!!!! J told me in English today that she'd seen me and Han kissing each other on Saturday night!!!!!!! She said she'd come out into the kitchen to get something to drink and had seen us disappear up to the end of the garden and kiss under the tree!

I said to her she was mistaken but she just laughed dryly and said, 'How many other Goth girls wearing matching corsets were there at the party? I know what I saw, Clem,' and I didn't know what to say, so just repeated that she must have been mistaken and it wasn't me. She said, 'It's cool. I got no problem with it, if that's what you're worried about!' and I didn't say anything, which was pretty much an admission of guilt.

I sat and stewed about it all through the lesson, but then kinda got cross about stuff and thought, well what the hell if she DOES know? I'm my own person, for God's sake—why should I freak about people knowing? I s'pose I was thinking about the fact Han reckons most of her college friends know now, so why the hell shouldn't mine? I've kept it secret from them for such a long time now (apart from Caroline) and I'm getting soooo tired and stressed with all the secrecy.

Anyway, after the lesson we went down to the common room and I told her that it WAS me and Han she'd seen. She just said, 'I know. I told you that already,' and I said, 'And you're okay with it? 'cos, you know, some people aren't,' and she said, 'I told you, it's cool,' and then added, 'Besides, I think it's kinda sexy,' and I nearly dropped the polystyrene cup of coffee I'd just got from the machine.

I chose to ignore that, but wondered if I ought to tell her mine and Han's relationship history, but she really didn't look that bothered about it at all, so instead I asked her not to say anything to anyone at school 'cos I wasn't ready for a whole heap of people to know, and she said she wouldn't. I hope she means it!

I also asked her about that Ethan boy she'd been with on Saturday and she told me he was her boyfriend, and I said the last time I'd spoken to her, which was, like, last year, she was going out with Gareth, and she just said, 'Oh him, yeah. I got bored with him,' and started casually flicking through the pages in her ring binder.

When I got home tonight I went up to my room and lay on my bed, thinking about things. I decided I want to tell Matty and Ems that I'm gay as well, especially as I've just come out to J today. Matty and Ems are two of my oldest friends and they're the only two of the old gang that don't know now, and that doesn't really seem fair on them, if that makes sense.

Just need to find the right time and place to tell them both now, though.

Wednesday 22 October

Couldn't sleep last night for thinking about stuff. There were all these things just going round and round in my head until I thought my head would pop. I was thinking about telling Matty and Ems about me being gay, and then suddenly thought that if I tell my friends then I really do need to tell Mum and Dad about it too. But I don't want to. Then I got thinking about why does being gay have to be so full of bloody pitfalls? Why? Just 'cos I'm not what's considered 'normal'?

(And what bollocks that is! I mean, what's normal anyway??)

Why do I have to feel like I've got to keep telling people about me, anyway? Straight people don't have to tell their friends they're straight, so why do I feel like I gotta tell MY friends and family that I'm gay?

Sheesh. But there's a part of me thinks I *ought* to tell Mum and Dad before I tell too many other people. I've never kept anything from them, never lied to them, and I dunno, I really do want them to know about Han especially because Han's my life and she makes me happy. Any parent wants to know their kid's happy, don't they?

But I'm scared. I'm scared of what their reaction's gonna be, and it's that fear that makes me not want to tell them. I just keep going over and over the same thoughts, knowing that I've gotta tell them, then wondering WHY I've gotta tell them, to thinking that I DO have to tell them and, blah, blah, blah. It's doing my head in. It's with me 24/7 at the moment. It's all I can think about and I just wish I knew what to doooooo!

Thursday 23 October

Was talking to J about Han today and it felt reeeeally weird! She was asking me, like, all these questions about when did I first realise I was gay and had I ever dated boys, and was Han the only girl I'd ever slept with? I didn't really like talking to her about it to start with it 'cos it felt strange. I told her a bit about Ben and how it hadn't felt right, and how I'd then met Han and how everything suddenly made sense, and so after I'd said the words 'gay' and 'my girlfriend' a few times it began to feel a bit more normal, and I loosened up a bit. Then she asked me if it felt dead different kissing a girl and I just kinda said that it felt nicer, 'cos all I could remember from kissing Ben was his stubble and the fact he tasted of stale Coke all the bloody time. I just told her that kissing Han felt softer, and that she smelled a lot nicer than Ben did, and how it had felt weird kissing Ben, like there was something missing, and I hadn't liked it at all, but that the first time I kissed Han it felt perfect and lovely and I'd liked it very much indeed.

She looked at me strangely and I wondered if she was disgusted by it so I shut up, but she just said, 'It sounds nice,' and all I could say in reply was, 'Yeah, it is. Very nice,' which seemed a bit of a pathetic way to describe something that, to me, is amazing and perfect and feels completely right.

Friday 24 October

J saw me poring over the draft edition of our school magazine today so I kinda told her that I was having an input into it and told her I was going to be the Agony Aunt, but told her on pain of death that if she told a soul I'd come looking for her 'cos Mrs. Schofield had told me it was all meant to be completely anonymous. After laughing for what I considered a bit too long, she just said to me that she thought I'd make a good Agony Aunt 'cos I had 'a kind face', whatever that's supposed to mean.

Saturday 25 October

Went into town with Han this afternoon 'cos I wanted some more clothes for school. I'm sick of wearing the same things week in, week out. It was okay last year 'cos we wore uniforms, but now we can wear what we want (within reason) I really struggle to find something new to wear every day, so Han took me into Goths and Cloths and said she'd help me find something in there that would 'blow the minds of all the square kids at St Bart's'.

I saw a wicked, like, black and red striped camisole top thing, which clung to all the right places. I figured it wouldn't be suitable for me to wear to school, but the way Han was looking at it, I figured it would be suitable for me to wear for her so coughed up the £10 for it. School can wait. Han can't!

Sunday 26 October

HRBH came home for the day so we all had lunch together for the first time in ages. I haven't seen HRBH since she went off to uni at the end of September, but she still managed to irritate me within ten seconds of her walking into the house when she kinda looked me up and down and said, 'Still having that identity crisis of yours then, Clem?' to which I replied, 'What identity crisis?' and she said, 'Thinking you're a proper skater,' and laughed a hollow laugh.

I looked down at my baggy cargo pants and skater shoes, and my wrist covered in leather and cloth bracelets, and adjusted my oversized beanie and just glared at her, wishing she'd bugger off back to uni 'cos the peace and quiet we've had in the house since she's been gone has been awesome.

Sometimes I think she must have been adopted, 'cos there's no way me and her came from the same egg. No bloody way.

Monday 27 October

At last! An interesting e-mail sent to the magazine! Actually, a VERY interesting e-mail!!! Someone calling themselves 'Confused and Curious' wrote in today and said that they thought they were something called 'Bi-curious' and they didn't know what to do about it. I wasn't sure what bi-curious was—the only thing that sprang to mind was someone that was intrigued about Biology or something, but that didn't really make sense, so I checked it out on Google and was interested to see it meant someone who's straight, but fancies trying something with someone of the same sex!!

I know nothing about this (it's not really the sort of thing we discuss round the dinner table at our house), so I read loads of stuff about it on the Internet so that I would be better able to reply to this person. After spending about 20 minutes reading about it, I came to the conclusion that I can only equate bi-curiosity as being like, if you've always eaten cabbage 'cos that's what everyone else eats, and it's seen as the 'right thing' to do, but then maybe one day you fancy sprouts, even though some people tell you it's wrong to want sprouts, and that you really shouldn't do it. Then you try the sprouts and realise that they actually taste nice, and it adds a bit of variety to your diet, and there's nothing wrong with eating them, despite what people might think.

I didn't really think this would be the sort of thing Mrs. Schofield would want to see in the school magazine, so I just sent a personal e-mail back to 'Confused and Curious' and more or less said that. I hope he or she understands what I was trying to put across, otherwise my career as an Agony Aunt might be very short-lived.

Tuesday 28 October

There was a programme on the telly tonight and two women in it were gay!!! I'd seen it advertised in the telly magazine and kept dropping hints over dinner that I wanted to watch it. I could have watched in my room, I know, but I was kinda hoping that I might plant some seed of inquisitiveness into my parents' heads, and it might kick-start a deep and meaningful conversation about sexuality and stuff.

Anyway, we watched it together and Dad cracked some dumbass joke about them 'not looking like proper lesbians because they weren't wearing dungarees and they didn't have a number 2 haircut.' I was disappointed that even Mum laughed at such a pile of stereotypical shit.

Am back to square one again over my decision to talk to them. Great.

Wednesday 29 October

The first edition of our sixth formers' magazine was published today!! I'd had no new letters for the problem pages (apart from the one the other week about dicks which we couldn't print) and the e-mail from 'Confused and Curious' arrived too late for this week's deadline, so I made up a few myself—one about periods, the other about worrying about exams—and answered them myself too. Actually, I'd nicked them from Sunday's paper so I hope no one notices any similarities, but

I had no choice 'cos Mrs. Schofield was breathing down my neck for something like some demonic dragon.

Thursday 30 October

We have a space on the coach when we go and see *Hamlet* next week so I asked Han tonight whether she wanted to come with us. She told me that 'she'd rather pierce her own nipples with a staple gun than have to sit through three hours of Shakespearean shit', so I think it's fair to say she won't be coming with us.

Shame. I kinda liked the idea of cosying up on the back seat of the coach with her, but instead I guess I'll have to put up with Matty texting her new boyfriend, some lad called Robbie, who's in her Maths class, all the way there instead.

#joy

Friday 31 October

Today was Halloween so I decided to wear the black and red camisole thing that I'd bought on Saturday 'cos it looks, like, really Halloweeny and spooky and all. Of course, the fact that I was going out with Han later tonight had nothing to do with it at all. Ahem.

We met up in town after school and bought this pumpkin, then we went back to her house to hollow it out and put it in her window, hoping it would encourage all the Trick or Treaters to come round so we could scare them all and tell them all to bugger off home to their mummies.

I'd been wearing my short leather jacket round town and when we got back and I took it off, Han took one look at my new top and whistled through her teeth at me, raising her eyebrow and giving me one of 'those' looks. There wasn't anyone in 'cos Han said her mum and dad had taken little Joe into town for a burger and then to the cinema to see some film, but just to make absolutely sure we were alone she yelled out throughout the house, in the garden, and up the stairs but no one answered. Han grinned her lazy grin at me and said, 'Seems we're all alone,' then took me by the hand and led me upstairs to her room.

She asked me to keep my new top on and I wondered briefly for a minute if that was a bit kinky, but then I figured if me keeping my top on turns her on, who am I to complain??! She obviously DID like me with my top on 'cos what started as just a bit of early-evening shenanigans turned into quite a session with Han being—ohhh, how can I write this in my diary without sounding rude?—VERY appreciative of what I was doing, and letting me know just how appreciative she was by being very noisy, which made me feel, OMG, like, amaaaaazing!

Anyhow, afterwards we were lying together in her bed and I was just thinking about having another go, when we suddenly heard someone moving around downstairs. So, me thinking it was her parents, and Han thinking it was a burglar, we got dressed and quietly went downstairs only to find her older brother Dan slumped in front of the TV with a can of beer in his hand.

He jerked his chin in recognition at me and mumbled 'urright?' to us both. Han said, 'I thought you were at uni?' and he just shrugged and said, 'So I came home for the weekend.' He supped at his can for a bit then casually said to Han, 'I don't mind where you do it, H, or when you do it, or who you do it with, but next time, just keep the bloody noise down, will you? I was trying to have a kip up there.'

After I'd finished choking and Han had slapped my back a bit, she said to him, 'What you talking about?' but she didn't convince me, let alone him! Dan said, 'It's no big deal, H. I don't give a crap what you do, I'm just saying keep it down next time, 'specially if there's someone else in the house.'

I think he must have seen the looks on our faces 'cos he laughed and said, 'And I'm not going to tell Mum and Dad, if that's what you're worried about,' and I almost felt weak with relief and felt even weaker with relief when Han hissed at him, 'Good, 'cos if they do find out, I'll know who to come looking for and I'll chop your bollocks off and hang 'em off the Christmas tree.'

And I knew she meant it.

Saturday 1 November

I'm still cringing with embarrassment that Dan heard me and his sister at it hammer and tongs yesterday. Han thinks it's funny now, but then I've always thought she had a warped sense of humour. Every time I think of what Dan said to us yesterday, I can feel my scalp prickling.

Sunday 2 November

Not that it would be a problem if her parents did find out, though. I guess they've got to find out sooner or later, but I figure it would be better if we broke it to them gently, rather than them finding out we're at it like rabbits all the time. I know her mum's a nurse, but there are ways and means of breaking something to someone, aren't there?

Monday 3 November

I texted Han today and asked her if Dan had said any more to her about *what happened* on Friday. She sent me a text back just saying, 'Chill! He's gone back to uni and oldies haven't killed me so he obviously didn't tell them,' so I texted her back again and asked her if he'd said anything to HER about it, but she just texted me and said that all Dan had said was that I was 'sweet' and that Han 'could do worse'.

I'm not quite sure how to take that, actually.

Tuesday 4 November

I got a reply back from 'Confused and Curious,' thanking me for my e-mail to him/her last week. It said that, whilst they thought the analogy of the cabbage/sprouts was unconventional, it was better than any advice they'd ever read on the matter before and that they were going to have a good think about it all.

I'm glad my first piece of problem solving has been a success. Watch out Dr Phil, here comes Clemmie!

Wednesday 5 November

There was a firework display down in town tonight to celebrate Bonfire Night, so me and Han got all snuggled up in thick coats and scarves and went down there.

The fireworks were awesome! Like, really loud so that I kinda wanted to put my hands over my ears, but I didn't 'cos I thought Han might laugh at me. She'd brought some sparklers with her and we wrote each other's names in the air with them and it was soooooo romantic!

Came home to find Barbara in my bed. That was soooooooo not romantic!!

Thursday 6 November

Poor Han's full of cold! She sent me a text this morning to say she'd woken up with a throat 'that felt like a cheese grater' and that she thinks she picked it up last night at the fireworks 'cos she's sure some little kid sneezed on her.

I rang her tonight and I have to say she sounded terrible! She's pissed off as well 'cos she's had to take her nose ring out 'cos she reckons it hurts like hell when she blows her nose with it in, 'cos she's, like, blowing it every two seconds. That made me feel well queasy. Not for the first time since I've known her, I'm soooooo grateful her EMO weakness for piercings has never rubbed off on me!

Friday 7 November

We went to Stratford on Avon to see *Hamlet* tonight and a really horrid thing happened. It started off okay—we caught the coach up to Stratford, and Matty was practically apoplectic with excitement at the thought of seeing Jude Law playing 'the Danish Prince', as she called it. I figured Matty had got her plays mixed up 'cos we were going to see Shakespeare, not some Danish play, so I kinda hoped she wouldn't be too disappointed when we got there, but never mind.

I was texting Han all the way up the motorway, telling her I wished she was with me. She's still ill so she just kinda replied that she was far happier slobbed out in front of the TV, with a hot drink and box of tissues, watching a repeat of last week's *X Factor*. I had a momentary pang of wishing I was home with her, but did my best to ignore it, figuring I was going to Stratford to be educated.

Anyway, the play itself was all right, I suppose. It was a modern version of *Hamlet* so it was a bit strange to see him being played with a beanie and a parka jacket on, but I'm glad they didn't stint on the skull, which looked eerily real. In fact, if I hadn't known better I'd have said one of the actor's dogs had just conveniently died a few days before the production. What I didn't realise, though, was that *Hamlet* was Shakespeare's longest play. Had I known that, I wouldn't have had two bottles of Coke on the way up and then had to spend the next God knows how many hours wriggling in my seat, needing a wee.

On the way back home, the coach driver stopped off at a motorway service station 'cos the oil warning light was flashing on and off on his dashboard, so he let us all get off and have a wander round the café inside while he got it sorted. Anyway, I took myself off while Matty was queuing for the toilet and rang Han to tell her what the play was like, and to ask her how she was. I'd positioned myself behind a pillar and was whispering sweet nothings to her and being all silly—as you do—and when I looked up, Matty was standing next to me!!!!

So I put the phone down real quick and Matty looked at me all funny, then started taking the piss out of me, saying things like how sweet it was that I was in love and she had no idea I WAS in love, and wasn't I a dark horse for keeping my boyfriend a secret from her? I felt my face getting dead hot, which just made her wind me up even more, and then she kept asking me 'who he was', and when I wouldn't tell her, she snatched my phone from my hand!!!

I got dead cross with her then and told her to give me my phone back, but she wouldn't. I didn't want to cause a scene in the service station so I just told her real quiet—and kinda menacingly—that I wanted my phone back right that minute or I'd twat her. Or words to that effect. But she wouldn't give it back! Instead, she said, 'So let's see who the last number dialled was,' and then there was like this slow-motion moment where she flipped my phone open, with me still trying to get the phone off her, and read the last name I'd dialled.

I kinda watched her face change from being all smiley and joking, to confused and then dead serious. Then she looked up at me and I guess it was obvious from the look on my face that what she was thinking was right. I was sooooooo fucking angry with her! I mean, what right did she have to take my bloody phone off of me and start pissing about with it anyway??

So I just told her to give me my phone back, and she gave it back to me without saying a word. I leant on the pillar that I'd been hiding behind to speak to Han and kinda just said, 'So now you know who I was talking to,' and Matty just went, 'Yeah, I do.'

Then we didn't say anything for a bit and it was really embarrassing, so I said to her, 'Is there anything you want to ask me?' and she just said, 'No,' which was really not what I wanted to hear. I felt like I wanted to cry, and could feel my eyes beginning to prick so I walked past her without saying anything and went back to the coach.

Anyway, once the coach had been sorted out and we'd set off again, I just kinda stared out the window, not saying a word to Matty, and she didn't say anything to me. Then, after about ten minutes, she turned to me and said, 'I didn't know you were like that,' so I turned to look at her and said, 'Like what?' and she said, 'Y'know.' Then she said, 'Or Han, for that matter,' and I said, 'Does it really matter?' and she said, 'I dunno.'

So we didn't speak again for about another ten minutes and I started to get cross again, so I said to her, 'Does this change how you feel about me, then?' and she looked at me strangely and said, 'I dunno.'

Great! Matty's been my mate for, like, over five years and she finds out one tiny detail about me, and now she's doubting our friendship. I said to her, 'I haven't changed! I'm still the same Clemmie that just sat next to you and watched Jude Law poncing about on the stage with a beanie and a dog's skull!'

And Matty just said, 'I didn't know you liked girls, thassall. You know, *like that*,' and I kinda said, 'Well I do,' and then I said, 'And there's not a whole lot I can do about it.'

Then she didn't say anything for, like, ages, so I just turned to her and said, 'Y'know what? You should be pleased for me rather than just sitting there ignoring me, Matty. I'm really happy and so is Han, and as long as it's not hurting you, or anyone else, then I really don't think it's fair of you to sit there just not talking to me, like I've done something wrong. 'Cos I haven't. This doesn't change who I am, Matty. I'm still Clem. I'm still your friend.'

But Matty just said, 'Yeah, but you're not who I thought you were, and right now I really need to get my head round that,' then stuck her iPod on, which kinda indicated that she didn't want to talk about it any more, which really pissed me off.

So we drove the rest of the way in silence and I felt more wretched than I've done in months. When we got back to school, she just got off the coach and didn't say anything to me, and I felt really alone.

Rang Han the minute I got in but her phone was off. I really need to speak to her.

Saturday 8 November

Spent the morning stressing about Matty. I texted Caroline last night and told her what had happened, and she texted me back this morning and told me not to worry, and that she'd have a word with her, and that Matty probs just needed to have time to get used to the idea.

WTF?

Then I rang Han and, after she'd sneezed about a hundred times down the phone at me, I told her what had happened last night and she pretty much said the same as Caroline had said, and then told me that 'It's never guaranteed that everyone you tell will be totally comfortable with your gayness, and you've just got to get used to the idea, Clem.'

I made some feeble comments about Matty being my friend since year 7, and that as far as I was concerned, nothing had changed, but Han just said that it just freaks some people out, and that was a fact of life.

Well, it shouldn't be. Now I'm dreading having to see Matty at school on Monday. I couldn't concentrate on doing the dumb essay on *Hamlet* that Mr. Harman kindly gave us to do as we stepped off the coach on Friday night. Wrote about 100 words but couldn't be arsed with the rest so spent the afternoon on the PS3 perfecting my freestyle skateboarding tricks.

I'm a teenager, not a pensioner. Essays can wait for when I'm dead. Besides, I need time to think about Matty.

Sunday 9 November

Woke up thinking about Alice today, and wondering how she is, and kinda wanting to tell her about what happened with Matty. I sent her a text asking her how college was going, not expecting her to reply, but she did. I felt really happy when I saw her name appear in my message inbox, and wondered briefly if she'd like to hang out today, but I didn't ask her. I figured it was better to take it one step at a time for now.

Her texts were short and polite, like she was talking to a teacher or something, not her previous BFF. She said that college was awesome, and it was the best move she'd ever made. She told me her course was great and she was getting good marks, and was predicted to do very well in her re-sits next year. I was glad.

I'm pleased she's happy. I'm glad she's moved on and that she's doing well at college, but I also feel a bit sad that it took going out with me, and me dumping her, for her to get to this point, if that makes sense. I feel eaten up with guilt that I managed to fuck her life up so spectacularly 'cos that's really not the person I am, but at least it sounds like she's happy again.

We texted each other on and off all day, which was nice. I ended by suggesting it would be good to get together again maybe one day, but she didn't reply. I kinda miss her.

Monday 10 November

Didn't see Matty at school all day, much to my relief. I'd thought of all these things that I would say to her if I did see her, but it all came to nothing, and, to be honest, I was relieved.

I did get another e-mail from 'Confused and Curious' today, though, which arrived in my in-box, completely out of the blue! I didn't reply to the last one 'cos I thought my work had been done, but he/she e-mailed me today to say they're still curious about experimenting with a 'friend' and did I, in my capacity as Agony Aunt, think it was a wise thing to do?

I replied and said I thought it might not be a good idea to pounce on the 'friend' in question without actually talking it through with them first, 'cos they were likely to twat them, and a beautiful friendship could be ruined.

I didn't use the word 'twat', of course. I don't want this person to think me an uneducated oaf.

Tuesday 11 November

It was Remembrance Day today so we all had to stand for a two-minute silence during our English class at 11 o'clock. I always get a bit embarrassed during these silences, thinking I'm gonna hiccup or fart or something, but it was okay today. I caught sight of J watching me from the corner of her eye and for one horrible moment I thought she was gonna try and make me laugh, but she didn't. She just kinda looked at me.

Saw Matty at lunchtime. It was dead awkward. I dunno if Caroline had been having a go at her, but she was a bit more talkative than she'd been on Friday—but not much—and managed to have half a conversation with me without actually using the word 'gay' once. She just said to me that she'd had no idea I liked girls, and that finding out the way she'd found out had been really shocking. It was on the tip of my tongue to tell her that if she hadn't nicked my phone off me like she had, and then refused to give it back to me, then she'd have never found out. But I didn't. Instead I just listened to her ramble on about how she didn't know any people 'like that' (!) and it all felt a bit weird to her, but that I was still her mate and she'd try not to let it change anything.

That was big of her! I said to her that I was still the same person as I was before she found out, and she nodded and looked a bit ashamed, but then asked me to give her time to get used to it. I said to her that as far as I was concerned, nothing had changed with me, and that I really needed her to understand that being gay was a huge part of who I was, and what I didn't need was for her to shut me out, or, worse, judge me because of it. I also told her that I'd happily talk to her about me and Han, how we got together and stuff like that. She nodded and said 'Yeah, maybe,' then kinda hugged me, a bit tentatively, and said she'd see me in English class later.

I think I feel a bit better about everything, but only a bit. Texted Han and told her I thought me and Matty were going to be okay. She texted me back and said, 'See? What did I tell you? I'm always right!!'

I hope she is right this time.

Wednesday 12 November

OMG what a straaaaaange day! So, like, basically I went to the common room after English today with J for a coffee, like we do most Tuesdays, but this wasn't like any normal Tuesday! There was no one else in the common room when we got there, so I thought it would be great to start some work in peace on a D.H. Lawrence book we've gotta have partially read by next Tuesday.

So we sat down with our coffees and J said to me, 'Thanks for your e-mails, by the way,' and I didn't have a clue what she was talking about so just kinda went, 'Eh?' at her, not really taking any notice of her. She said, 'Your advice e-mails. Thanks,' and I STILL didn't know what she was on about, so just blithely slurped on my coffee and kinda went 'Eh??' again at her. She laughed and said, 'My e-mails. About me being, uhh, curious. Y'know,' and I nearly spat my coffee out across her lap.

So I looked at her with wide eyes and spluttered, 'You??? The e-mails were from you??' and she shrugged and said, 'Yeah,' like I'd just asked her if she wanted another coffee or something. So I just stupidly said, 'You're kidding me, right?' and she just laughed at me!!

I said, 'So you're wondering what it would be like, um, to get it on with another girl?' (like, durr) and she said, 'Well, yeah. Like I said, I'm curious. I've only ever been with guys before so it'd be cool to see what the other side's got to offer.'

At this point the pile of papers that had been on my lap slipped onto the floor, so I spent the next two minutes scrabbling around on the floor like an idiot while she just casually carried on drinking her coffee and thumbing through her D.H. Lawrence.

When I'd plonked myself back on my chair, she turned to me and said, 'I s'pose I've got you to thank for pricking my curiosity, really. You intrigue me, Clem,' and it was all I could do to stop the papers falling off my lap again. I said, 'Intrigue? How?' and she said, 'I dunno, you just do. Have done since I saw you kissing your girlfriend at Matty's party, and now I know you bat for the other side, well, that adds a bit of an extra something to you, as far as I'm concerned.'

I said to her, 'But you've got a boyfriend!' and I thought I sounded a bit like a flustered old maid, but she just laughed and said, 'Yeah, but that doesn't stop me from wanting to try some cabbages and sprouts, does it?'

I took a big gulp of my coffee and said, 'So when you said about wanting to experiment with a friend, who did you mean?'

She just held my gaze a bit longer than I felt comfortable with and said, 'Who did you think I meant, honey? I didn't mean Rosie, did I?'

I guess not. Rosie's lovely and all, but I can see she's a bit too cardigan and slippers for J, bless her. Anyway, just as I was about to say something else to her, some people came into the room just then so we never got to finish the conversation. I went off to my History lesson just hoping and praying that:

She was joking,

She'll forget about it,

She'll change her mind,

All three.

Decided to keep this to myself at the moment 'cos if Han gets even so much as a whiff of it, there'll be rivers of blood running through the corridors of St Bart's by the weekend.

Dear God, has the world gone mad? My life has more ups and downs at the moment than a porn star's arse.

Thursday 13 November

Thing is, I don't actually fancy J any more. She's as fit as the proverbial, granted, but I don't fancy her—at least I don't think I do. But if she came on to me, what would I do? I've got the willpower of a chocoholic round PMT week—all that crap with Alice back in the summer showed that—but then I was hurting over Han. Me and Han are the strongest we've been in months and months, and I don't want to do anything to mess that up.

Besides, I could just be J's muse, couldn't I? I could just be her, what was it she called it? Her experiment. She'd experiment with me, then drop me like a hot potato, leaving me feeling used.

Satisfied, but used.

Friday 14 November

Managed to avoid J all day 'cos I didn't have any lessons with her. I'm glad 'cos I didn't think I could cope with her looking at me the way she's been looking at me and her making suggestions to me again. Not sure what I'll do next week when I have to sit next to her in bloody English!

Had lunch with Matty and it was okay, actually. Yeah, it was a bit awkward to start with, and she didn't ask me anything about Han, or about me, and so I didn't push it with her. I suppose she didn't feel comfortable talking about it, but, to be honest, that's her problem, isn't it? I'll tell her stuff if she asks me, but there's no way I'm going to volunteer information to her. I was just grateful that she wanted to have lunch with me at all, even if that sounds pathetic.

I just want things to get back to normal, and if that means skirting round the subject, and never mentioning the words 'gay', 'lesbian', or 'girlfriend', then I guess I'll do it. I figure she'll talk to me about stuff when she feels ready to. Again, her problem. Not mine.

Saturday 15 November

Went out with Han and some of her friends tonight. It was wicked! We went to Pizza Hut and there was, like, about eight of us! This Goth boy Freddie that Han's always on about from her Film Studies group was there too. It was the first time I'd actually met him close up and he looked dead scary! I thought I'd got used to EMOs, what with having gone out with one for over a year, but he was something else! He had bars and rings and bolts coming out of just about every hole, and I didn't really say much to him all evening 'cos he was busy talking to other people. I did notice, however, that he couldn't take his eyes off Han, so I think I'm gonna have to keep MY eyes on HIM.

Sunday 16 November

I've decided to try and ignore what J said to me on Wednesday. I think she was just trying to shock me, see what my reaction would be. I think she might be that kind of person. If I don't react, or show that I'm shocked, or interested, or even the least bit keen, she'll get the idea and hopefully try out her curiosity on someone else. That is, if she was even telling the truth about being curious in the first place…

#headfuck

Monday 17 November

J told me today that she thinks I'm 'cute' and that she can see what Han sees in me!! She also said that if I ever got bored with Han I knew where she (J) was, and that she'd be waiting for me.

She was looking extremely fit today but I just kept telling myself that I had a girlfriend who loves me very much and that J was just playing with me. When I went for a wee at lunchtime I looked at Han's photo on my phone and felt a bit better. I sent her an 'I love you' text as well while I was weeing, and felt even better.

#multitasking

Tuesday 18 November

Went over to Han's house after school tonight. Han finished college at, like, 3 o'clock today (how?!) and texted me to say she was bored and wanted me to come over. How is she able to finish college at 3 in the afternoon? How is that fair, when I have to stay until 4 bloody p.m.?

Anyway, I went to hers on my way home, texting Mum and telling her I was staying on in the library until 5 'cos she has, like, major stresses about me going to people's houses during the school week, thinking I should be spending my time studying.

Well, mother, I did spend my time studying tonight. I studied Han's chest extremely carefully—both visually and physically—for a good hour this evening. I studied it wisely, and thoroughly, and longingly, and I can now declare the results: Han's chest was most fine, thank you very much.

Wednesday 19 November

I made the mistake of telling J that I sometimes go skateboarding down the park at the weekends. Boy, what a dumb thing to tell her!

She said, 'You skate? My God, that's, like, SO fricking hot,' and kinda looked at me up and down, like a judge inspecting a prize poodle at a dog show and just nodded, saying, 'Soooo hot,' again.

I think it's official. I think J's gone crazy.

I mean, how can she think being a skater is hot? More to the point, how can she think a short, scruffy git like me, who dresses in baggy, scruffy gear and a baggy scruffy beanie when she skates, could possibly be hot? Han sure as hell doesn't think so! She's already told me that, while she's okay about buying me stuff for my 'skating obsession' (her words, not mine) she doesn't want me coming anywhere near her when I'm dressed up for going skating in case she's seen out with me (which is a bit insulting if I'm honest, but I figure even EMOs have their pride).

Thursday 20 November

Finished school early today 'cos we had a free last lesson, in which we were supposed to go and do some study leave for some essay or other that we've gotta hand in next week. J asked me if I wanted to go up to the library and do some work but I thought I'd make the most of being let out of prison (school) early and go meet Han down at college.

I found Han in the refectory with Freddie and some of the others, having coffee. She squealed and jumped up when she saw me, wrapping her arms round me in a bear hug and whispering something I didn't catch into my hair, and I was stoked that she seemed so pleased to see me.

Friday 21 November

J sent me a text tonight, which said 'Sooo thinking about you.' I think she must have been a bit pissed because some of the letters were jumbled up, and she sent it at, like, 12 a.m., but I got the gist of what she meant.

This is so freaking me out! I lay in bed thinking how ironic it all is, and how strange life can be sometimes, 'cos if this had happened, like, 18 months ago I'd have been sooooo happy, but then I didn't have Han, did I? At the beginning of last year I would have given anything for J to say what she'd said to me yesterday, but now I've got Han and I love the bones of her, and I've never given J a second thought in all the time I've been with Han, but then J comes out with something like that and now I'm all confused.

Actually, if it had happened when I was going out with Alice last summer I'd have been happy 'cos, let's face it, you wouldn't kick J out of bed for spilling crumbs, if you know what I mean. But that's just a bit mean to Alice, isn't it?

Aaaargh! Why can't life be easy???

Saturday 22 November

Ems and Ryan have got engaged!!! Ems texted me last night and told me that Ryan had popped the question while they were out bowling down the Mecca. She said he'd just hit his third strike of the evening when he turned round and said to her, 'We should get hitched. D'yoo fancy it or what?' and Ems said it had been so romantic she could have died and gone to heaven right there!

Anyway, they're going shopping for an engagement ring today and EVEN BETTER, they're having a party at Ryan's house in two weeks' time and we're all invited!

S'pose this means I'll have to buy them an engagement present, though.

Something dead nice happened tonight as well. Matty rang me and apologised for being 'such a twat just lately'. She told me she'd been out with Caroline today and they'd talked about me a lot, and Caroline had told Matty to 'grow up' about me and Han, and to 'get over herself' 'cos I was one of her oldest friends and she should be supporting me rather than being weirded out by me. Go Caro!!!

Apparently Caroline told Matty to remember all the laughs we've all had together over the years, and then she said to her that it must have been really tough for me, not only having to come to terms with being gay in the first place, but then for having to keep Han a secret from everyone for such a long time, especially all through school, and that the only reason I didn't ever tell my friends was because I was worried about what sort of reaction I'd get. Then, according to Matty, Caroline told her off for giving me just the sort of reaction I'd been dreading, and she said she (Matty) should feel ashamed for embarrassing me and letting me down, and not being more understanding. Blimey!

So, Matty said everything Caroline had said to her had been spot on, and that she was sorry to me for not being a better friend, and that she really wanted to make it up to me. She asked me loads of questions about me and Han, like how long we'd been seeing one another, and asked me if I was happy, and when had I first realised I liked girls, and stuff like that. She asked me if there was any part of me that still liked boys, and then we had a right laugh about Ben; Matty said now she understood why I was never gutted when we broke up, and why I didn't give a toss when she started going out with him soon after.

I went to bed feeling so happy. The last thing I ever wanted was for any of my friends to be weirded out by me, and I never wanted to lose any of my friends just because I'm gay. I thought I might have come close to losing Matty, but the last words she said to me before we finished our conversation were, 'You'll always be daft, Clemmie, whether you're gay or straight, and that's why we all love you. Don't ever change.'

I think she meant it as a compliment.

Sunday 23 November

I sent Drummer Joe a text and asked him if he wanted to go over to the skate park, adding that I wanted to talk to him about 'women trouble'. He's the only one I can really trust not to blab anything to Han about all this business with J, so I was dead relieved when he said he'd meet me over there.

I figured I might as well tell him everything, so I told him about how J was the first girl I really ever fancied, and how I'd cried myself to sleep over her and blah, blah, blah, and about how since I'd been with Han I'd never given her a second thought but now she was coming onto me and it was puddling my head.

So he said, 'But do you actually fancy her any more?' and I told him that I didn't think I did, but then it's difficult to tell when a fit girl is coming on to you. So he said, 'Well then, have you told her you're not interested?' and I suddenly realised that I hadn't actually ever told J I didn't fancy her and I didn't want to get involved with her. So Joe said, 'So it's easy! Just tell her you're with Han, you're happy with Han, you're not interested in J and that if she wants to experiment, then she should go experiment with someone else.'

Everything seemed so much clearer then, and I went home feeling less worried and more relaxed about stuff than I have done in weeks, all thanks to Joe! Who'd have thought it, hey? I think he's wasted on my sister!

Monday 24 November

J put her hand on my leg today!!!!!!!!!!! We were in the common room after English and we'd sat kinda to the side of the room behind a small screen but it meant that no one could see us. I was trying to put together some notes from the lesson we'd just had, and she was reading through a chapter of the *Moll Flanders* book we're doing at the moment, then all of a sudden she put her hand on my leg!!!

I wasn't sure what a girl's supposed to do when she has a hand land on her leg, so I just left it there for a bit, then she started stroking it!!! I looked down at her hand like it was something I'd never seen before, and she just said to me, 'Am I making you feel uncomfortable?' I thought, well no, actually, it's quite nice, but figured the correct answer was 'yes', so I said 'Yes,' and she took her hand away. I kinda looked at her out of the corner of my eye and she turned and looked at me and said, 'Just showing you I'm still interested,' and started chewing on her pen and smiling at me which made my face burn crimson with embarrassment.

I felt a whoosh of something inside, which I hoped wasn't wind, and sort of smiled weakly at her, kinda like I was smiling for a passport photo, and just blurted out, 'Sooooooo, *Moll Flanders*. Misunderstood victim of circumstances or just a slapper?' and she just sighed and said, 'Oh Clemmie, Clemmie. You are sweet when you blush, y'know,' and carried on reading her book.

I tell you what, I for one can't WAIT for the bloody Christmas holidays so I can get away from this maelstrom of hormones otherwise known as Justine 'I'm Fucking With Your Mind' Button!

Tuesday 25 November

Okay, so J is coming onto me, like, dead strong and I don't know what to do about it! After I'd been so unresponsive with her in the common room yesterday I kinda thought she'd take the hint that I'm not interested and go amuse herself with someone else. But, nooooooo!

Today, right, she got me by the drinks machine in the common room and told me again that she thought I was cute and that she couldn't stop thinking about me and that every time she sees me, all she thinks about is kissing me! She said, 'You told me that kissing a girl was nice, so I want to try it myself, see if what you said is right,' so I just kinda went, 'uh-huh' like some dumbass, then she said, 'I think about doing it with you, Clem. You have very kissable lips, y'know?' and she looked me up and down and bit her lip, just like Han does when she wants some, and it made me feel a bit squishy inside.

Thank God Kirsty Chamberlain came bumbling over looking for some change for the tampon machine in the toilets 'cos I tell you what, you could have cut the atmosphere with a knife up to that point.

I don't know what to doooooo!

Wednesday 26 November

Do you know who I wish I could talk to about all this?

Alice.

Alice of old would have understood. She would have had a laugh with me about it, and would have told me not to stress so much about it. Or she would have had a word with J. Whatever. Alice would just have been someone to lean on. But I don't have Alice to lean on any more, do I?

Thought about texting her and spilling, but I knew I couldn't. Then I thought about texting Caroline and telling her, but Caroline can't keep a secret for more than five minutes, and I couldn't guarantee she wouldn't tell Han, so I'm stuck stressing about it alone, aren't I? Great.

Thursday 27 November

Han reminded me that we still hadn't bought anything for Ems and Ryan's engagement present and said that, bearing in mind we'd been invited to their party, we ought to show willing and get them something. I had to agree. I don't know Ryan's family from Adam, but if we're going to go to their house and wolf all their party titbits and drink all their alcohol, I suppose the least we can do is buy them a gift. But what do you buy a newly engaged couple? This is a tricky one. You can't buy them jewellery 'cos you'd have to buy his 'n' hers matching trinkets, and Ryan doesn't strike me as the necklace-wearing type. You can't buy them stuff for their house 'cos Ems has already told me they'll be living at Ryan's mum's when they first get married 'cos they can't afford a house yet. So what else is there?

Anyway, Han met me after school and we went into town together. I was slightly worried that J would be coming out of school at the same time as me and see Han and make some comment, but luckily for me I didn't see J at all for the whole day. And the present? We plumped for a silver picture frame and a pair of mugs with 'Just Engaged' written on them. Okay, tacky I know, but it was a 3 for 2 so we got a bath towel bundle free, which me and Han split 50/50 and took home to our respective mums and earned lots of gratitude for and, in my case anyway, an extra helping of treacle pudding at tea. Result!!

Friday 28 November

J did it again today. So, we went to the common room again after English, and Matty came with us so I thought I'd be safe—y'know, safety in numbers and all that—and everything was fine until Matty said she was going. J was wearing this, like, dead short skirt and I was trying sooooo hard not to look at her legs, so I told her I had to go too, but J said she wanted to ask me something about this coursework we're doing at the moment so I stupidly stayed. When Matty had gone, J said she was glad she'd gone so we could be alone, and then asked me something about 'had I had any more thoughts about showing her what she was missing?' which made my legs go to jelly.

I took my chance, though, and remembered what Drummer Joe had said to me on Sunday so I said to her (quite firmly, I thought) that I thought this charade (good word, huh?) had gone on quite long enough, that I had a girlfriend and I was very happy with her, and I had no plans to cheat on her just so J could satisfy her own curiosity.

I sat back feeling quite pleased with myself, but all J did was arch an eyebrow at me and say, 'Oh Clemmie, Clemmie, Clemmie! You are sweet!' which got my mad up a bit, so I said to her, 'I'm not sweet, I'm just in love with my girlfriend and I don't want to be part of any experiment you want to have.'

J just laughed and said, 'Honey, you're not an experiment! Okay, maybe a few weeks ago I would have said different, but it could be fun, don't you think?' and she crossed her legs slowly, so that I had to make sure I fixed my eyes dead on her face and not on her legs.

Then I remembered something else Joe had said to me on Sunday and snapped at her, 'Yeah, but I don't fancy you. Sorry,' and she raised that damn sexy eyebrow again and said, 'Oh you will, you will,' and smiled at me, which made my ears go red, and I was just about to say something to her about stop treating all of this like a game, when she looked at her watch, sighed, and said she had to go, getting up and leaving me sitting there gaping like some sort of fish caught in a net.

I was furious with myself—and her—that nothing seemed to have got through to her, but at the same time I kept thinking about her short skirt and arched eyebrow. Sent Han a text telling her I loved her and she replied about 10 minutes later telling me she loved me back x1000000, so I felt a bit better and a lot less guilty.

Saturday 29 November

Sent Drummer Joe a text and told him that I'd spoken to J yesterday and told her I wasn't interested but she hadn't seemed to have taken any notice and had carried on flirting with me.

He sent me a message back saying he thought he really should meet J 'cos once she clapped eyes on him, she'd forget all about coming on to me!!!! Y'know, just when I was beginning to think Joe was okay for a boy, he comes out with a pile of shit like that and just reminds me that underneath his fairly sweet and understanding exterior, he's still a cock like all the rest of them.

Sunday 30 November

Han texted me this morning and told me she'd bought me a present in town yesterday, and would I like to come over and see it? I thought that was dead sweet of her, so I went over to her house after lunch and after I'd chatted to her mum for a bit, I went up to Han's room. She told me she'd bought me some lingerie so I looked around for a bag with smalls in it, but instead, Han locked her door and took her top off, revealing the most stunning bra I think I've ever seen in my life.

I said, 'I thought you'd bought me something?' and kinda still looked round her room for a bag.

She said, 'I bought you this, silly,' and pinged her bra straps (how did I ever get to have such a hot girlfriend??!!) and looked at me all seductive.

I think I understood the meaning behind it (more so after she'd pulled me to her and pressed herself to me) even if I was just a little bit miffed that when she said she'd bought me a present, what she really meant was, she'd bought herself a present but I'd still get to look at it, enjoy it, play with it, and get exhausted by it. Kinda like a Wii Fit.

She told me it was something called a balcony bra which, as she put it, 'squished, pushed up and enhanced' what she already had. I like balcony bras, I've decided. To be honest, standing up there in Han's locked room, I'd have quite happily set up a chair and parasol on that balcony and rested there all day.

What a girl!

Monday 1 December

Han told me today that Freddie asked her out!!! She came over to our house after college and we were sitting up in my room just chilling on my bed, and she just, like, mentioned it in passing! So casually!

So I said, 'Err, and what did you say to him?' and she just kinda looked up from this magazine that she was flicking through, and said, 'I told him you and I were dating,' and then carried on reading! Just like that!

I said, 'So now he knows we're not straight?' and she just nodded. So I said, 'And is he cool with that?' and she just went, 'Oh, totally. Why wouldn't he be?' and I didn't really have an answer to that.

I mean, I sorta guessed that he liked Han 'cos on the two occasions when I've seen him with her, he can't take his eyes off her, and I can understand why he'd want to ask her out, 'cos she's hot, but…

Grrrrr! It felt like Will the Bloody Photographer all over again! So, remembering what Han had said to me when I'd been unhappy over Will, I asked her if she liked Freddie, and she laughed and leant over and kissed my cheek and said, 'There's not one ounce of me that thinks he's anything other than the scruffy Goth that I go to college with, so you have no worries on that score either,' and winked at me, and of course that immediately made me feel squishy inside. She said, 'And I told him you're the love of my life and he said if he'd known he'd never have asked me out, and then he said he was sorry, so if you're stressing about it, don't!'

I felt a bit better when she said that. Then she dragged me over to her and we had this marathon kissing session on my bed and I felt a hundred times better!!

Tuesday 2 December

Great Aunt May bought me a Hannah Montana advent calendar this year, which was very nice of her. I tried to tell Mum that I was too old for Hannah Montana but she told me not to be such 'an ungrateful wretch', which was charming of her, wasn't it?! Despite my misgivings, I still took a slightly perverse pleasure in opening today's flap and chomping the head off the chocolate Miley Cyrus that was hidden inside.

Wednesday 3 December

J sent me a text tonight saying she was 'thinking about me'.

Aaaaaargggggghhhhhhhhhhhhhhh!

I sat and stared at her message for what seemed like hours, just trying to figure out exactly what she was playing at, then I got annoyed with her for sending a message like that to me. So I sent her a message back saying, 'Why are you doing this?' and sat in bed waiting for her to reply. She sent one back again saying, 'Doing what?' which was infuriating!!!!

I replied and said, 'Messing with my head. Told you I'm not interested, so just leave me alone, ok?' Then she sent me one back saying, 'But I can't stop thinking about you' (!!!!!!!!!!) and another one straight after it saying, 'And I'm not messing with you.'

I figured if I replied again we'd just end up texting each other all night, and I didn't want that. I was just about to delete them but stopped myself for some reason. Maybe I'll delete them tomorrow.

Thursday 4 December

Couldn't sleep last night for thinking about J. I feel like, I dunno, I feel like I'm cheating on Han even though I haven't done anything with J. I s'pose it's because me and her are having all these conversations and Han knows nothing about them, it makes me feel like I'm doing the dirty on her. I hate keeping secrets from her! God knows it was bad enough when I was first seeing Alice, but then I didn't want Han to think I was dating Alice just to get back at her. Nah, scrub that. I didn't want Han to know about Alice 'cos I knew what Han thought about Alice and I suppose a small part of me thought Han would think it was funny, me and her going out with each other.

But how can I ever tell Han about J? How can I tell her that another girl's coming on strong to me? She'd kill her and hang her up like a string of fairy lights in the town centre as a warning to any other girl, that's for sure.

This is so fucking unfair of J to do this to me!!! How many sleepless nights have I had over that girl in the past and now, the one time I've felt really settled all year, she goes and does this to me! Why couldn't this have happened when me and Han were apart?! I'd have had her like a flipping shot then!

(Sorry, Alice.)

Friday 5 December

Went to Ems and Ryan's engagement party tonight with Han and Caroline. It was at Ryan's parents' house so I felt like I had to be on my best behaviour 'cos both his parents would be there, and his grandparents and all his aunties and uncles and cousins. Ems's whole family was there too, so it was a bit of a squeeze 'cos Ryan's house is only an end terrace with 2 bedrooms and a conservatory, which is really just a lean-to but which Ryan's mum kept calling 'ahh conservatray' in this funny posh accent which Ryan said she always puts on when there's strangers in the house.

Alice was there too, with some girl that Caroline told me later is on the same course as her at college. It was neat seeing Alice again. I haven't seen her since August, and I thought she looked okay, to be honest. She looked pretty happy, even though she wouldn't come near me all evening, or speak to me, or even acknowledge I was in the same room as her. I worried that Ems might notice and ask me questions, but she was too busy wrapping herself round Ryan all evening to even see what was going on.

Anyway, me and Han gave the happy couple our presents and they both seemed very happy with them. Then Ems showed me, Han, and Caroline the engagement ring Ryan had bought her. She said Ryan couldn't afford a dead expensive ring 'cos he only works in the trainer department in a sports shop now he's left school, and it's not very well paid, so he'd got a cheap ring out of the catalogue. She said it did have a jewel in it and we were all ooh-ing and aah-ing at it while she proudly showed it off, but the stone was so small I struggled to see anything remotely resembling a gem and my eyes were dazzled by metal that was more mustard-yellow than gold.

Alice left before anyone else did, and I can't say I was sorry, to be honest, 'cos it was a bit awkward being there with Han, and a small part of me kept stressing that the two of them would have a massive fight or something, which was a ridiculous thing to think, I know. But everyone else seemed to have a good time and we were all given a glass of fizzy wine to toast the pair of them, but I think it must have been cheap 'cos I had heartburn for the rest of the evening.

Saturday 6 December

Woke up early with sodding indigestion from Ryan's cheap wine last night, so texted Joe and asked him if he wanted to come down to the skate park with me 'cos I figured the fresh air might do me some good. Besides, Han had gone to visit family today and the thought of spending the day alone and writing stupid essays all afternoon chilled me to the core.

Met Joe down at the park and it was, like, really busy, but I didn't really care 'cos I've kinda got a lot better recently so I don't feel so self-conscious bombing it up and down the ramps (and falling off) any more. We'd been there about an hour and a half and we were just taking a breather up at the top of one of the ramps when Joe nudged me and told me there was someone watching us.

I peered towards where he was jerking his head and nearly fell off when I saw it was J!!!! She was standing behind the fence, leaning against a post, legs crossed at the ankles, her hands in her jeans pockets and JUST WATCHING ME.

Like some freaking stalker!!!

FFS!

I said, 'Oh crap, it's J,' like proper stressed about it, and Joe's eyes nearly popped out of his head.

He said, 'THAT'S J??? You never told me she was a babe! Please tell me you think she's hawt, or I'll lose every ounce of respect for you right here and now.'

I said, 'Of course I think she's hot, you prat! I spent the best part of two years lusting after her at school, but that was then. It's all different now.'

Then Joe just looked at me strangely and said, 'You don't fancy THAT?'

Thing is, diary, I just dunno! I mean, yeah, she's fit and everything but I know she's just messing with me, so what's the point getting drawn in? Whatever happens I'm just gonna end up looking stupid, especially 'cos I know it's all just a game to her. But seeing her standing there at the park today just totally weirded me out.

Anyway, Joe kept pestering me to go speak to her but there was no way I was going down to her 'cos that's just what she wanted. I think Joe was toying with the idea of going down himself, but I guess the thought of HRBH finding out that he was spotted talking to a fit girl was enough to stop him. Can't say I blame him; HRBH scares the shit out of me and I've known her all my life!

There was, like, NO way I was going to do any skating while she was still watching, so I just kinda sat up there, picking at my fingers and occasionally glaring down at her until she must have taken the hint that I wasn't going to either perform for her or talk to her, and she wandered off.

I just wish I knew what her game is! She's totally messing with my head.

#SoooStresssssssed

Sunday 7 December

Great Aunt May and Great Uncle Elvis came to us for Sunday lunch today. I was telling them all about Ems and Ryan getting engaged and about their party on Friday night and Great Aunt May was very interested when I told her Ryan's granddad was there too, and started asking me loads of questions about him and adjusting her wig in an agitated manner when I was answering her. She asked me if he'd gone grey yet (of course he has!!! He's 81!!!!!!), then she started staring far away and rambling on about the fact when she knew him he had thick, black hair, a bit like 'a jaguar's pelt' and said to me that he probably looks more 'like a wolf now he's gone grey', but I couldn't really tell whether he was a jaguar or a bloody wolf 'cos the only sight I had of him the other night was him sitting in a chair in the corner nursing a pint of pale ale all evening.

Then she started sighing and sucking her teeth, so I got up from the table and got myself some more roast potatoes from the kitchen. Sounds like there's definitely a bit of history between Great Aunt May and Ryan's granddad but, quite frankly, I really don't want to know, and I'll bet poor Elvis doesn't want to, either!

Monday 8 December

HRBH is back from uni for Christmas. Since when did Christmas holidays start so early???

She arrived home this evening looking like she'd just spent the last three months backpacking across Africa, took one dismissive look at me, dumped her bags in MY room (okay, so it used to be hers) and told me to 'shift my crap out by bedtime' before flopping down in front of the TV and flicking up and down the channels on the remote control.

It's not HER room any more! It's MY room! Waited until Mum came back from her meditation class to have a moan but Mum wasn't having any of it, just telling us to sort it out between ourselves 'cos she was chilled from her meditation and refused to get stressed again!!!

Sometimes I wonder what the point of my mother is.

Tuesday 9 December

Gobbled back Lilly Truscott AND Amber Addison out of my advent calendar before breakfast today and then felt a bit sick.

Joe stayed over at our house last night so I came downstairs this morning to find him standing in the middle of our kitchen wearing my sister's dressing gown, scraping burnt toast into Barbara's bowl. He looked at me through bleary eyes and asked me if I was still stressing over J or whether I'd sorted stuff out with her yet, so I told him that she was still coming on to me like some sort of oversexed lusty maiden, and that her turning up at the skate park had been, like, the final straw.

He lowered his voice and said, 'So she knows you're gay, right?' and I nodded. So he said, 'And she started coming on to you once she found out you were gay, right?' and I nodded again, so he thought for a minute and said, 'Look Clem, I'm no expert in women. I might be going out with your sister,' and he looked over his shoulder to make sure HRBH wasn't within earshot, 'and God knows she's no good indicator of what a normal woman should be like, but it seems to me that this J bird just wants to test out her sexuality with you, use you as her experiment, so why not have a crack at it?'

I rolled my eyes at him and said, 'She just wants to experiment? No shit, Sherlock!! I know she just wants to experiment with me, but how can I do that to Han?'

Joe said to me, 'But if you give in to her just this once, give her what she wants—or what she thinks she wants—she might just leave you alone afterwards. She might not even like it! It's gotta be worth a try, hasn't it?'

I said, 'I s'pose so. I dunno. It's weird, isn't it?' and Joe said, 'Weird, maybe, but women are complex characters, Clem. Sometimes they just don't know *what* they want, sometimes you've got to show them the way, take the upper hand, show them you're boss and give them what they want. Women like to know their partners are in control, you know.' He carried on scraping burnt toast into Barbara's dish then said, 'Right, I better get this up to your sister. Can you see any black bits on it? If she sees any she'll grumble at me and send me back down to make more.'

So much for being the boss, eh, Joe?!

Wednesday 10 December

Managed to avoid J until lunchtime when she slipped me a note while I was queuing for lunch. She just kinda pushed this piece of paper into my hand then walked on by, turning to look back at me over her shoulder, just to frazzle me even more.

The note just said, 'Thought you looked hot Saturday, Skater Girl.'

I screwed it up and put it in my bag, but however tight I scrunched it up, it wasn't as screwed up as J apparently is. Or as screwed as I'd be if Han ever caught wind of any of this.

#HatingThis

Thursday 11 December

Went to a Christmas market with Han in town tonight and had a really romantic stroll around the stalls in the darkness until we got fed up with being pushed and shoved everywhere, and being hassled into buying fairy lights and stuff from the stall holders. I did manage to lose Han for ten minutes so that I could buy her this dead cool necklace that she'd seen on one of the stalls and that didn't require me to take out a mortgage to buy, so I was pleased that I at least managed to buy her one present while we were out.

We left early and walked home together, taking a detour along the canal towpath. Han was looking shit hot 'cos she'd Goth-ed herself up to the max in defiance to what she calls the 'commercialism of Christmas'. She was wearing gear that would scare the most hardy of souls, with her full-length distressed leather coat, walloping great black boots (unlaced, of course), loads of smudged black eyeliner and black nails and loads of black lipstick. She looked awesome.

We had, like, this fabulous kissing session in the darkness of the towpath, which was well sexy. I felt so in love with her I thought my heart would pop, especially when she draped tinsel round my neck and told me she adored me, and all my worries about J just seemed to disappear in an instant.

She went off home, turning every now and then to blow me kisses and I returned to Normal Land where I found HRBH slumped in front of the TV with Drummer Joe, watching some programme on the Discovery Channel about African tribeswomen making cooking pots out of mud and their own spit, or something.

HRBH looked briefly at me and frowned, telling me I had 'black round my gob' and I felt my heart nearly fall out of my arse. I wiped my mouth and realised I had some of Han's lipstick still on my lips, so made some feeble excuse about eating liquorice down at the market. Joe looked at me with a comical expression on his face, but HRBH didn't bat an eyelid, so I think she believed me.

I tell you what, I'm turning into a dead accomplished liar!

Friday 12 December

A weird thing happened tonight. HRBH came into my room this evening while I was on my laptop chatting to Han on MSN, and she said if ever I wanted to talk to her she'd be 'there for me'.

I closed my laptop lid down slowly (habit) and eyed her suspiciously 'cos:

a.) My sister, like, never comes into my room unless it's to have a go at me,
b.) She never wants to talk to me,
c.) She's not nice, and when she acts nice, it immediately makes me suspicious.

So I looked at her for a bit and kinda went, 'uh-huh,' like I was waiting for the next bit where she shouted at me for leaving my Vans outside her room, or breathing the same air as her or whatever, but she just stood there and said again if ever I wanted to chat, just let her know.

Chat? With HRBH? The day she says anything more than two words to me is the day hell will freeze over.

Saturday 13 December

OMG what a totally crappy night I had tonight! So, like, I went to Caroline's Christmas party at her house with Han, and the whole gang was there—Ems, Ryan, Matty, Alice, Marcie (with Ben—yuk, yuk, yuk)—all festooned in tinsel and mistletoe and shit like that. J was there too, wrapped around Ethan, who looked a bit like the cat that got the cream, but I noticed J kept looking at me, especially 'cos I was there with Han, even though we weren't really making a show of ourselves, if you know what I mean, primarily 'cos Ryan's twat of a friend Charlie was there and I figured if he took so much as one look at a pair of girls kissing, he'd have to change his boxers.

Anyway, Caroline had opened up a litre bottle of crème de menthe, which she says her aunty gives her mum for her birthday every year, even though her mum can't stand the stuff. It looked like, and tasted like, toothpaste, but toothpaste with a kick, and after the third or fourth sip of it, it actually began to taste quite nice. Han obviously thought so 'cos she was drinking it like it was going out of fashion, but it was beginning to make me feel a bit sick so I stopped after about the fifth shot, but I noticed Han sitting in the corner of the room talking to Caroline's mum's orchid, absolutely wasted and reeking of alcoholic mint.

I went upstairs for a pee, then went into Caroline's room to find Han's hoodie 'cos I thought I could take it downstairs and put it over her, All Han was wearing was a short skirt and vest-top thing and I figured if she didn't move for the next hour she'd be cold, not to mention that half the room could see right up her skirt the way she was sitting. I'm kind like that, you see. Anyway, I was just coming out of Caroline's room when J came in!!!!!!!!!! She was on her own, looking a bit pissed like I was, but no way wasted like everyone else, and she, like, came into the room, shut the door behind herself and leaned against it so I couldn't get out.

She did that thing that she keeps doing to me, like arching her eyebrow and chewing at her lip, so I just said to her that I had to get Han's hoodie down to her 'cos she was cold, then winced for sounding like some trussed-up old wife fretting about her elderly husband. J was still leaning against the door, but then she reached out and took my hand and pulled me over to her, so I just kinda mumbled 'don't' at her but she didn't seem to hear me 'cos she was still holding my hand and looking at me *in that way.*

She must have spotted the leather necklace that Han had given me when we were in Scotland in the summer and which I wear, like, ALL the time, 'cos then she reached over and started touching it and telling me it 'looked kinda sexy' on me and, I dunno if it was the crème de menthe or what, but my breath suddenly started getting dead hot and I could feel myself getting dizzy. She said to me, 'You're not an experiment, Clem, I keep telling you that. I haven't been able to take my eyes off you all night,' and if it wasn't for the pink flock wallpaper in Caroline's Mum's room and the picture of a poodle sitting on a bicycle on the wall next to me, I could quite imagine that I was in a scene from *A Streetcar Named Desire* or something like that.

I said something dumb like 'But your boyfriend's downstairs,' and she just puffed out her cheeks at me in exasperation and said, 'So what?' and moved her hand around the back of my neck and started running a finger up and down my back, giving me goose bumps on my arms. She leaned closer to me until we were, like, a centimetre apart and I could practically feel her lips on my lips, when someone tried to open the bedroom door from outside, like, quite forcefully, so we both moved out of the way and, OMFG, Alice came in looking not at all pissed!!!!!!! J still had her arms round me, but dropped her hands from my back and I stepped back looking dead startled; Alice copped one look at us both, laughed a sarcastic laugh and said I was 'priceless' before grabbing her coat and walking back out again.

I looked horrified at J, who was just standing there inspecting her nails and smiling to herself, and with my head still swimming with crème de menthe and God knows what else, shot off downstairs and was relieved to see Han still sitting talking to the orchid but no sign of Alice. J came downstairs and went over to Ethan, shooting me a glance and kinda smirking at me, and I felt furious with her. Then I started feeling furious with myself 'cos I know I came within a second of kissing her while my lovely, beautiful (if not extremely rat-arsed) girlfriend was downstairs making polite conversation with an exotic house plant.

Did my best to sober Han up a bit before she went home, then came home myself and wondered about texting Alice about what she'd seen, but figured if I didn't make a fuss about it then she wouldn't get suss. After all, what HAD she seen? It's not as if I actually kissed J, is it?

Sunday 14 December

4 a.m.

Can't bloody sleep.

J sent me a text yesterday evening which just said 'Next time' on it. I've been churning stuff over and over and over again in my head. Would I have kissed J if Alice hadn't have come into the room on Saturday? Even now, if I close my eyes I can still see her, leaning against the door, pulling me in towards her. What would have happened if Alice hadn't wanted to leave early?

Just sent Alice a text, even though it is 4 a.m. and she'll still be asleep. Just said 'Hi Alice, how are you? Did you enjoy the party?' and now I'm waiting for her to reply.

10 p.m.

Well, Alice sent me a text back at lunchtime today saying, 'Seems like you had a good time. Hope your gf doesn't know though.' I sat and stared at her message for ages before replying with one that said, 'What you saw wasn't how it looked,' and she sent one back saying, 'Whatever.' Huh? What does she mean? Such a cop-out answer! Does it mean she doesn't believe me, or does it mean she doesn't care what I got up to at the party? One thing's for sure, I hope to hell she doesn't start dropping hints to other people, hoping it'll get back to Han. She hates Han enough to want to hurt her, I know that for sure.

Monday 15 December

Didn't see J at school today, which was sooooo frustrating! Had lunch with Matty and she was saying what a good night it was on Saturday, then asked me if Han was okay 'cos she said she was 'Like, totally wasted, wasn't she? Last time I saw her she was dancing on the coffee table to Usher, so she must have been wasted 'cos she always used to say that listening to Usher brought her out in an angry rash.'

I said, 'She sobered up when we got outside and the cold air hit her,' and left it at that. I kinda wanted to tell Matty about J as well, but, to be honest, I didn't even know where to begin, or if Matty would even believe me. I mean, I sometimes can't believe it myself, that one of the hottest girls in the school is apparently crushing on me and got me up against a bedroom door on Saturday night.

I mean, what the freaking fuck? It even looks stupid just writing it down!

I sent Alice another text when I got home from school tonight, just kinda asking her not to say anything to Han about what she'd seen on Saturday night. Actually, scrap that. I didn't *ask* her, I *pleaded* with her not to say anything.

Alice replied, just before I was going to bed, and said she didn't give a toss what I did any more 'cos I 'was nothing to her' and that she wouldn't waste an ounce of her breath even speaking to my 'bitch of a girlfriend', so perhaps I can safely say I'm off the hook? Let's hope so, anyway.

Tuesday 16 December

Had sort of a rude dream about J last night. She was pole dancing round our rotary drier in the garden and giving me loads of 'come hither' looks. I started walking towards her and tripped over Uncle Buck's run, then got taken to hospital in a wheelbarrow that was being pushed by David Beckham in his LA Galaxy strip. J was leaning up against Caroline's bedroom door and waving me off, telling me she'd wait for me.

What a strange dream!

I daren't tell Han.

Wednesday 17 December

We got our Christmas tree today! Han said she got hers, like, last week but will Dad get ours any more than a week before Christmas? Noooooo! He says the needles always fall out two days after we've bought it and reckons that's 'cos Mum insists on having the thermostat on the central heating 'cranked up so high it makes the wallpaper peel', and the poor tree can't stand it.

He's got a point. It must be such a shock to the system for a poor pine tree, sitting happily in a forest for 50 weeks of the year, only to get hacked down, shoved into a house that's as hot as a sauna and then, to add insult to injury, gets covered from head to foot in so many bright, sparkly lights it puts Times Square to shame.

HRBH and Joe deigned to join us from her room and help finish off putting the last of the tinsel on it. Once Dad left the room to fetch the hand-held vacuum to suck up some loose needles, HRBH asked me if I was okay. I said I was fine, that I was decorating the tree. Then she asked if there was anything I wanted to tell her. I said, no, I didn't need to tell her I was decorating the tree, she could see that for herself.

So then…and this totally weirded me out…she said (again) if there was ever anything I wanted to tell her, or talk to her about, she'd be there for me. I noticed Joe was looking dead shifty when she was saying this, and then he left the room.

I don't like it when HRBH acts nice. It's not her. The fact that Joe looked uncomfortable when she was saying all this can only mean one thing, can't it? He's done something to piss her off and she wants to talk to me about it, but HRBH being HRBH, she can't just come out and actually tell me, so she has to do all this reverse psychology shit and get me to talk to her first.

I think it's about time my sister realised I'm not as daft as I look.

Thursday 18 December

Not that I look daft, of course. Sometimes, if I put a pair of glasses on and pout in the mirror, I can look half-intelligent.

I told Han today that HRBH is freaking me out by being nice. Han reckons it's either gotta be hormonal, or that HRBH is on drugs. Or both.

Friday 19 December

It was the last day at school before Christmas today and I can't say I was sorry, 'cos I really need some time away from school and from J right now.

Finished school at, like, midday, so went over to college and waited for Han, then went into town with her to buy some Christmas presents. I dropped, like, MAJOR hints at some clothes which I'd seen and that I quite fancied, but I was disappointed that she didn't suggest we split up at any point, because that meant she had no intention of going back and buying them for me.

She didn't point out anything she wanted, either, so I have precisely five days to figure out what the hell to get her. Sometimes I loathe Christmas.

Han hasn't looked at me strangely, or threatened to kill J, or started playing menacingly with knives around me, so I think I can safely say that when Alice said she wouldn't waste her breath telling Han about me and J, she was telling the truth.

I feel so relieved, I think I could cry.

Saturday 20 December

Ohhhh weird day alert! So I went bowling down the Multiplex with Han, Ems, Ryan, Matty, and Caroline this afternoon. And who did Matty invite as well? J!!! With Ethan!!! I could have killed her, I really could! (Not that Matty knows anything that J's been doing to me, so, upon reflection, I guess killing her would be a bit extreme.)

Anyway, J was wearing this, OMFG, really low-cut top with the skinniest jeans I've ever seen, which looked like they'd been spray-painted onto her, and every time she bent over to select a ball, I could see right down her top so I had to keep looking away. I think she knew I was looking at her 'cos she kept taking her time, and there was only so long I could gaze around the Multiplex before my eyes rested back on her and her magnificent cleavage.

And, right, whenever it was my turn to bowl, she'd stand, like, reaaaaally close to me so that I couldn't concentrate, so then I got a dead low score and got all ratty. When I passed her after bowling a particularly crappy round, she grabbed my arm and whispered, 'Am I putting you off your stroke?' and I nearly tripped over my feet and landed in Ryan's lap.

I was terrified that Han would see that my face went red every time I so much as looked at J, or if J brushed past me, and I can't really say I had a brilliant time. That really pissed me off 'cos I usually love going bowling, but how could I enjoy it today with J fingering the holes in her bowling ball seductively and looking at me like she wanted to eat me alive every five flipping minutes, while her boyfriend stood less than a foot away from us, apparently oblivious to his girlfriend flirting with me??

Sunday 21 December

Great Aunt May and Great Uncle Elvis (hehehehe) came over for Christmas lunch today, 'cos apparently they both wanted to spend Christmas Day at Autumn Leaves. Father Christmas was visiting and they didn't want to miss him. That's what Dad told me anyway. Okay, so it was four days early, but I didn't care! It meant I get to have two Christmas lunches, which is fine by me. I don't think Mum was too chuffed though, 'cos I'm SURE I heard her muttering about 'If I have to stuff one more bloody turkey in my life, I swear I'll go round the bend.' Sometimes she has no festive spirit at all!

Anyway, Great Aunt May and Great Uncle Elvis seemed to enjoy themselves. They kept saying about how much they were looking forward to spending their first Christmas together 'and many more to come', which caused a raised eyebrow between Mum and Dad. I thought it was dead sweet. I couldn't help but think of me and Han, and about how many Christmases we're gonna spend together. And then 'cos I'd been thinking about her, I missed her, so I texted her and then I rang her before lunch, and then we had a bit of a rude conversation on my phone up in my room and then I had trouble looking anyone in the eye over the sprouts at lunchtime.

Everyone seemed to want to be dead boring and sit around watching TV this afternoon (or in Melvis' case—haha—have a doze in front of the TV). I got dead bored and, 'cos Han couldn't hang out with me this afternoon, I took Barbara for a long walk along the canal, and it was really nice for one major reason: I saw Alice. She was walking back along the canal with her dad, and I had one of those moments where I saw her walking towards me, and I knew that I couldn't turn around and walk away again 'cos that would be too obvious. So I knew I was going to have to pass her and speak to her, and I felt dead nervous 'cos I was worried she might blank me, or start having a go at me about what happened at the party. But she didn't.

Instead, we all kinda said, 'Hi' to one another and it was a bit awkward, what with her dad standing there too, but eventually Alice asked him to walk on and said she'd catch him up. We sat down on a bench on the towpath, and I asked her how she was and how college was going, and what she was doing for Christmas and polite stuff like that, and I felt really sad, like I always do when I remember how we used to be.

Anyway, Alice said that she was doing great at college and was going to take her exams early 'cos she was doing so well…and then she told me she was sorry for saying I was nothing to her in her text last week, and that she hadn't meant it, and that sometimes she missed talking to me!! I felt my throat tighten when she said that, and then everything kinda came tumbling out. I told her I missed her too, and that I was sorry I'd ruined our friendship and that I knew it was all my fault 'cos I'd been such an arsehole and that there wasn't a day went by when I didn't feel guilty for what I'd done.

Alice said that she hated me for a long time after we broke up (ouch!) and that she'd thought I was a complete wanker for what I did at Caroline's party, but that she'd figured that was just the way I was (WTF?) and I'd never change. On the positive side, she said that going to college had really helped her though, 'cos she'd made a whole new bunch of friends there, and that there was a boy in her English class who she'd just started seeing, and that she was 'really happy'. She said, 'I sometimes wonder if I went a bit nuts over you, and that I got confused between our friendship and wanting something more.' I didn't really like her suggesting I might have made her a bit nuts, but ignored her comment anyway.

I asked her a bit about this boy, and she said he was called Tim and he was really nice, and that it was 'early days' but he seemed to like her as much as she liked him. I kinda wanted to ask her if her going out with me was just her experimenting with her sexuality, but then when I thought about experimenting I remembered about J and felt myself going red just remembering everything that had happened at Caroline's party, and stayed quiet.

Anyway, me and Alice chatted for about half an hour, and when we parted, she told me to 'stay in touch'. I will. I'm just relieved and pleased that she's apparently forgiven me for what I've done; okay, I know things will never be the same between us ever again, but perhaps now we can go some way to getting back to how we used to be. Today was a start at least.

Monday 22 December

We got invited to the new neighbours' house for evening drinks tonight. I didn't want to go, but for some stupid reason, Mum thought it would be 'nice' for me and HRBH to 'show our faces', so we both got dragged over there grumbling and pouting, and grizzling about the fact we both had lives and didn't want to spend the next four hours or whatever being bored to tears. It fell on deaf ears.

The new neighbours seem very strange, I've decided. There were some other neighbours there as well, people we've not spoken to in years, so the conversation was all a bit stilted to begin with. We all drank mulled wine (yuk, yuk, yuk) and ate mince pies (yuk, yuk, YUK) and sat around trying to make polite conversation. The weirdo son was there, looking at me, and at one point, I swear to God, he offered to show me his *Glee* poster in his room. Yeah, right!

Anyway, after about two hours of total boredom, the husband of the house got some small bagpipes out and spent, like, half an hour pumping them up and down under his arm before he could get a half-decent tune out of them, by which time I'd completely lost the will to live.

I think Mum and Dad had had enough too 'cos we were back home by 10 p.m., which is unheard of for them. One whiff of free alcohol and the pair of them are usually being carried out, feet first, way after midnight. Perhaps they're maturing at long last.

Or perhaps, like me, they were just bored shitless.

Tuesday 23 December

Went into town to buy Mum and Dad's presents today. The shopping centre was heaving with people wearing Santa hats and dangling bits of mistletoe from their heads, or people from offices falling out of pubs and bars with tinsel wrapped round them.

I walked past the wine bar where I'd been for lunch a few times back in the summer with my work experience people, and bumped straight into Felicity, Ed, Call Me Dave, and a few other people from my internship whose names I've conveniently forgotten! They'd been having their Christmas lunch in there and were all heading back to the office for the afternoon, but the minute they spotted me they tried to drag me back into the wine bar for 'just one more drink'.

I declined. I've managed to blot out any memories of working in the stupid place, and had no intention of renewing any friendships. Besides, I didn't like the way Call Me Dave was looking at my chest, and didn't want to have to explain why I'd never rung him. Weirdo.

Anyway, I managed to buy Mum and Dad a present each just before the shops closed. This year Mum's getting a rolling pin, and Dad's getting a tyre pressure gauge thing for his car. Both cheap, functional and, most importantly, easy to wrap.

While I was in town I also managed to buy Han one more present to add to the necklace I'd already bought her the other week. I bought her a dead sexy, dead lacy, black bra that I found on the Sale rack at the lingerie store—cheap, functional and, most importantly for me, easy to UNwrap. Ha, ha, ha!!

Wednesday 24 December

OMFreakingG! I came out to my sister today!!!!! On Christmas Eve!!!

So, right, where do I start? Okay, so I went over to Han's this morning to give her her Christmas presents and ended up spending, like, three or four hours there 'cos me and Han had some time up in her room away from prying eyes when we swapped presents (amongst other things, haha!) and then I got chatting to her parents downstairs afterwards and stuff like that, so I didn't end up coming home until way later in the afternoon.

Anyway, I had such an awesome time over at Han's 'cos we got talking up in her room about 'us' and 'the future' and about how next year was gonna be our best year yet now we were totally over all the silly shit we'd gone through this year. We lay together on her bed, Han stroking my hair and telling me just how special I was and how much she loved me and all that. She said she thought we'd 'come out of all the crap we'd been through even stronger than we were before' and how much she just 'loved being with me'. It was well cute and I honestly found it hard to believe there were times over this last year when I was so sad over her I couldn't eat and couldn't sleep 'cos right at that moment I felt so happy and proud and loved up, it was unreal.

Anyway, I kinda floated home on a cloud of Hannah Happiness and when I got in HRBH was lying out on the sofa watching *The Snowman* on TV and trying to make Barbara, who was sitting just in front of her on the floor, catch peanuts in her mouth. When I saw her (HRBH, not Barbara) I tried to leave the room without her seeing me, but she spotted me and beckoned me to her, like a queen summoning her servant to scrape her bunions or something. Not that the Queen has bunions. I don't think.

She said, 'How was Han?' and I kinda just went, 'Yeah, okay.'

HRBH said, 'She home for Christmas?' and I said, 'Yeah. Why?'

'Just asking,' she said.

Hmm.

I sat on the chair by the fire and kinda watched her warily from the corner of my eye as she carried on idly tossing peanuts to Barbara, who seemed to be enjoying the game more than HRBH was (probably just grateful for five minutes' attention from her. God knows she normally never bothers).

And then—OMFG!!!—then, HRBH said, 'You like her, don't you?'

So I said (deliberately), 'Barbara? Yeah, I like Barbara,' and HRBH did that rolling of her eyes that she does to perfection and said, 'Nawww, Han. You like Han, don't you?'

So I said, 'Yeah, she's a mate,' hoping to God that HRBH couldn't see my heart beating in my neck 'cos it was kinda going at a hundred miles an hour now. I wanted to get up and leave, but you know how it is? If I'd have got up, then it would have looked so bloody obvious that I didn't want to talk to her about it, so I figured I'd just try and ride it out.

Big mistake!

HRBH said, 'I've been talking to Joe...'

Joe! I made a mental note to rip his head off and shove it up his half-pipe next time I saw him. Anyway, just as I was thinking of the most painful and slow way to take Joe's head off, HRBH completely threw me by saying this:

'You're more than friends, aren't you? You and Han, I mean.'

I didn't say anything. I just kinda looked at her out the corner of my eye and nodded slowly, waiting for her to give me a total bollocking.

She didn't!

She said, 'I guessed as much,' and then...get this...SHE SMILED AT ME!!!!!

That totally freaked me out.

HRBH NEVER SMILES.

She said, 'I didn't know you were into girls. I mean, you went out with some boy once, didn't you?'

I told her that I'd only really figured out that I was into girls a few years back, and that it'd been Ben that'd actually confirmed what I'd kinda already known, and that meeting Han had been the final piece in my confused and complicated jigsaw, and that it was only once I'd got with Han that everything finally made sense.

I said (and my voice suddenly developed this frog in it), 'You won't tell Mum and Dad, will you?' and HRBH said she wouldn't, and that it was nothing to do with anyone else anyway. Then she asked me how long we'd been together and when I told her, she raised her eyebrows in a *that long and you've never told me?* sorta way. She asked me if I loved Han and I got dead embarrassed and told her that, yeah, I did. Very much.

She said, 'Well, I think it's sweet, my little sister in love.'

WTF?

Did aliens come down in the night and abduct my sister and replace her with this person who was in front of me? Give me back my snide, grumpy, sarcastic, whinging sister at once!!!

I kinda mumbled a thanks to her and then she looked down at where she was sitting and said, 'But if I ever find out you and her have *done it* on this sofa, I'll tighten the strings on your hoodie so flipping hard it'll make your eyes pop out,' and I knew everything was going to be okay. Aliens hadn't abducted her after all.

Thursday 25 December

Christmas Day!!!

Woke up and my first thought wasn't 'It's Christmas Day' but, strangely, 'OMG, my sister knows I'm gay!' I texted Han late last night and told her that I'd had a heart-to-heart with HRBH and that she knew everything, and Han texted me back and said, 'She knows everything? Please tell me she doesn't know we did it on the sofa back in the summer. I don't want to spend Xmas Day in hospital!!'

I told her HRBH was being very sweet about everything and Han said pretty much what I'd been thinking ever since I'd told HRBH and asked me whether my sister had had a personality transplant.

So, anyway, Christmas Day was awesome!! I got a text off Alice wishing me a 'Merry Xmas', which made my day; we ate far too much turkey again, dressed Barbara up in her favourite festive dickie bow tie, and I actually managed to keep one present unopened until just after the Queen's speech! Result!

Everything was going swimmingly until I got a Happy Christmas text from J at about 6 p.m., which kinda mucked things up 'cos I'd managed not to stress about her all day. She said she was at Ethan's house, being bored to tears, and wished she was with me, back at Caroline's house, pressing me up against the door. Then she said she was looking forward to the Christmas party that Matty's gonna have at her house this Saturday 'cos she knew that would be the night she got her wish. 'I know you won't be able to keep pushing me away forever,' she wrote.

I read the text and felt dead sorry for Ethan. How shitty it must be not to know that your girlfriend thinks you're 'boring' and is spending her evening texting someone else, telling them what she wants to do with them. I read the message again then deleted it quickly, in case Han ever got to see it, and made sure no one had seen that my face had gone, like, totally red reading it.

#stressed

Friday 26 December

I told Han today that I didn't want to go to Matty's party tomorrow night but she said she'd been looking forward to it all over Christmas Day and that she couldn't wait to 'let her hair down after being stuck with her 'rents for the last three days'.

The thought of Han going to a party without me is, well, unthinkable, so I guess I'll go. If J really meant what she said, and is going to try and kiss me, then I'll have to do everything I can to make sure she doesn't get me on her own, which pretty much means sticking to Han like glue for the evening.

I texted Joe and told him what J had said. He just replied with a text that said, 'Wow! Can I come and watch?'

He's such a shithead sometimes. Why I even allow myself to be seen out with him is a mystery.

Saturday 27 December

Today was, like, the WEIRDEST day ever! Tonight was Matty's party and I'd been absolutely-bloody-dreading-it. I'd tried to wriggle out of it again with Han, by telling her I was getting a headache and wasn't sure I'd be up for going out, but she said that she was bringing Freddie along too, and there was NO WAY I was going to let her be alone with him all evening. Okay, so she's told him she's not interested, but he's a boy. They don't ever take no for an answer (apparently) and I figured all it would take would be for him to get wasted on cheap beer and then try it on. With my girlfriend.

Anyway, so me, Han, and Freddie all arrived together and I was dead pleased to see J wasn't there, so I was kinda hoping she'd changed her mind. We drank, like, LOADS of beer 'cos Matty's dad had done a run to France in his van a few days before Christmas and there was still boxes and boxes left over. Okay, it tasted like crap, but Matty reckoned each bottle worked out at about 20p, so we all figured we could get pissed as farts for under a quid. Can't complain at that!

I started to relax after about an hour 'cos it was obvious that J wasn't coming, so I lay out on some bean bags with Han over in a dark corner away from prying eyes. We took silly photos of each other on our phones and just kinda pissed about for a bit, blowing across the tops of our empty bottles and making stupid sounds, occasionally stopping for a quick kiss when no one was looking, 'cos all they'd do is make dumbass remarks to us.

Freddie had left us alone the second we'd got there, which I'd been dead pleased about, and had headed straight for the beers and any available girl standing on their own. I occasionally saw him disappearing out into the garden with one girl and coming back with another, but I didn't care; all I cared about was that Freddie was leaving me and Han alone, and that J wasn't coming, so I didn't have to stress the whole evening.

And then I saw her. J, I mean. She arrived in the room with some boy who wasn't Ethan draped over her arm and, OMG, I swear it was like something from one of them films, like *Brief Encounter* or *Shrek* or something, when our eyes met across the gloom of Matty's parents' front room and locked on each other. I was still sitting on the bean bag in the dark with Han and she was kinda leaning against my neck and making me laugh, but all the while she was doing it, I was aware of J watching us, with this kinda funny smile on her face and I just KNEW she was going to try and do something at some point over the course of the evening, and so it was up to me to make sure she didn't get the chance.

Then Han suddenly said she was going to go to the toilet and then get us another beer each on her way back and got up and wandered off upstairs. I tried to get up and follow her, but 'cos the bean bag was so squishy I couldn't get up, and kinda just floundered for a bit like a tortoise on its back. I saw J watch Han disappear up the stairs and before I could do anything, she came sauntering over to me and I felt like a budgie trapped in a cage while a cat wandered ever closer towards it with its claws out.

She flumped down next to me on Han's bean bag and kicked her legs out in front of her, and I had to try sooooooo hard not to look at them. She kinda just went, 'Hey' to me, then looked around the room, saying, 'This is a bit of luck, isn't it?' or something like that, while I just sat, stiff with nerves and watched the stairs for any sign of Han's feet coming back down (and the rest of her as well—not just her feet) thinking that if she knew what J was planning, she'd attach a string of fairy lights to her and plug her in to the mains, Christmas spirit or no Christmas spirit.

J reached past my head and switched a lamp off that was near us, plunging us both into total darkness, so that all I was aware of was her breathing next to me. Then she started nuzzling at my neck, running her hand up and down my thigh while I just lay there, feeling totally trapped, just like I'd felt when she'd pinned me up against the door at Caroline's party. Unlike at Caroline's party, though, I kinda liked it, and kept flicking my eyes towards the stairs, hoping that Han wouldn't come back. Then J fished a sprig of mangled mistletoe out from God-knows-where and dangled it in front of my face, making some comment about a 'Christmas kiss' while I just lay there like a complete dumbass watching the mistletoe go back and forwards like I was being hypnotised or something.

And then she leaned in and kissed me! OMFG she kissed me! And the weird thing was, I sooo knew she was gonna do it, but I didn't do anything to stop her, 'cos she was looking dead hot, and smelling dead nice, and I knew she really wanted it, and that kinda made me really want it too.

I'm ashamed to say, diary, that I kissed her back too. So I'm human. Bite me. Call it animal instinct, call it *hot girl kissing me, whatamma gonna do?* Or just call it me being an arsehole, but I kissed her back, and I really, *really* liked it. She just kept kissing me over and over, and did this amazing thing like nibbling and sucking at my bottom lip between kisses, which made me feel dead funny *down below* and made me instinctively reach a hand up round her neck and pull her closer to me.

When she'd finished kissing me, and I was lying there staring up at her with my hand still round her neck, she looked down at me, smiled, and said 'Nice. Very nice,' and sort of licked at her lips, which made my insides go mushy, like they go mushy when Han raises her eyebrow at me.

I said (or more, kinda squeaked), 'Was it as you expected?' and she said, 'No,' and leant down and kissed me again, and whispered in my ear, 'It was better.' This time she lay across me a bit more, pinning me down hard onto the bean bag, and she put her hand up my top, which Han does sometimes when she's kissing me as well. But J's hand felt different, more forceful maybe—I dunno.

Then she suddenly pulled herself off me, sat up, tidied up her hair, looked back at me, still lying there in a mushy, horny heap, and told me I was a 'hot kisser' and that we'd 'do it again soon', then got up and sauntered off to the kitchen.

I'd never felt so puddled in all my life! Okay, well I have, of course, 'cos I felt lousy with all that stuff when Han dumped me, but you know what I mean. I kinda lay there, staring up at the ceiling and feeling like I'd been used and abused by one of the hottest girls in my school, then Han came back, wearing a pair of reindeer antlers and flopped down next to me, laughing about the fact that Freddie was 'getting his face chewed off out in the kitchen by some fit girl from your school', who I could only assume was J.

Sometimes I think the whole world has gone mad and I'm the only sane person left.

Sunday 28 December

Han has just sent me a text this afternoon saying that Freddie had told her he was now going out with J!

Han wrote, 'Wasn't she the one you used to crush on, like, years ago?' and I replied with a 'dunno' text. What could I say? 'Erm, yeah, she was the one I fancied for years and, oh, who I just happened to kiss last night while you were out of the room, because she wanted to see what it was like to kiss a girl, and chose me.' I feel guilty enough as it is that I wasn't strong enough to resist her, and I feel like the biggest cow in the world that I kissed J while my girlfriend was upstairs having a wee. And the fact I enjoyed it.

I needed to get my head round all this, so I spent most of this afternoon up in my room, thinking about stuff. J has been coming on to me, like, for the last two months and when I finally give in to her, she immediately goes off and kisses Freddie in the kitchen afterwards! I knew that would happen! I just bloody knew it! I've known ever since she first came on to me that she didn't mean it, and it was all a game, and I tried to stop her, but would she listen? No.

Then I got really angry with her for messing with my head, because she must know I can't ask her why she kissed Freddie at the party as well 'cos then that'll sound like I fancy her, won't it? I sent her a text, telling her she was a headfuck and that I hated her and that if she so much as breathed a word to Han about anything, I'd come looking for her.

Okay, I wouldn't have to look far 'cos I'll see her at school again next week, but the threat was clear enough and I hope she understood that I was pissed off with her. I'm still sitting up in my room now, waiting for her to reply, getting more and more angry with her, about how she could think it was okay to mess around with me like that.

<u>6 p.m.</u>

Still no reply. Why is that? Is she ashamed of what she did? I mean, ashamed at how she's pissed around with me, rather than ashamed of having kissed me?

Whatever. The smell of reheated turkey coming up from the kitchen is forcing me back downstairs again.

8 p.m.

I mean, just who the fuck does she think she is? I hate her! I hate her more than I've ever hated anyone in my life (even more than Susan Divine).

11.40 p.m.

Just going to bed now. J still hasn't texted me back. I don't know whether to laugh or cry.

Monday 29 December

I gave in and texted J again this morning. She had, like, TOTALLY ignored my text from last night and I was, like, TOTALLY going up the wall stressing about stuff, so I just sent her a text asking her if 'she was done with me now?'

She sent me a text back just after lunch saying sorry for messing with me for so long and that it had been 'a laugh'. I was sooooo fucking angry with her! A laugh? She calls all that stress she's put me through 'a laugh'? So I texted her back and told her to leave me alone from now on, and she texted me straight back and said she would.

She said, 'I just wanted to know what it'd be like to be with a girl and now I know, so thanks. It was fun, though, wasn't it? Looking forward to the next one already! BTW, am going out with Freddie now. See you @ school next week.'

FFS!

After I'd picked up my phone—which I'd thrown across my bedroom in a tantrum—from the floor, I texted Drummer Joe and told him everything that had happened, and what J had just said to me about it just being 'a laugh'.

His text came back about an hour later. It just said, 'hahahahaha.'

Arsehole.

Anyway, I figured I'd wasted enough of my time stressing over J, so went back downstairs, and thank God my day suddenly got better when Mum and Dad told me they're going to Aunty Marie and Uncle Bob's annual NYE party again this year. Aaaaand just like last year and every other bloody year before it, they asked me if I wanted to go, but I figured I was done with their annual party two years ago when Mum came home with a pair of used boxer shorts. Enough already.

Besides, apart from last year, in previous years I didn't have a totally awesome girlfriend waiting to give me the longest kiss of my life on the stroke of midnight, did I? So my decision to not go again this year was a total no-brainer.

Mum and Dad foolishly asked HRBH if she wanted to go to Aunty Marie's too (I think they probably did it more out of parental duty than actually *wanting* her there). The look of relief on Dad's face was hilarious when she said (quite scornfully actually) that she was going to a rave with Joe and probably wouldn't be home until around 5th January.

HRBH sidled up to me in the kitchen later and said it was good that there'd be no one home 'cos it meant I could invite Han over and we could have NYE to ourselves, and it would be really nice and romantic for us with no one disturbing us, and then she said she hoped I had a really awesome time.

WHO'S STOLEN MY SISTER? GIVE HER BACK AT ONCE!!!

So with the house empty until at least 3 a.m., not only will I get the longest kiss of my life from Han, but with any luck, the longest shag too. Hahahaha!!!

Tuesday 30 December

Han sent me a text just before I went to bed last night that said, 'We should get married!'

I hope she was joking!

Still fuming with J. Am going to give her such a stare when I see her again next week, the total cow.

Wednesday 31 December

OMFG! Han wasn't joking!!! I ignored her text, just kinda texting her back to say 'hahaha, very funny,' you know, like you do, but she was dead serious!!

She rang me up and sounded a bit hurt 'cos she said I'd not taken her text seriously, but that she'd really meant it. I waited for her to start laughing and tell me she was taking the piss, so I deliberately didn't ask if she was gonna go down on one knee later or anything like that. But she didn't laugh, she just told me she'd been thinking about it for ages, and when she came over later she'd talk to me properly about it.

I spent, like, ALL day thinking about it, wondering if it really was just some kind of special Han joke 'cos when we texted again later in the day she didn't mention it. Anyway, she came over at about 6 and had her tea with us, and she looked smooooking hot! How I kept my hands off her over the sausages was anyone's guess. She was Goth-ed up to the max 'cos she said she wanted to make an effort for NYE, and was dressed, like, from head to toe in black leather, her hair looking like she'd just got up (which must have taken her hours to do) and so many accessories she was jangling like Jacob Marley shaking his arms at Scrooge on Christmas Eve. She looked amazing!

Anyway, Mum and Dad *finally* went over to Aunty Marie and Uncle

Bob's annual New Year party at about 7, telling us both not to expect them back much before 1.30 a.m. (I was hoping for more like 3 a.m., but never mind), and 'cos HRBH had already gone to Joe's in the afternoon, me and Han had the whole house to ourselves, and it was AWESOME!

We had this dead profound conversation about 'us' and how much we loved each other and then Han said how sorry she was for everything she'd done to me over the year, and I said how sorry I was for getting together with Alice (I conveniently ignored the bit about kissing J the other night, 'cos as far as I'm concerned it never happened) and then we had this awesome kissing session on the sofa and we said we'd never do anything to hurt each other ever again and that we were for keeps forever and ever and then (and I can hardly believe I'm even writing this)…

She asked me to marry her!!!!!

Okay, so she didn't go down on one knee, but then you can't expect a girl whose legs are covered in chains to do anything other than sit very carefully, but she did take both my hands in hers, look dead deep into my eyes, and tell me I was the most amazing thing that had ever happened to her and that there was no way she was ever going to risk letting anyone else have me again. My mind briefly flickered to J, and I wondered if she was getting it on with Freddie tonight, then quickly flickered away again as Han took her friendship bracelet off and asked me to take mine off so we could swap (we never did get round to buying those commitment rings, did we?) as a sign that we were engaged.

It was on the tip of my tongue to tell her that I hadn't actually accepted her proposal yet, but then I kinda thought, *Yeah, right! Who am I kidding?*

Hannah Harrison wants to marry me! Of course I'm going to bloody well marry her!

She told me she loved me and that she wanted to spend the rest of her life with me, then she *finally* asked me if I'd say yes. I said yes straight away, dear diary, and I'm not ashamed to admit that I felt like crying. I didn't, of course. I'm now a fully fledged skater girl (Joe said so, so it must be true) and skaters don't cry. It's in the rules.

Anyway, I have to say, for the first time since I was, like, 10, I didn't stay up until midnight and watch the fireworks in London on the TV. Let's just put it this way. I was up the stairs and having my own fireworks under a duvet with my new fiancée (squeeeeeee!) before Big Ben had the chance to even bong once.

Thursday 1 January

So that's it. I'm engaged. I'm just ordinary, old Clemmie Atkins and I'm engaged to the most awesome, adorable, cute, sexy, HAWT girl in the entire world.

WTF?!

It's mad! It's more than mad. It's madder than a mad thing from Madchester. But at the same time it's brilliant. I mean, what a year! What a freaking year! It's been another 365 days of more ups and downs than a lift in Harrods (Okay, 366 days. So it was a leap year. Sue me), and I feel like I've been on a bloody roller coaster for all of it, but what a freaking year it's been! I've plunged to the depths of depression and despair when Han and I broke up, to feeling a cow when I got with Alice, to acquiring a Great Uncle Elvis (high five, Uncle Elvis!!!), and then finally being back on top of the world when Han and I got back together again (despite being totally weirded out over J).

And then just when I think it can't get any better she proposes to me!

What a girl!

I love her sooooooo much it hurts, and the fact she wants to commit to me for the rest of our lives makes me know she loves me just as much. I can do anything with Han by my side; I can achieve anything I want in life, I can go anywhere, do anything, be who I want to be. No one can touch us, no one can hurt us, and no one can judge us. What we do is up to us. Our love's special and there's not a single person on the planet that can take that away from us.

As long as she's with me, we're invincible.

I wonder if there's anywhere any higher than the top of the world? 'Cos now I'm engaged to Han I think I'm up there, head held high, standing with my arms outstretched, soaking it all in, yelling from the top of my voice that I love Hannah Harrison, and she loves me.

And I tell you what, diary, there's no way any bugger's ever gonna drag me back down again.

About the Author

KE Payne was born in Bath, the English city, not the tub, and after leaving school she worked for the British government for fifteen years, which probably sounds a lot more exciting than it really was.

Fed up with spending her days moving paperwork around her desk and making models of the Taj Mahal out of paperclips, she packed it all in to go to university in Bristol and graduated as a mature student in 2006 with a degree in linguistics and history.

After graduating, she worked at a university in the Midlands for a while, again moving all that paperwork around, before finally leaving to embark on her dream career as a writer.

She moved to the idyllic English countryside in 2007 where she now lives and works happily surrounded by dogs and guinea pigs.

Soliloquy Titles From Bold Strokes Books

Another 365 Days by KE Payne. Clemmie Atkins is back, and her life is more complicated than ever! Still madly in love with her girlfriend, Clemmie suddenly finds her life turned upside down with distractions, confessions, and the return of a familiar face… (978-1-60282-775-2)

The Secret of Othello by Sam Cameron. Florida teen detectives Steven and Denny risk their lives to search for a sunken NASA satellite—but under the waves, no one can hear you scream… (978-1-60282-742-4)

Andy Squared by Jennifer Lavoie. Andrew never thought anyone could come between him and his twin sister, Andrea… until Ryder rode into town. (978-1-60282-743-1)

Sara by Greg Herren. A mysterious and beautiful new student at Southern Heights High School stirs things up when students start dying. (978-1-60282-674-8)

Boys of Summer, edited by Steve Berman. Stories of young love and adventure, when the sky's ceiling is a sbright blue marvel, when another boy's laughter at the beach can distract from dull summer jobs. (978-1-60282-663-2)

Street Dreams by Tama Wise. Tyson Rua has more than his fair share of problems growing up in New Zealand—he's gay, he's falling in love, and he's run afoul of the local hip-hop crew leader just as he's trying to make it as a graffiti artist. (978-1-60282-650-2)

me@you.com by KE Payne. Is it possible to fall in love with someone you've never met? Imogen Summers thinks so because it's happened to her. (978-1-60282-592-5)

Swimming to Chicago by David-Matthew Barnes. As the lives of the adults around them unravel, high school students Alex and Robby form an unbreakable bond, vowing to do anything to stay together—even if it means leaving everything behind. (978-1-60282-572-7)

Speaking Out edited by Steve Berman. Inspiring stories written for and about LGBT and Q teens of overcoming adversity (against intolerance and homophobia) and experiencing life after "coming out." (978-1-60282-566-6)

365 Days by KE Payne. Life sucks when you're seventeen years old and confused about your sexuality, and the girl of your dreams doesn't even know you exist. Then in walks sexy new emo girl, Hannah Harrison. Clemmie Atkins has exactly 365 days to discover herself, and she's going to have a blast doing it! (978-1-60282-540-6)

Cursebusters! by Julie Smith. Budding psychic Reeno is the most accomplished teenage burglar in California, but one tiny screw-up and poof!—she's sentenced to Bad Girl School. And that isn't even her worst problem. Her sister Haley's dying of an illness no one can diagnose, and now she can't even help. (978-1-60282-559-8)

Who I Am by M.L. Rice. Devin Kelly's senior year is a disaster. She's in a new school in a new town, and the school bully is making her life miserable—but then she meets his sister Melanie and realizes her feelings for her are more than platonic. (978-1-60282-231-3)

Sleeping Angel by Greg Herren. Eric Matthews survives a terrible car accident only to find out everyone in town thinks he's a murderer—and he has to clear his name even though he has no memories of what happened. (978-1-60282-214-6)

Mesmerized by David-Matthew Barnes. Through her close friendship with Brodie and Lance, Serena Albright learns about the many forms of love and finds comfort for the grief and guilt she feels over the brutal death of her older brother, the victim of a hate crime. (978-1-60282-191-0)

The Perfect Family by Kathryn Shay. A mother and her gay son stand hand in hand as the storms of change engulf their perfect family and the life they knew. (978-1-60282-181-1)

Father Knows Best by Lynda Sandoval. High school juniors and best friends Lila Moreno, Meryl Morganstern, and Caressa Thibodoux plan to make the most of the summer before senior year. What they discover that amazing summer about girl power, growing up, and trusting friends and family more than prepares them to tackle that all-important senior year! (978-1-60282-147-7)